THE SILENCE BETWEEN BREATHS

Passengers boarding the 10.35 train from Manchester Piccadilly to London Euston have no idea that their journey is about to be brutally curtailed. Holly has just landed her dream job and Jeff is heading for his first work interview after months of unemployment. They sit next to each other. Among the others travelling are Nick with his young family who are driving him crazy; pensioner Meg and her partner setting off on a walking holiday and Caroline, run ragged by the demands of her stroppy teenage children and her demented mother. And in the middle of the carriage sits Saheel, carrying a deadly rucksack...

THE SILENCE BETWEEN BREATHS

by

Cath Staincliffe

Magna Large Print Books
Long Preston, North Yorkshire,
BD23 4ND, England.

British Library Cataloguing in Publication Data.

A catalogue record of this book is
available from the British Library

ISBN   978-0-7505-4437-5

First published in Great Britain in 2016 by Constable

Cover illustration © Alison Burford/Arcangel by arrangement with
Arcangel Images Ltd.

The moral right of the author has been asserted.

Published in Large Print 2017 by arrangement with
Little, Brown Book Group Limited

Magna Large Print is an imprint of Library Magna Books Ltd.

Printed and bound in Great Britain by
T.J. (International) Ltd., Cornwall, PL28 8RW

For Tim. Again. For ever.

CHAPTER ONE

April 2015

Jeff

Jeff pelted up the ramp towards Piccadilly station, dodging round all the people dragging suitcases or pushing buggies. He couldn't miss this train. He couldn't. His heart hammered in his chest, a pain there, so it hurt to breathe. He ran in through the automatic doors and up to the bank of electronic departure boards, forcing his eyes to slow down, to concentrate. London? London? London Euston? There! *10.35. Platform 7. On time.* Shit! His eyes flew to the clock at the base of the screens. *10.32.* No! It said on the website the doors closed two minutes before departure. He turned and raced to the gate. He could see the train, but the platform was empty.

If he missed it now... The thought made him feel sick. No interview, no hope of a fresh start. And he'd be sanctioned.

No money.

He reached the first carriage, hit the door-release button.

He could hear his mum going on about it: 'Missed the train. Honestly, Jeff, I sometimes despair, I really do.' His gran, disappointed but trying to hide it. Maybe she'd understand, make

9

him feel all right about it. More than his mum ever would.

If he hadn't had to go back for his phone, if he hadn't had to charge it in the first place, he'd have been all right. But he'd missed the bus and the next one was late. He'd done a survey once when he was getting the bus for a week-long skills course the Job Centre had forced him to take. In the morning it was late four times. Eighty per cent of the time. Jeff had emailed the company, pointing this out. He got a reply eventually saying his feedback was valued and they were continually striving to improve their service.

The train made a noise, a whirring sigh. Jeff jabbed the button again and the door opened. He climbed on with shaking legs. He was sweating now. Brilliant. He'd turn up stinking and that'd be a great first impression. 'What about the Manchester lad?' they'd say.

'The one with the BO? I don't think so, do you?'

He'd used half a can of his stepdad's deodorant. *48 hours,* it said, *bio active ultra.* What did that even mean?

Jeff felt in his coat pocket for his ticket and seat reservation. They weren't there. He felt the blood drain from his face. He went through each pocket in turn. An announcement came over the PA: 'Any passengers not intending to travel with us today...'

For a moment his vision blurred in panic. He felt the waves rising, the shivering, clenching in his head, in his guts. No. Not this. Not now. Calm, he told himself. Just calm down.

He went through every pocket again. Phone.

Key. Lighter. They'd kick him off. Oh, God. They'd make him get off at the next station and that'd be the end of it. Baccy, papers. Phone. Oh, shit! Relief drenched him as he opened his phone case and pulled the tickets out. Tucked in there, along with the tenner Nana had given him. 'It probably won't buy you more than a butty and a brew,' she said, 'but there you are.'

Jeff took off his specs to read the reservation: B22. He glanced around. This was coach A.

The train began to move as he made his way through the coach. Other people were taking their seats. There was a putrid smell near the toilet. He was still out of breath. In coach B a family of four were blocking the aisle with enough gear to stock a car-boot sale. The woman, who was holding a baby, smiled and said, 'Sorry,' as the bloke loaded stuff into the luggage area. The little kid with them was asking a ton of questions and not waiting for any answers.

Finally they were done. 'Come on,' the dad said, 'Nineteen, twenty, twenty-three, twenty-four.'

Jeff followed them. He was boiling. He'd shed a layer, soon as. He scanned the numbers on the edges of the seats. Everything was unfamiliar. He'd not done many long train journeys: no need. And no money.

Ahead, the family found their seats and started a debate about who would sit where.

'You sit where I tell you to, Eddie,' the dad said to the little kid.

And the little kid said, 'But I want to look out.'

Jeff counted off the numbers, passed a guy on his own in 15, and on the other side, in 17, a

11

middle-aged woman on the phone, and behind her was Jeff's seat: 22. By the window. Facing backwards. With a girl in it. A woman. A mass of shiny black curly hair, dark skin, pink lipstick, lots of makeup. Wearing a black-and-white-checked skirt and jacket, little ankle boots.

'That's my seat,' Jeff said.

She looked up. 'Sorry?'

'You're in my seat.' Jeff held up his ticket. 'B twenty-two.'

'The reservations aren't working,' she said.

'What?' Jeff said.

She pointed a manicured finger at a small LED panel above the window, which was showing blank. 'The reservations are off.'

'That's still my seat,' he said.

'You can sit there.' She nodded to the vacant seat beside her.

'It might be reserved,' Jeff said.

'I don't see anyone,' she said.

'They could get on at Stockport,' Jeff said. 'And if they've got a reservation and I'm sitting in their seat then they've every right to ask me to move. Like I'm asking you.'

'Are you serious?' she said.

Jeff didn't reply. He felt the heat creep up his neck and into his face. He unzipped his parka and stuffed it up on the luggage rack.

'Right then,' she huffed. She made a show of putting her magazine and water into a bag that was the size of a trunk, metal studs and rivets on it, like some piece of medieval furniture, then slammed up the tray table and climbed into the aisle.

12

'Thanks,' Jeff said to his neighbour. Though he didn't know why. Wasn't that she'd been particularly helpful. The opposite in fact.

The little boy began to snivel. 'I want the window.'

'You won't get anything if you make that noise,' his mum said.

Jeff sat in the seat, which was still warm. He felt pervy thinking that. Why had he even noticed it? He opened the tray table and set his phone down. He took off his specs and rubbed them on his shirt.

She sat down next to him, spent some time rummaging in her bag – you'd need a headlamp and a map to find anything in there – pulled out the magazine and water again. And her own phone.

Jeff closed his eyes. His back was stiff as a plank, his jaw tight. *Calm. Calm.*

He could smell her perfume. Or shampoo or something. It was sweet, like honey, but with some spice in too. Like those things his nana stuck in oranges at Christmas. Began with a C ... or an L? He opened his phone, launched the browser, typed in *orange Christmas spice*. Picked a link, ignoring the ones that were obviously cakes, tapped on the picture. Cloves, they were. And the thing was called a pomander. It reminded Jeff of the ebony mace in *The Elder Scrolls V: Skyrim,* a nifty piece of kit. Whatever the girl was wearing, it was a nice smell, not too strong. His mum wore perfume by the bucketful, powerful enough to choke any person inhaling the fumes. A walking chemical weapon.

Did he smell? Jeff leant down towards his phone as though he was examining something close without the zoom and sniffed as near as he could get, without looking like a total tit, to his right armpit. He caught the greeny smell of his stepdad Sean's deodorant and, thankfully, nothing worse. He couldn't sniff his left side without drawing attention. Maybe later. He could go to the bog and do it. Mind you, with the reek in there...

He wanted a smoke. Two hours, eight minutes, the journey was. No chance till then. If he'd not forgotten his phone, he'd have got the earlier 86 and would have had time for a rollie on the walk between Piccadilly Gardens and the station. That was if the earlier 86 had come on time. But if it was still like it had been in November then he would have had only a one-in-five chance of its being on time. Two hours and counting.

The kid across the way was still scriking, and Jeff felt like telling the dad to just swap seats and shut him up. Kids love looking out of the window. The twins always wanted to sit at the front upstairs on the bus or by the windows in the car. Quite often Jeff would end up in the middle, a sister either side, knees up to his chin, blocking the sight line from the rear-view mirror, to keep the peace. They weren't much bother, the twins. Happy most of the time in each other's company, only occasionally bugging Jeff to play on the Wii with them or to let them have a go on one of his role-play games. They had their own made-up language, which Jeff thought was totally cool and drove his mother demented. Not that there was far to drive her. Maybe demented wasn't quite right. 'A drama queen,' Nana said to him on the quiet. 'Don't let it get to you, lad, she always was a drama queen. Centre of her own universe. She can't help it.'

The announcement came that they were pulling into Stockport and Jeff sat up straighter, watching.

'Waiting to see me get kicked out?' the girl said. Woman.

He didn't know if she expected an answer.

'That you?' She nodded to his left hand, the tattoo. JEFF. Letter on each finger, blurry ink, a muddy blue colour. He'd done it himself when he was seventeen and in a bad way. If he was ever dead rich he'd have it removed. His mum had gone ape when she'd seen it. Totally ape. Sean had had to calm her down. She'd wanted to take Jeff to A and E, convinced he'd get blood poisoning. Went on about it so much he'd begun to feel queasy.

Jeff gave a nod, turned his hand over to hide it.

'In case you forget?' she said. Like he hadn't heard that before. 'Short for Jeffrey, is it?'

'Just Jeff,' Jeff said.

She gave a little grunt. Not impressed.

Her lips were full, a darker outline round the edge. Her teeth really white. He wondered if she bleached them, had them done at the dentist, maybe. Jeff's were stained a bit, from the smokes, but they cleaned up all right when he had a scale and polish.

'What's yours, then?' Jeff said, before she could go on.

A man in a long black coat and a white scarf, carrying a leather laptop bag, stopped beside them and said to her, 'I think that's my seat.'

Jeff felt disappointed. Which was stupid.

'The reservations aren't working,' she said, 'so no one knows what's reserved and what isn't.'

'Well, I know this is my seat,' the bloke said, 'because it's printed here on my coupon. C twenty-one. So you'll have to move.'

'This is B twenty-one, mate,' she said crisply. 'You want to get yourself into the next coach before someone nicks your place.'

'Oh, good God,' the man said, as though it was her fault he'd got it wrong, and he swept off with his laptop bag banging the seats.

'Knob,' she muttered. Then, 'Do you have to do that?' she rounded on Jeff, startling him. 'With the leg. We won't get there any faster.'

He never noticed when he was doing it. Jiggling, his mum called it. Like biting his nails. Where did she get off on telling a complete stranger what to do? Jeff put his heel hard on the floor. Looked out of the window.

'It's Holly,' she said.

'What?'

'My name. It's Holly.'

'Figures,' Jeff said, glancing at her. 'Prickly as hell.'

Her eyes went even larger than they already were and her mouth hung open.

Jeff swallowed. Bad move, he thought. What were you thinking, dickhead?

Then she laughed, a big hoot of a laugh, loud enough to stop the kid crying for a minute. Jeff

16

felt himself start to smile and his cheeks glow warm again.

'You cheeky sod,' Holly said, through her laughter, her eyes dancing.

Jeff felt the knot in his stomach loosen. He'd got the train. He hadn't missed it. He hadn't lost his ticket. There was no delay. All he had to do now was sit tight and go over his practice interview questions.

It's all going to be all right, he thought.

Holly shook her head and picked up her magazine, her chuckle dying away.

He got out his headphones and opened his phone, launched *Grand Theft Auto* to see if he could complete his final mission. It's going to be all right. There was practically no chance he'd get the apprenticeship but it was a start. Yeah, he could live with that.

Caroline

'Tickets from Manchester and Stockport, please.'

Caroline got hers out. She was pretty sure they wouldn't let her transfer it but she'd ask all the same. The inspector got closer. He checked the young man across the aisle, who was lucky enough to have a forward-facing seat, then turned to her.

'I missed the ten-fifteen,' she said.

'Sorry, not transferable. Advance tickets are

only valid for the exact service stipulated,' the man said.

'A single, then,' she said. She'd no idea what it would cost, buying at the last minute like this.

'One hundred and nineteen pounds,' the man said.

Her heart dropped. She'd have to put it on her credit card. She had thought about cancelling the trip when she realized she'd probably miss the ten-fifteen, her taxi stuck in roadworks then delayed by a diversion. But she had been looking forward to this weekend away, away from her mother, away from the kids, from the endless grind of crises and caring, work and worry, ever since last summer when her friend Gail had said she was planning a trip over from the States and would Caroline like to catch up while she was here? God, would she!

The last family holiday, to Crete, had been a shambles. Paddy and Amelia had reached an age when they regarded time spent with their parents as little short of torture. They had refused to go on trips and had complained about the rooms, about the heat, about the food. Even the beach had been ruined by an invasion of jellyfish, and the resort was full of elderly people and young families with no other teenagers in sight.

One night they had spent a fortune on steaks at a restaurant only to have Paddy claim his was like leather. Back at their rental apartment, Trevor had cracked open a beer and gone out onto the veranda. Caroline felt hot and bloated: she was going through the menopause and it was bloody horrible. She'd been to the loo and come back to find Paddy and Amelia microwaving pizza. 'For Christ's sake,' she'd said, 'I just shelled out a hundred and twenty euros and now you're eating more junk.'

'It was crap,' Amelia had said, 'just like this place is crap.'

'The whole holiday is crap,' Paddy said. 'Why did we have to come?'

'Your dad and I wanted a break, and all you've done is moan and complain and act like spoilt brats the whole time,' Caroline had said. 'You selfish little shits.'

Paddy had flinched but recovered quickly, Amelia had smirked, as if she'd won some victory, and Caroline had felt wretched. She'd tried to rein in her rage. 'I'm sorry. I just think if you could please make an effort...'

'You forced us to come,' Amelia said. 'It was a stupid idea. Why should we pretend we're enjoying it when it's so rubbish? Like totally sad.'

'Do what you want, then.' Caroline flung out an arm towards the pizza box. 'But at least clear up after yourselves.' Tears stinging her eyes, she'd pulled open the fridge door and got out a bottle of white wine, poured a large glass and taken it outside.

'Trouble in Paradise?' Trevor said.

'They're driving me up the wall,' Caroline said.

'I got the gist.'

'You could have put in a word of support.'

'Would it have helped?'

She'd sighed, looking across the garden, with its coarse grass and spiky shrubs spotlit by solar-powered lamps, to the darkness of the sea beyond. 'Maybe not the situation, but at least it'd have been two against two.'

He had taken her hand, squeezed it. He was so even-tempered, Trevor, almost passive, a detachment that felt like a luxury she would never have. She sometimes felt she worried for both of them. She understood that the trauma and drama of his job as a paramedic gave him a different perspective, and he never suffered the angst that the kids drummed up in her.

'Were you ever that horrible?' she asked.

'No, meek as a lamb, I was.'

Moths and flies danced around the orbs of light among the plants.

'We shouldn't have brought them, but if we'd left them at home...' She shuddered. 'Let's go into town tomorrow, just you and me, pretend we're on our own.'

'Good idea.'

Her resentment had lingered for the rest of the holiday.

Now Caroline passed the inspector her credit card and he put it into the machine.

Her phone rang again and she glanced at the display: *Mum*. And let it ring. She needed to concentrate on paying for her ticket; her mother would ring back. Her mother always rang back. It was hard, these days, to concentrate on several things at once. They didn't tell you that about the change of life, or not as often as they told you about hot flushes and mood swings. Your thoughts could become mushy and muddled; there was a new forgetfulness.

The man asked her to check the amount and

enter her PIN. She'd even forgotten that last week. Couldn't recall if it was 4140 or 4104. Today she got it right and waited for the tickets to print.

There was a child crying and a man remonstrating with him. Someone else was laughing.

Caroline's phone went again. *Mum.* 'Hello, Mum.'

'Are you there?'

'Yes,' Caroline said.

'Where are you?'

'I'm at home,' Caroline said.

'I can't see you.'

'I don't live at your house,' Caroline said.

'Who is this?' her mother said.

'It's me, Caroline.'

'What do you want?'

Caroline took a breath. 'I'll see you soon, OK? Bye now.'

There had been no worrying background noises at her mother's end of the line, nothing to suggest she'd gone walkabout. That was what Caroline feared most, more than the prospect of the crumpets burning and starting a fire in the kitchen. Worse than a fall down the steps was the prospect of her mum wandering in traffic. There were large printed notices on the inside of the back door and the front door, saying, STAY IN THE HOUSE. VISITORS COMING.

The carers went in four times a day, to get her up and dress her, make breakfast and supervise her taking her medication, to do lunch, then tea and more medication, and then bedtime – which could be at any point between six and eight thirty.

Their appearance each time was a complete

21

and utter surprise to Phyllis.

Caroline's phone rang. *Mum.* 'Hello, Mum.'

'Is that you, Caroline?'

'Yes, Mum, hello.'

'It's me,' her mum said.

Caroline closed her eyes. 'Hello,' she said again.

'I wanted to ring you.'

'Yes,' Caroline said.

There was a long silence then, 'Is your father there?'

Not for the past twelve years. 'He's out,' Caroline said.

'Where's he gone?'

'To work. He'll be home later.'

'Can you tell him to bring some buttons? For tea.'

'Buttons. Will do. Bye for now.'

It's like the Talking Heads song, Caroline had emailed Gail at Christmas. *I keep thinking, how did I get here? What happened? Where did it all go?*

Don't beat yourself up, Gail had replied. *You've got two lovely kids – even if they are the devil incarnate ATM – a good man, a job you love. It could have been worse.*

And it could be a whole lot better, Caroline thought. Ah, well, things would change again. Maybe in ten years' time, with the kids through university all independent and adult. Her mother... Well, she wouldn't dwell on that. But maybe then she and Trevor could see a bit more of the world, fulfil some of their dreams. Visit Cuba and Mexico.

She had imagined herself moving to South America after graduation, making use of her

Spanish degree. She and Gail setting up something together: a language school or a holiday retreat where people could study and relax, or an exchange programme. The specifics were never clear. Then Gail had met Ethan, headed off to the States for a road trip with him and stayed.

Caroline had had to pay rent and bills so she'd taken a teaching job in a high school. Trevor had asked her out and, after a few months, moved in with her. One year, in the summer holidays, they'd made it to India, the next Thailand, before taking out a mortgage on their first home. Then the kids had come along.

She got out her Kindle. The weekend stretched ahead. She and Gail would drink too much and talk themselves hoarse, telling each other things they would never share with anyone else, not even their husbands. They'd complain and gossip and reminisce. For a whole forty-eight hours she would be Caroline. Not someone's mother, or someone's daughter, not someone's carer or wife or teacher. Just Caroline. Herself.

Naz

Naz checked up on the stock as the catering manager put the float into the till. Naz had spilt some coffee on his uniform jacket on the journey up. He had rubbed at it with cold water but the stain had spread.

He took off his name badge and pinned it over

23

the mark. It was a bit low on the jacket but better than before. Red wasn't a good colour for a uniform. When he opened his own restaurant, he'd have to think about that, what colour the uniforms should be. Most places it'd be black, innit. Black with a white shirt or those black tunics with the stand-up collars. But maybe the uniforms should go with the type of food. Naz wanted to do fusion, Indian and Western mix.

'Curry and chips?' his mum said, when he was explaining it one time. 'They already have that at the chippy.' She didn't get it. But she'd see, when he had a nice swanky place with thick white tablecloths and locally sourced ingredients.

'Halal, will it be?' That had been his big sister, winding him up.

'It's not going to be a curry house,' he said. 'It's going to be top rate, Michelin.'

His sister had choked on her food. She'd found it all hilarious. They always had to poke fun. Like when he'd got this job, which had taken for ever. He'd passed his catering HNC and applied to half the kitchens in Manchester, Stockport and Trafford, but got no offers. Meanwhile he'd helped out in the family shop. Then he'd finally got an interview. And they'd offered him the job. Full-time. No zero-hours malarkey. Solid.

'Train presentation assistant,' he'd announced to the whole family over tea.

'Which is what in plain English?' his dad grouched.

'Be pleased for him,' his mum said.

'I am, or I would be if I had a clue what he's actually doing.'

24

Naz wanted to stop the bickering before it started. 'Keeping things in order,' he said. 'Making sure everything is tidy and where it should be.'

'He's the cleaner!' His sister had clapped her hands. Everyone laughed.

His mother stopped giggling, wiped her eyes, then patted his hand. 'Well done. A job is a job and we're pleased for you, aren't we?' She'd stared at his dad.

Naz had helped himself to more dhal and rice.

'It's a rung on the ladder,' his dad had said.

'That's right,' his mum agreed.

'He clean the windows too?' his sister said. Naz ignored her.

'And a wage,' his mum said.

Naz had grinned.

'Oi, Naz!' the catering manager said now. Naz jumped – she'd a screechy voice. 'Chop-chop.'

'All ready.' Naz gathered up his bags.

'What's your badge down there for?' the catering manager said.

'A spill, innit.'

The catering manager pulled a face. 'Right. Time to feed the poor and huddled masses.'

She said that every time. Naz had no idea why or what it really meant. He waited while she made the announcement that the on-board shop was now open and listed all the things they sold.

If the restaurant went well, though, he might get his own TV show. Like Reza Mahammad on the Asian Food Channel. He ran the Star of India in London; he was the chef and the owner.

Maybe Naz could do cookbooks and merchandise, too. A range of sauces or ready meals.

A YouTube channel.

It happened, didn't it, the rags-to-riches stuff? Like a cousin of his mum's had started off with a market stall selling shoes and now he ran a whole supermarket chain in Pakistan.

Naz looked at his badge again. He wondered if he should swap it back. Or take his jacket off altogether. His shirt was clean.

'Earth to Naz,' said the catering manager.

'I'm going,' Naz said.

The train took a bend fast and the cans and bottles rattled in their shelves.

He'd need a name. He still liked Dawood's or Dawood's Dining. Or maybe Naz D's for the more street end. Same when you got people like Dynamo doing the magic on the streets, just an ordinary kid. Wouldn't work for the Cordon Bleu crowd. Maybe two ranges: high-end and a street-food spin-off. He smiled. He liked that idea. He really did. But would it confuse people?

He stepped into the next carriage and spoke clearly: 'Any rubbish, any empties or waste, thank you?'

Meg

Someone shrieked with laughter and Boss began barking. 'Quiet!' Meg yanked his lead, signalled him to lie down

'Boss.' Diana added her own reproach, still fussing about taking off her jacket and scarf. 'Can you?' She couldn't reach the overhead luggage rack.

Diana had been short to start with, Meg thought, but age was shrinking her – in one direction anyway. Meg gritted her teeth, nudged Boss out of the way and edged across the seat. She paused before levering herself into a standing position.

'Sorry,' Diana sighed, 'it's just–'

'It's fine,' Meg said. But anyone with a tin ear would have heard the exasperation in her voice. She shoved the clothing up with her right hand, ignoring the needle of pain in her shoulder.

'You're not taking yours off?' Diana said.

'Plainly,' Meg said.

Diana blinked.

'Come on, sit down,' Meg said. 'Tickets.' She nodded to the inspector coming their way. He stopped to check the group of businesswomen at the table opposite them, all fancy haircuts and dark suits. Clones, Meg thought. She'd never worn a suit in her life.

Diana sat down with a thump, more than filling the aisle seat. Boss wriggled between their feet, finding some space.

'Who's this, then?' the inspector said. 'Hello, hello.'

Boss looked up, tongue out, eyes full of canine adoration. Tart, thought Meg.

'I'd a Springer Spaniel before, lovely dog,' the man said. 'You taking her to see the sights?'

'Him,' Meg said.

'Him,' the man said. 'Good boy.'

Meg felt Boss's tail thud on her foot. She bit

27

her tongue.

'Walking holiday,' Diana said, 'the South Downs Way. We're starting in Winchester, then walking to Brighton. We'll have a couple of days at the seaside.' She passed him their tickets.

'So how far's that, then?'

'Sixty-five miles,' Diana said.

'You must be fitter than I am.' He stamped the tickets and handed them back.

Boss panted, looking up at the inspector as though he was the Second Coming.

Meg stroked the dog's head.

'We've done the Pennine Way but not all in one go,' Diana said. 'And before that Offa's Dyke and the Santiago Way in Spain – it's like a pilgrimage.'

Meg cleared her throat. She'd talk to anyone, Diana would. Prattle on about this and that. And people warmed to her. The weekly shop, the trip to the library took for ever, Diana's sociability making up for Meg's lack of it. Not that Meg went that often, begging off time in the studio at the back, *I just wanted to... I was thinking of...* The beginnings of any excuse and Diana would chime in, 'You stay. I'm perfectly happy going on my own.' But Diana wouldn't really be on her own: she'd be out and about with the great and the good of Buxton. Never mind that Diana had to drive in there every day for work as it was: five days a week, forty-odd weeks a year for at least twenty-five years, working in the procurement department of the High Peak Borough Council. Procurement. Just the word made Meg want to stick pins in her eyes.

'We both use walking poles now,' Diana was

28

saying. 'It helps with the knees.'

Will I manage? Meg wondered. She was getting breathless more and more often, weaker too. The guides rated the route as moderate. It was too late to back out now. And the holiday had been a making-up present after the most God-awful row. Diana in tears and Meg telling her to fuck off, that she was sick of being nagged, sick of Diana, her interfering and meddling, sick of the sight of her.

Of course, Meg had been pissed. She should have left the cottage before it had got to that point, gone out to the studio as soon as she felt the anger flickering inside her.

She had slept on the sofa that night, Diana in their bed above. Meg had been frozen, even with a log burner going, the sleeping bag and blankets. Cold and shivery and, as her anger had cooled, flames to ash and cinders, the shame had come, congealing thick, like grease.

She had lain on her back, staring at the old beams, the drab white plaster between them, listening to the night sounds, the wind snapping at the roof and the cry of a fox. Close to dawn, she heard crows and sheep from the farm next door. Boss got out of his bed in the kitchen, his claws clacking on the stone flags.

Meg had fed the stove and let Boss out, then made some tea for Diana and taken it up. The bedroom was icy, the heating only just coming on.

'Hello,' Diana said, her tone flat. She hoisted herself into a sitting position, tugged the pillow up behind her back.

'Tea?' Meg said.

'Thanks.'

Meg passed Diana her cup. There was a drilling pain between her eyes and her stomach was roiling.

'Are you not having any?' Diana said.

'I'll put some coffee on.'

Silence fell, apart from the birds outside, and a cow lowing.

'I'm sorry,' Meg said.

'It's just–' Diana said.

'I know,' Meg said. 'I'm a stupid bitch, Diana. You should know that by now.'

Diana gave a weak smile. Meg was not forgiven yet.

'What would you like to do?' Meg said. 'A break? Christmas in Venice? Berlin?'

'I don't want to put Boss in kennels again,' Diana said. 'He hates it. I hate it.'

'Something here, then,' Meg said. She really didn't care. Would've worked fifty-two weeks a year if she could, quite happy with the solitude. Which was how yesterday evening's row had started: 'We don't do anything together,' had been Diana's complaint. 'I'm just like your bloody housekeeper, except you don't pay me.'

'There's always the coastal path,' Diana said, and sipped her tea, 'the south-east.'

'That'd be good,' Meg said.

'If we wait until the spring, take a week.'

'Great.' Meg caught Diana's free hand and leant in to kiss her cheek, holding her breath as she felt the bile rise in her throat. 'You book a holiday week,' she had said, drawing back. 'We'll take it from there.'

30

'You've still got charcoal on your face.' Diana smiled, her eyes almost disappearing as her plump cheeks rose.

Meg had moved to look in the mirror. It was old, tarnished, a piece she'd salvaged when they'd moved in. She rubbed at the black smudges on her chin and cheekbone. I look like a hawk, she thought, hooded eyes, nose sharp and hooked, face gaunt. Her white hair stuck up at all angles. She had been a brunette most of her life. Now she was seventy, it was like looking at a negative of herself, only with more wrinkles. Haggard. Her eyes were still blue, bloodshot this morning but not rheumy. Small mercies. Oh, who cares? she had thought. Vanity was such a waste of energy but it had always been there. A looker, her dad had called her. A real looker.

'I hope the weather stays good for you,' the ticket man said now, as he moved away. Boss turned round twice, bumping Meg's legs, then sank to the floor.

'What a nice man,' Diana said, and shifted in her seat, her thigh warm against Meg's.

Meg grunted.

Behind them a child was wailing. Meg considered turning off her hearing aid. She leant her head against the window and gazed at the land they were passing. Flat, the Cheshire plain. Rich farmland. Cows, crops and hedgerows, ponds and wide fields, some strung with pylons.

It would be good to see the sea, to walk the chalk hills. She thought she'd manage one way or another, and when they came home, she'd have to find a way to tell Diana the truth.

Nick

'Shall we stop the train?' Lisa said. 'Shall we all get off and not go to London?'

Oh, good God, woman, Nick thought. We discussed this. Don't make threats, or promises, that you can't follow through on.

'No,' Eddie sobbed.

'Well, if you don't stop crying...' Lisa said. 'Evie's not crying, is she?'

Because she's asleep, you daft cow.

Eddie flung himself away from Nick, leaning his head on the armrest by the aisle, his shoulders jumping with each sob.

Nick looked up at the ceiling. He had known it would be a disaster. He'd suggested that if they had to go to the wedding...

'She's my sister, Nick. Of course we have to go.'

...at the very least they leave the kids with someone but, oh, no, the kids were welcomed, insisted on even. Who in their right minds wanted uncontrollable toddlers ruining their special day? But Lisa wouldn't listen to reason and here they were. Forty-eight hours of tantrums and hassle, all playing out in public. There was a pause in Eddie's weeping: had he fallen asleep? Nick opened his eyes.

Oh, for fuck's sake. The coloured girl opposite was playing peek-a-boo, hiding her face behind her hands, then parting them. 'Boo!'

Eddie laughed.

'Right,' Nick said. 'You've stopped crying, so you can sit by the window now.' He lifted Eddie, ignoring the fresh objection, 'I want to play', shuffled himself to the left and put his son down in the window seat.

'Good boy,' Lisa said.

Eddie looked bewildered, obviously unsure whether he'd won or not.

Nick didn't acknowledge the coloured girl. He'd already seen more than enough: flashy clothes, slathered in makeup. Lips that size, why would anyone want to draw attention to them by daubing them with lipstick?

He was going to vote UKIP in May. No question. The rest of them were all in it to line their own pockets, kowtowing to Europe. Eddie's nursery celebrated Chinese New Year. What was that all about? They'd do Ramadan too, and probably even the Jewish thing, Passover or whatever. English culture was being totally swamped. You celebrate St George's Day and you were as likely to be called a racist as a patriot.

Like all that mess with Clarkson. Best show on the telly, sold all over the world. A great British export with 350 million viewers. The man excels at what he does, but the loony lefties who've taken over the BBC play the political-correctness card at the first opportunity.

'Dad, a tractor,' Eddie said.

'Yes,' Nick replied.

'I want to go on a tractor again.'

'We will,' Lisa said. 'In the summer we'll go to the farm again.'

Nigel Farage talked common sense, and he was honest. His opinions might not suit everyone, not the bleeding hearts and the immigrants, but someone had to stand up to Brussels. Someone had to say, 'Enough is enough. If you want to come here, you contribute, no freeloaders, you integrate, you speak English, you don't take jobs from British workers.' Nick would ban the veil, like they had in France. The state of them, men in pyjamas, the women in floaty trousers and sandals. Sandals – even in the snow. If you used the word 'Paki', you got called a racist. It was just an abbreviation, like calling a Mancunian a 'Manc'.

'I'm hungry,' Eddie said.

'Can you get the sandwiches?' Lisa said to Nick.

He checked his watch. 'It's only eleven.'

'I'm a bit peckish, too,' she said.

Nick stood up and walked down the aisle. Someone had put a case on top of their holdall. He had to lift that down. Lisa should have told him to bring the holdall down to the seats – it would fit in the overhead rack.

Nick wasn't a racist, he was a realist. These mosques were breeding grounds for terrorists and the security services didn't have a clue. Let them go to Syria, any that wants to, that's what he'd do. Give up their citizenship if they were so keen on Sharia law and all that.

Back at the table, Eddie had moved into the outside seat and was pulling faces at the coloured girl. She was pulling them back, tongue poking out, thumbs in her ears, fingers waggling. And

Lisa was just sitting there, not doing anything about it. Encouraging it.

'Budge up,' Nick said to Eddie.

'I'm playing.'

'You're hungry, and your dinner's here. Now move,' Nick said.

He put the bag on the table and Lisa began to unpack it. Crisps, cheese and tomato rolls. She sorted Eddie out and gave Nick his, sat back and smiled.

'Horses.' Eddie jabbed his finger on the window. 'Horses.'

'Don't talk with your mouth full,' Nick said.

'Yours is full,' Eddie said, spraying wet crumbs over the table.

Nick swallowed quickly and was about to reply when Lisa said, 'Just eat your dinner. Then you can have a choccy bar and do some colouring-in.'

Nick checked his watch. Eleven ten. He felt the hours stretch out ahead, the whole of today, this evening, then the wedding, the meal, the evening do. Another night. The journey home. The utter bloody pointlessness of it all.

They were alongside a canal. Nick saw a road bridge ahead, a car heading up it. He imagined himself in the car, on his own, driving away. Leaving all this: the messy table, the kids, Lisa and the baggage. Just heading off.

Work was OK. He would still show up, or find an equivalent job somewhere else, a small town say, a market town. Somewhere with traditions to be proud of. He'd join the local cricket team, do some off-road biking, quad bike even.

He crammed the rest of the sandwich into his

mouth; no taste to it. He'd a craving for some-thing hot and salty and filling, steak and kidney pie or sausage and chips. The things that Lisa refused to cook, or only as a special treat since the doctor had warned him about his cholesterol level.

'Apple?' Lisa said, holding one up. Nick shook his head, leant back against the seat. Closed his eyes.

'Daddy's going to sleep,' Eddie crowed.

Nick clenched his jaw. Kept his eyes shut. He heard Lisa tell Eddie to shush and eat up his Wispa. He listened to the clatter of the wheels on the tracks and tried to shut out everything else. To forget everything else. To escape into the clack-clack-clatter and the rocking of the train. And the blessed darkness.

Rhona

Rhona had nearly rung in sick, but she knew if she did that Felicity would pounce on it as evidence of her lack of commitment, her failure to reach her personal targets as set out in her last performance review. She'd be all over her like a rash.

'You don't mind sitting backwards?' Felicity said, not so much a question as an instruction.

Rhona shrugged, 'No problem.' She noticed that Felicity hadn't asked Agata if she'd sit back-wards.

Rhona had taken time off recently when Maisie had chickenpox. And when she'd returned, Felicity had given two of Rhona's biggest clients to Agata, the Polish girl.

'The best way to ensure continuity of service,' Felicity said, when Rhona had queried it. And Felicity gave that smile, a wide beam, eyes flashing. Like an attack dog just before it strikes. Daring Rhona to be awkward, to protest.

Rhona didn't dare confide in Agata. Agata was smart, ambitious and as good as Rhona, if not better, at what she did, and the way Felicity worked was to isolate individuals for either favour or censure. Divide and rule. As line manager, she kept each of the team in her orbit and encouraged them to come to her and her alone, with questions or concerns. Rhona saw all of this, knew all of this – even understood the irony that the recruitment agency was itself riven by poor staff relations – but could think of no way out. Not until she'd secured another position, in Manchester or nearby. But that would mean a reference from Felicity and she could imagine how mealy-mouthed she would be.

Rhona pulled out the brochure for today's recruitment fair. They had a stand from one p.m. to eight. The plan was to stay at a budget hotel near the convention centre and travel back in the morning.

Rhona hadn't yet told Felicity that instead she would be getting the train straight back at the end of the day. She was still working out the best way to break the news: invent a phone call during the afternoon saying her overnight sitter had cancelled, or slip away from the others on the way to the hotel and text Felicity, explaining she was going straight to Euston, a domestic crisis. Surely staying overnight in a Premier Inn couldn't count as essential to her career development – though Felicity could easily put some spin on it, team-building time.

'Rhona?' Felicity said.

'Sorry?' Rhona said.

Felicity must have asked her a question and she'd missed it.

'I was telling Agata about the graduate fairs, our expansion in that field.'

Rhona's palms were warm, moist, she could feel sweat underneath her breasts. She undid her suit jacket. 'Aye, it's going well,' she said. She opened the brochure. Her eyes slid over the words, the images. *Sectors, positive attitudes, people solutions.*

Agata laughed at something Felicity said and Felicity smiled at her. A genuine wee smile, nothing like the blast of artificiality and vicious bonhomie she treated Rhona to these days. She couldn't let them force her out. She had to be strong. She had a fixed tenancy agreement so she'd be expected to pay the rent even if she lost her job. And the chance of winning a constructive-dismissal claim was slim, even if Rhona could stomach the thought of trying it.

Felicity knew exactly how to manipulate the situation so that there was never anything concrete for Rhona to document. The consultancy had their own guidelines on effective management and policies to prevent bullying in the workplace. Like all the other advice on offer, it said to keep a record but that was impossible.

A yawn grew in the back of her throat and she tried to resist it but failed, covering her mouth and feigning interest in the view in the hope that Felicity wouldn't notice.

'We keeping you up?' Felicity said, eyes bright.

'No.' Rhona tried to laugh. 'Just a bit stuffy in here.'

'You look tired,' Felicity said, head tilted to one side, brow creased in fake concern.

'I'm fine.' Rhona smiled, making it as broad and bold as she could. She never talked about Maisie at work, not these days, in case she gave Felicity any extra ammunition.

It was such a slog on her own. Her mum had come down from Glasgow for a couple of weeks when Maisie was first born. Since then she'd visited for a weekend or so when she could. The grind didn't get any easier. Day in, day out, getting Maisie washed, fed, dressed, then to the childminder. Picking her up, hours later, when she was cranky and tired. Home for bath and bedtime, which Maisie would drag out for as long as possible. Countless times when Rhona fell asleep beside her daughter, waking suddenly at one or two in the morning, her work suit crumpled, her chin tacky with drool. The weekends were a blur of chores and attempts at quality time. There was never anyone to pick up the slack, to take a turn. Never a lie-in or a couple of hours to herself. Beneath all the pressure and the work of parenting, Rhona felt a pull of love for Maisie that was inexplicable, visceral, a bond as strong as chains.

Sometimes in the bleakest moments she

wondered if she would have gone ahead with the unexpected pregnancy, the result of a fling with a stranger after a marriage party, if she'd known then what she knew now. She couldn't answer the question. The gap between before Maisie and after Maisie was so wide, immeasurable.

At least now that Maisie had started school Rhona didn't have to spend quite so much of her income on childcare.

Felicity was right. Rhona was tired. Shattered. She had been awake much of the night, Maisie wheezing and snatching at breath.

At close to three a.m. Rhona had almost called an ambulance, but then Maisie's breathing had improved and she'd slept until Rhona had woken her at seven thirty.

'You OK, chicken?' Rhona had asked.

Maisie gave a shrug of her thin shoulders.

'I'm taking you to school today,' Rhona said. 'Lesley will pick you up and you'll stay at hers for tea.'

Maisie nodded between spoonfuls of cereal. Her appetite was OK: that was a good sign.

'Why are you taking me?'

'Because I'm going into work late and I'm coming home late,' Rhona said.

'I'm wheezy, Mummy.'

Rhona's heart sank. 'You sound OK to me.'

'And I'm too tired.'

Of course she was tired – there were dark smudges under her eyes. But tomorrow was the weekend, time to catch up on sleep then.

'You've got your inhalers, haven't you?' Rhona said.

40

'Yes.'

'Show me.'

Maisie dug in her pocket and produced the blue inhaler.

'And your brown one?'

It was in the other pocket. 'Good girl.'

As she fastened Maisie's coat, Rhona half expected a tantrum, with the snot-drenched sobs that could trigger another attack, but Maisie was biddable.

Rhona almost hadn't mentioned it to Miss Blackledge – she could imagine the teacher telling Rhona she would have to look after Maisie herself, that it was irresponsible to send an ailing child to school.

'She was a bit chesty last night but she's got her inhalers,' Rhona said.

'It's tight,' Maisie whined. 'It hurts and I'm too tired.'

Rhona sighed and exchanged glances with Miss Blackledge, who gave her a knowing look.

'Maisie, I'd like you to come and help me take the register today, put in the ticks. Would you do that for me?'

Maisie nodded.

'Thank you,' Rhona mouthed. She had walked away, tension stiff across her back, drained already and dismayed at the prospect of the day ahead, being picked on by Felicity.

Now Rhona looked at Agata. 'Have you been to London much?'

'I was there for two years when I first came over.' Just the faintest trace of an accent, unlike Rhona's brogue, which Felicity had once described as impenetrable.

'Did you like it?' Maybe Rhona should look for work down south, more opportunities, but there everything cost more. And accommodation would be a complete nightmare. They said everyone but the rich was being forced out of London.

'Very much. Nearly as much as Manchester,' Agata said, and they all laughed. To Rhona it had sounded completely insincere.

A child was crying and the sound grated on her nerves, making her think of Maisie. She squashed the thought. She must focus on work. It was after eleven now: she'd be back home in twelve hours.

Rhona kept laughing, as though Agata was the wittiest woman on the planet, while she thought desperately for something else to say.

Saheel

Saheel had no idea if the seat next to him had been reserved. The system was down so it was impossible to find out. He had put his rucksack there straight away to deter anyone looking for a place, and no one had asked him if it was taken while they waited to leave at Piccadilly. Further down the carriage, people were squabbling about seats, the train was almost full. He'd done the journey a fortnight before. Then the reservations had been working and the seat next to him was reserved from Stockport, seven minutes away. It wasn't this exact seat, B15, but further down on the same side, B26. That time the person who'd reserved the seat hadn't shown up. Saheel had wondered why. If they'd had a crisis or something, been taken ill or had car trouble on the way to the station or if it was more mundane. Like businesses reserving seats way in advance to get cheap tickets, then using only some of them as their plans for meetings and travel changed. The train company would be quids in because the tickets weren't transferable.

His phone rang and he looked at the display. *Kulsoom*. His sister. He felt his guts tighten in irritation. He let the call go to voicemail. That girl was seriously out of control. She had no respect, no humility, no dignity. His parents were partly to blame, not setting a good example, not bothering to go to mosque, letting Kulsoom dress as she pleased. Aged thirteen and she was allowed to go here, there and everywhere, with no proper supervision. Who knew what types she was mixing with, what ideas she was getting? Kulsoom should stay at home. His mother should not be working, either. Saheel loved his family, of course he did, but they brought him shame. It was unnatural, blasphemous, the attempt by women to ape men. It had to be crushed. And proper rules put in place. That was something the Saudis understood. Rules for everyone: men and women. Look at his brother Arfan, neglecting his studies and hanging around with a bunch of losers, acting like a hoodlum, playing at making music.

His parents claimed they were proud of Saheel, over the moon at his A-level results, then at the unconditional offers to study chemistry at university, at his marks so far – top of his class in his first year and again this year so far. But if all that really mattered to them, how come Arfan hadn't got more than a cuff round the ear and a talking-to when he'd messed up his GCSEs so spectacularly that he had to resit? It was like one rule for Saheel, another for the rest of them.

When they pulled into Stockport, Saheel waited, fists clenched, willing the passengers boarding to keep walking past him and find places elsewhere. The woman opposite was sitting on her own too, shouting into her phone. Not angry, just loud, as though she was deaf or the other person was.

His wish was granted. Only Macclesfield and Stoke-on-Trent to go now. He rolled his shoulders back, flexed his legs.

In front of him a family was sitting at a table, bickering over sandwiches. The little boy stood up on his seat and looked over the top at Saheel. Saheel ignored him: he really could do without the attention. The kid went on staring at him, even said hello. Then the father said, 'Get down!' and he must have yanked at the boy because he disappeared like a shot.

His own phone pinged, a text notification. Kulsoom: *wen u home?* He shook his head, tongue pressing against the back of his teeth.

He was calm. A calm that he knew he could maintain if he didn't start looking into the future. In fact, he noticed when his mind strayed towards what lay ahead, it slid away, bounced off. It was as if a barrier, a magnetic pole, was repulsing him. It was a good thing, he thought, protecting him from any doubts that might try to take root. It was too late for doubts.

He stared out of the window at the new-built red-brick houses with narrow windows, the old sheds, warehouses and car parks, with cars glinting in the sun. And prayed to Allah for victory.

Holly

The kid was colouring in. Imagine having a dad like that, Holly thought, on your back all the time, cold and disappointed. Least, that was the way he'd come across. Maybe he'd had a bad night, maybe the baby had kept them all awake or he'd lost his job or his mum had just died. Maybe the rest of the time he was relaxed, enjoyed playing with the little boy, delighting in him. Yeah. Right.

She was restless, had read the same page in her magazine three times without taking any of it in.

Beside her, Jeff of the naff finger art was clicking on his phone, earbuds in. Gaming, she guessed. Yawn.

She fluffed at her curls, checked her own phone and scanned her Twitter feed, retweeted a funny photo of a kangaroo being chased by a rabbit, then watched a video of passengers who'd been on a plane that had made an emergency landing at Gatwick. Another showed a man chucking a rock at a car and the rock bouncing back to knock him out cold. It made Holly laugh.

Outside, the sky was blue with big white clouds, like in a kid's drawing. The sun shone bright, sparkling on the water where the fields were flooded. She could hear the women at the table behind chatting, one recounting some holiday horror story 'And the villa was locked, it was midnight and we couldn't even get in.'

The woman in the seat in front, oldish, dark blonde hair streaked with highlights, answered her phone and said, 'Hello,' then, 'I'm at home,' plain as you like. She even repeated it. Perhaps she was off for a dirty weekend. Or pulling a sickie.

Holly leant forward, hoping to hear more, opening her water bottle again, and she heard the woman say, 'I'll be back soon, Mum. See you later.' Which kind of killed the stories Holly had been dreaming up. Stone. Cold. Dead.

As she lifted the bottle, the train pitched to the left and Holly went with it, she leant to the right to compensate, and the train shook sharply right, then left again, and Holly chucked water over Jeff. Whose first thought was obviously to protect his phone, 'cause he moved like lightning, lifting up his arm. Then he pulled out his earbuds and glared at her.

'So sorry,' she said. 'It's only water.'

Jeff stared down and she did too, at the dark patch on his crotch. Holly looked away quickly, fighting the impulse to laugh.

'It'll soon dry,' she said.

'I look like I've—'

He did.

Totally inappropriate words zinged in her head. *I'd offer to rub it for you but...*

Get. A. Grip.

'So where are you going?' Holly said tightly.

He raised his eyes. His eyebrows were dark, unruly. 'London.'

Comedian. 'You're on the right train, then,' she said.

'That's a relief,' he said.

'Work?' Holly said.

'Interview.'

'Whoo-hoo,' she said. 'For?'

He hesitated.

'State secret, is it? MI5? You can apply for them online, swear down.'

'Apprenticeship,' he said. He blinked, took off his specs. His eyes were this intense blue, sapphire, maybe, or lapis lazuli, like the stone. She remembered that from the design and decor module on her degree course: how colour created mood, how to use it with a theme to tie elements together, giving cohesion, clarity. She'd used that blue, lapis lazuli, with gold for a charity ball design.

'Apprenticeship in?' Holly said.

'IT coding.'

Bound to be something like that. He was a geek, only had to look. The frowsy hair, the specs. The way he couldn't meet her eyes, too, that awkwardness.

'You like that, the coding?'

'Yeah,' he said, though he didn't sound very sure. 'I think it'd be all right.'

Holly laughed. 'You might want to sound a bit

47

more enthusiastic in the interview. Or is it a done deal?'

'No, no, only stage one. There's two interviews, then you do an assessment session, practical.'

'So what have you been doing before?' she said. Hard to tell how old he was. Could be anywhere from eighteen to twenty-three, twenty-four.

'Not much,' he said. 'What about you?' He was blushing. Poor kid, he really didn't like being in the spotlight.

'Just got a new job. Event-management assistant. They're sending me down for training – health and safety, weekend course. So this afternoon I'm hitting the shops.'

'Event management? Parties and that?'

'Can be anything, parties, product launches, conventions, weddings, fundraisers. Anything at all.'

'Cool,' Jeff said.

'It's hard work,' Holly said.

'Yeah?'

'Swear down. It's not all champagne and party poppers. Not for those working on it. We've got to organize every little thing: venue, catering, car parking, stationery, branding, entertainment, corporate hospitality, comfort facilities...'

He looked puzzled.

'Toilets,' she explained, 'baby changing, chill-out zone, first aid. It's manic, I tell you, but you have to keep it all under control. I can't believe I finally got something. I left uni in June, right, and applied for six jobs a week, all over the country. Sometimes more. I got three interviews in all that time until last month when I applied for this.'

'Thirty-nine weeks, that's two hundred and thirty-four jobs. Less than two per cent,' he said.

'What?'

'Ratio of applications to interviews. One point two eight per cent, so nearer to one per cent, actually.'

'Human calculator,' Holly said. He went pink again. 'I could do you a mock interview, get some practice,' she offered.

'No, you're all right.' He looked panicked. Put his specs back on. 'There's some stuff...' He tapped his phone. 'Stuff, you know, things to go over.'

Crap liar.

'OK.' Holly glanced as quickly as she could at the water on his trousers. 'You could always use the dryer in the toilet,' she said, 'if it–'

'It'll be cool.' Jeff put his earbuds back in and swiped at his screen.

Trust her to get stuck next to an antisocial geek. Some job interview role-play would have passed the rest of the journey nicely. Or even a bit of conversation. Holly stretched. Maybe she'd go to the shop, get a mocha.

He sat, stooped over, both thumbs flying across the screen. His hands were large with slim fingers, nice hands if it weren't for the bitten-down nails and the rubbish tatts. All that maths genius stuff. Who thinks like that? OK, at work she'd know her budget, could figure out numbers attending, catering price per head. With a calculator.

Last year had been the year of the geek. Those movies about scientists, Alan Turing and Stephen

Hawking. Eddie Redmayne had beaten Benedict Cumberbatch to the Oscar. Not her type, none of them. Thing was, 'her type', when she did hook up with anyone, never really lasted. She liked them good-looking, someone with the wow factor. It'd be fine for a few months, then either she'd get bored or they'd start moaning that she was always out, that she put friends and work first, that she was only interested in herself. Or they'd go off and shag someone else. Never. A. Good. Move. At which point she pressed the reset button: young, free, single.

And so much freer now. In time the job would mean she could leave home, rent a place of her own. If she worked hard, which she would, she'd work like a dog, there'd be promotion, more money. Maybe one day her own company.

She smiled. Well happy. So, right, she'd get a mocha or a cappuccino and then have a look online, see what the trends were for the coming summer season, work out where she might try down Oxford Street. Bit of retail therapy, shop till she dropped. *You go, girl.*

Kulsoom

Kulsoom had rung Saheel, then texted him, and he'd just blanked her. She made herself a hot chocolate and got a Mars bar out of the tin. Maybe she should leave that – there were only two left. She put it back, took her drink into the

50

living room and clicked on the TV. Someone was burbling about Zayn Malik leaving One Direction.

It *was* a teacher-training day, though, wasn't it? Like a holiday. And holidays were for treats, weren't they? Kulsoom went back and fetched the sweet, unwrapped it and dipped the end into her mug, held it until the chocolate had melted and the toffee was soft, then put it into her mouth. Bliss. She sucked the melted layer off and it was all smooth and rounded, like the shape of an ice-cream cone or a lolly. She dipped it again.

Saheel should know she wouldn't ring if it wasn't a total emergency. She couldn't ask Mum or Dad, they were at work, and Arfan had gone round to his mate's to play *Call of Duty*, even though he was supposed to be revising and staying at home with Kulsoom 'in case'. Like she needed babysitting. That was so lame. Like she wouldn't know what to do if there was a disaster. She'd be better than Arfan if there was a fire or someone collapsed outside and Kulsoom had to call an ambulance, do CPR and be in the papers, then get a special award and all that shit.

Besides, she liked being in the house on her own. She could get on with her project without anyone butting in and telling her to do stuff or move or clear up. Except she couldn't now because her stupid lame computer had crashed. She'd told Dad it had been going slow for ages and freezing and maybe had a virus and he just said, 'We're not made of money. You're not getting a new one while that is still functioning.'

'But it's not–'

'It's probably corrupted,' Arfan had said.

She stared at him to see if he was winding her up. That was the sort of thing Saheel said all the time: they were corrupted, decadent. If you breathed the wrong way you were an infidel.

'Make sure you have everything backed up and then if it dies we can do a reset,' Dad said.

Well, it had died. And she couldn't do a reset, even if she'd known how, because the stupid dumb thing wouldn't even turn on. So she needed another computer.

There was a travel segment on the telly about holidays on long train journeys, the Orient Express and the Maharajas' Express in India. Then they were talking about Asian cities and there was Rawalpindi. Kulsoom groaned and shuddered. She ate another mouthful of the Mars bar, the toffee clinging to her back teeth.

She hated Pakistan. After their trip last year, which had been her first, she'd vowed she would never, ever, ever go there again. It was too hot, it smelt rank and she'd spent the whole time being picked on by all the aunties, who'd thought it was their job to turn her into some sort of house slave who couldn't think for herself. They even hit her. Slapped her arms or her head and shouted at her. She'd gone to her mum in tears, and Mum said she'd speak to them: they didn't understand how different life was in the West. 'They're calling me names too,' Kulsoom had said, wiping her eyes fast because she was angry more than anything else, and it was child abuse and Pakistan should have ChildLine.

Mum had talked to the aunties, and they had

spent the rest of the time glaring at Kulsoom, who stayed close to her mum. She wished her grandfather would hurry up and die so they could just go home. She hated her cousins, who called her a dirty girl and other words she didn't understand. One spat on the floor when Kulsoom went past. That was dirty, that was filthy, but no one smacked her.

The whole family hated it, really. Well, maybe not Saheel so much: he was being such a Goody-Two-Shoes. It was easier for her brothers but they still had to watch what they said when the older generation were around.

All because her grandfather had been taken ill and Dad had been called back, and he'd felt guilty because he hadn't taken the family over since just after Arfan was born so none of them had even met Kulsoom. She wished it had stayed that way.

She made her hands into a megaphone. 'Don't go to Pakistan,' she told the women on the screen. Kulsoom remembered getting to the airport in Lahore for the flight home and her mum had started to sing some weird song about country roads taking her home and her dad had got the giggles. Saheel had scowled and made a point of going to find the prayer room as they went through to the departure lounge.

Slumped on the sofa Kulsoom shook her hips, and her belly made that sloshing sound, like a hot-water bottle. She had two weeks to get the project finished and she needed every second because it took hours to get enough photos for just a couple of minutes. Miss Weston had said,

'Why not make it with Flash or another software program, use graphics, and you can still tell the same story?' But Kulsoom had wanted it to be stop-motion. She'd wanted to use Plasticine for the animals. She'd wanted it to be old school, even though it would take ten times longer. She'd done the titles and wanted to upload those photos and get that bit edited. Make sure it came out how she wanted it before she started on the story.

She didn't know where Saheel was. He could be at uni doing experiments. Or he could have gone to the mosque. Probably had, Friday after all. She texted again. If he didn't reply it was his own fault and she'd just borrow his laptop and do what she needed. He wouldn't even know unless he came in when she was in the middle of it.

She burped and finished the Mars bar. She picked up her mug and drained the hot chocolate. Checked her phone. Nothing.

Kulsoom went and put the bolt on the front door. If Saheel came back soon then he couldn't get in. And she'd be able to take her memory stick out, close down his laptop, put it back in his room, then let him in. She could say she'd been scared about burglars. Arfan might get into trouble then, though. But that was his fault, really. She'd only say that if she really had to.

And if Saheel realized somehow what she'd been doing, she'd make him see that she hadn't had a choice. The project was brilliant, even Miss Weston said so. The concept, the ambition of it was close to A-level standard, that was what she'd said, and Kulsoom was only in year eight. And when everyone saw what an amazing filmmaker she was, and she won awards and the Oscars, and her films were on TV at Christmas every year and boxsets, then he'd see how it important it was, wouldn't he? They'd all see. He should be pleased to have a genius in the family, and the least he could do was lend her his laptop when her PC died.

CHAPTER TWO

Jeff

When Holly came back from the shop with a drink, Jeff realized he was thirsty, hungry too. Someone somewhere in the coach was eating something hot. It smelt like chips but he didn't think they'd do chips on the train – pasties maybe or paninis. He had planned to wait until after his interview to buy some scran, because if he got really stressed and felt like throwing up, it'd be easier to keep it together on an empty stomach. But maybe he was overthinking it.

He imagined greasy sausage rolls, cloying flapjacks, cheese and onion crisps, then checked for any of the usual signs of nausea: a rush of saliva in the mouth, that clutching sensation in his guts, sweat on the back of his knees and his neck. Nothing. He could risk it.

Could he, though?

His stomach growled and he held his breath,

but Holly obviously hadn't heard anything over the noise of the train. It wasn't just the wheels on the tracks that made a noise but the air conditioning too, roaring away. If his stomach did that at the interview, sounding like a drain, oh man, it would be total humiliation.

He'd hang on for another ten minutes, and if he still felt hungry, he'd go and buy something. He Googled stomach noise, rumbling they called it, and read a bit about diseases and conditions – coeliac, Crohn's, diverticular disease, but not all the symptoms fitted – and then his phone vibrated. A text from his gran: *hi jeff hope u do really well toady I well b thinkin of u v proud of*

Then another: *hi jeff I HOP u do rally well toast I will b thik i*

Jeff groaned. Waited. Sure enough, *dunno wot is wrong with this PHone but hav fun in London do dont worry just do ur best lol x nana goin 2 town this aft wot do twins want 4 bday*

She never used punctuation and it drove him up the wall. And he'd told her 'lol' meant 'laugh out loud' but she wasn't having it.

He sent a short reply: *Ta Nana. No ideas for twins. Soz x.*

His stomach gurgled again.

'Eat something decent.' That was what his mum had said last year when he got ill. 'No wonder you're throwing up. You'll get an ulcer with all the junk you eat. And obese.'

'Obese?' Sean had said. 'Look at the size of him. He's a beanpole.'

'Well, he should be obese,' she said.

'It's my metabolism,' Jeff said. 'I burn it up.'

'You chuck it up. Oh, God!' She'd clapped her hand to her mouth, eyes on stalks. 'Is it bulimia? He's bulimic.' She'd turned to Sean. 'He's blooming bulimic.'

'I'm not,' Jeff said.

She always had to make things even worse than they already were.

'Then what's going on?' she said.

If she'd still been shouting it might have been different but she'd said it quietly, gently, and Jeff's eyes had stung. Then he couldn't hold back the tears but he couldn't explain either. It was all such a fucking mess. All of it.

'Christ, Jeff, what is it?' she said.

But he couldn't speak. He'd just kept wiping his eyes and choking and she'd gone to hug him. Then he'd heard the twins coming in and he hadn't wanted them to see him like that. So he'd gone upstairs and got into bed with all his clothes on because he couldn't stop shivering, and the only way he thought he'd be able to deal with it was if he was asleep and not thinking, not feeling.

Remembering it now, he felt echoes of those feelings, distant, paler, weaker, but they didn't overwhelm him any more. He'd learnt in the counselling sessions that it was possible to think of them, even to mention them, without every-thing crashing down around him. He held out his hand. Hardly a tremor.

'You're not thinking of having the other one done too, are you?' Holly said. Her mouth was puckered up in a grin, her eyes flashing a chal-lenge.

'No,' Jeff said. He decided to go on the

offensive. 'You not got any tattoos?'

She lifted her knee, the one next to him, twisted her leg. He saw the hummingbird just above her ankle.

'Nice,' he said.

'It is,' she agreed, looking at it for a few moments, her foot still raised.

She hadn't got any tights on, or stockings, just bare legs, high heels, skin the colour of treacle toffee. Jeff felt a bit dizzy. He swallowed – his throat was really dry. 'I'll just...' He pointed to the aisle.

'Sure,' she said, still smiling.

Was she laughing at him? Messing with him? She was. Was she? He checked his trousers, the dark patch still visible but who would be looking there anyway? And if he swung his arms a bit, he could hide it some of the time.

Holly stood up and Jeff clambered out.

The little boy said, 'He's got long hair like a girl.'

His mother told him to shush.

'He has, Mummy, look.'

The dad was pretending to be asleep.

Jeff set off past the woman on the phone, who sounded like she was close to losing it, talking a bit too slowly with that heavy sort of patience, one hand clutching her hair. The guy on the opposite side of the train, only a young guy, had a full beard. They were all the rage, that hillbilly style, though this guy was Asian so he probably wasn't rocking the same image as the hipsters.

Jeff had never tried to grow a beard, not sure he had what it took. When he'd been ill he'd not shaved and all he'd got was a sprinkling of bristles scattered around. Not the sort of thing you could cultivate. There was probably a gene for hairiness, or was it just down to hormones? Because people changing gender, they took hormones, didn't they? Male or female, depending on which way they were going. Were hormones down to genes, though? He'd look it up.

Jeff reached the end of the carriage and realized he'd come the wrong way. This was coach A. Coach C (for café) was the other direction. He felt himself blush. A beard might be good for that, hiding the blushes. He wondered whether he could cover his mistake with a visit to the bog first but the smell was still rank and he didn't like to think what might be in there. It could well put him off his food.

He walked back past the bearded guy and the stressed phone woman, by Holly and the family. Why hadn't he noticed which way Holly had gone when she'd been to the shop? She wiggled her fingers at him. Had she said nothing on purpose, waited for him to make a knob of himself? Had he said he was going to the shop? He couldn't remember.

There was a dog sitting in the aisle, a brown spaniel. As he got closer it jumped up at him, shoving its nose in his crotch.

'Boss!' the old women with it shouted, and the dumpy one said, 'I'm so sorry.' And the scrawny one said something to the dog, who slunk under the seats straight away.

The businesswomen at the table on the left all made 'Aw' noises, obviously on the side of the dog.

Jeff said, 'Cool, no worries.' And escaped past them. His heart was going too fast but it was just the suddenness, the shock, that was all.

He reached coach C. Maybe they did have chips: something smelt brilliant.

His phone vibrated: Gran. *did u get my text x*

Yes. No idea 4 twins x he replied. Then he looked at the sandwiches.

He picked a BLT and asked for a coffee.

'Four pounds fifteen,' the woman said. 'Milk and sugar's there.'

Jeff helped himself. He'd still have five pounds eighty-five left from Gran's tenner.

Back at his seat, he took everything out of the paper bag. He ate the sandwich first, watching the scenery, a tractor ploughing a field, the next field dotted with dark brown molehills.

He eased the plastic lid off the coffee, tore open the packets of sugar and poured them in. The milk was in long, thin, plastic sachets, a bit like you got for ketchup and mustard. He read the instructions, studied the diagram: 'Tear here.'

Carefully he pulled, like it said, and a jet of milk squirted all over his hand and onto the tray table. *Fuck!* He squirted the rest into his drink.

'Designed by sadists,' Holly said. 'I always get a latte or a cappuccino so you don't have to use them.'

'There must be a knack to it,' Jeff said, trying the next one, which made even more of a mess, some of the milk landing on his shirt cuff.

'The knack is not to use them,' Holly said.

Great. So now he'd smell of sour milk and his hands were all sticky, too. He'd have to go and

60

wash them when he'd finished his drink.

He patted the lid back onto the cup.

'Want a wipe?' Holly said.

'What?' Jeff said.

She rummaged in her bag and brought out a pack of hand wipes. 'Be prepared,' she said.

He was about to refuse, then thought of how he'd rather clean up without getting out again to find another bog, so he said, 'Cool, yeah. Thanks. They teach you that at event management, did they?'

'Of course. Hand wipes, safety pins and a sonic screwdriver.'

He liked the *Doctor Who* reference.

The wipe smelt of lemon and something a bit medical, like pine or menthol.

He opened his phone, Googled hormones and genes and beards, found out that the things were linked but you had to have the hairy genes in the first place; Asian people had less hair and Native American men didn't have beards.

His email notification sounded, a job alert from one of the sites he was registered with. Customer services assistant, details on the vague side but it did say minimum wage. Maybe he didn't need to apply; if he got accepted as an apprentice he could ditch the job search. But how likely was that, realistically? He should try anyway. He filled in the form, cutting and pasting stuff about his educational achievements, his referees, work experience (N/A), along with chunks from his CV altered to fit the categories on the form.

Imagine if he got offered both. Hah! Fat chance.

'Stay positive,' his mum used to say, when he got really down about the future, or the fact that he didn't have much of a future. That all he could see was months and years of trying for shit jobs that paid shit money, living at home for the rest of his life, Billy No Mates, while everyone he knew got decent jobs and got married and had their own place and made a life.

That was a joke, her telling him to stay positive when she could've set herself up in business as a doom-monger, one of those mythical people... Cassandra, was it? Always trying to warn people about disaster. He typed in Cassandra. Yep – gift of prophecy but never believed.

He checked over the job application and sent it in.

Jeff drank his coffee. He wondered if anyone had written to complain about the milk sachets, how they were a really crap design and should be scrapped. Someone should. Maybe he would. He began composing it in his head. Dear Sir/Madam, I recently travelled on the 10.35 service from Manchester Piccadilly to London Euston...

Caroline

Caroline's phone rang again. She should switch it off. Or not answer it, then check her voicemail. She had promised herself that she *would* switch it off, once she'd met Gail, then check every few hours. The carers would be going in and, with it being the weekend, more of the neighbours would be around. They knew the situation and would help raise the alarm in case of a crisis. Caroline glanced at the display but it wasn't Mum: it was an unknown number.

'Hello?'

'Mrs Thornicroft?'

'Yes, hello.'

'This is Alaric Jenkins, from Xaverian Sixth Form College.'

'Yes.' Her heart sank. Paddy or Amelia?

'I'm afraid Amelia isn't in college. She's missed her morning sessions.'

Caroline considered for all of a millisecond whether to lie and say Amelia was at home with a tummy bug and she, Caroline, hadn't remembered to notify the office. But it was too late for that, really. Amelia was on a final warning. If Caroline did invent excuses, Mr Jenkins would probably know it. And the situation needed facing head on.

Caroline had made the same sort of calls to parents of her own students. She knew how it worked. Sometimes it was something apparently trivial – the end of a relationship or a shift of friendship group – that saw the decline in attendance. At others, the student was struggling, floundering on the wrong course, fed up with education in general or reacting to troubles at home.

'Oh dear,' Caroline said. 'I really thought she was improving. I don't know where she is. She left for college at the usual time.'

'We'll need to speak with her again,' Mr Jenkins

said. 'I'm afraid this means she'll be asked to withdraw.'

'Yes.' Caroline was furious with Amelia. And sad, too, that she was chucking it all away. Without A levels, getting a decent job would be very hard. These days even graduates were competing for work as baristas and waiters and sales assistants.

'I'm away for the weekend now,' Caroline said, 'but I'll speak to her and we'll be in touch on Monday.'

'Thank you. We'll talk then.'

Bloody Amelia. Bloody, bloody Amelia. Caroline tried her daughter's number but there was no reply and she didn't trust herself to leave a message.

As soon as she hung up her mother was on the line again.

'Mum?' Caroline said.

'Who's this?'

'Caroline.' She pressed her spare hand against the back of the seat, her knuckles white. The train rattled through a deep cutting, the embankment sides steep, covered with dead grass leached of colour.

'I can't find them,' her mother said.

'Find what, Mum?'

'The things.'

'They'll turn up, I expect,' Caroline said.

'Nobody's here.' Her mother's voice grew tremulous. 'I haven't eaten for days.'

'Someone will be there soon,' Caroline said, 'to give you your lunch.'

Silence.

'Mum?'

'Who is this?'

Oh, for fuck's sake. Caroline drew a long breath in through her nostrils. 'It's Caroline.'

'I haven't seen anyone all week,' her mother said. 'Where have they all gone?'

'They'll be there soon,' Caroline said. 'I'll ring you later. Bye, Mum.'

She hung up. Her finger hovered over the power-off button.

Half an hour, she thought. Perhaps she could turn it off for half an hour then check. Before she did, she texted Trevor: *Amelia AWOL again. Mr Jenkins wants to meet Mon. Will call you tonight x.* She didn't expect a reply; Trevor would be run off his feet, the job getting harder all the time as the service was slashed back to the bone. Efficiency savings they called it – double-speak for cuts. There was a constant battle to try to retain the ambulance service within the NHS but private firms continued to circle, hungry and ruthless. Non-emergency transport had been flogged off to the lowest bidder, a bus company, a couple of years earlier. Their track record since had been pitiable.

'It was never meant to make a profit,' Trevor would say. 'The NHS has been fighting to break even ever since it was founded. So they want to take a struggling service, hack it up and sell the parts. Then it's run as a business. It's a service, the clue's in the name, to serve us at times of need.'

But there was money to be made, so the money from the tax revenues, the money that we all put

65

in, would now line the pockets of the corporations who called the shots. The same ones who wanted to avoid tax and lobbied and bribed government officials and moved their centres of production around to minimize labour rights and costs and maximize profits.

They think the NHS is a Commie plot over here, Gail had emailed when there was all the hoo-ha about Obama's health-care reforms.

What on earth would Amelia do now? Was the poor attitude to her studies a direct reaction to her mother working in education? Was she cutting off her nose to spite her face?

Amelia had shown such flair early on, an aptitude for geography, biology and sport. So far her antics hadn't infected Paddy. He had always been the more settled and was on track to get his A levels. He'd applied to uni and had accepted conditional offers from Warwick and Portsmouth. He was insolent and moody at times, but less so when his sister was away. Perhaps the separation would help them both. Paddy would go off and start an independent life, and Amelia would find her feet, one way or another.

Caroline had read all the studies about adolescent brain development, how the parts of the cortex responsible for impulse control, decision-making and planning didn't mature until the twenties while those parts involved in emotional responses, in pleasure and instant gratification, were heightened during the teens. Adolescence was genetically engineered to be a time of greater risk-taking and thrill-seeking. That made sense – it matched the anecdotal information that everyone shared. But it didn't actually make it any easier to deal with the manifestation of it.

Caroline thought of her own teenage years. She could still remember the peaks and troughs of emotion, the impatience, the overwhelming importance of her friends, her disdain for her parents, the ill grace with which she carried out the chores expected of her. All at her mother's bidding: peel the potatoes, set the table, do the ironing.

There were no explosive arguments – it was as if Caroline didn't feel she had any right to be openly obstreperous – and when her mother criticized her (often) or reprimanded her (less often), Caroline would swallow the resentment and curse her silently. She'd known that the only escape was a place at university where, once she'd achieved her goal, she combined an odyssey of experimentation, recklessness and hedonism with the dedication required to pass her course.

'My mother never hugged me,' she'd told Gail one night, as they sprawled on the floor, sharing their life stories, drunk and stoned, talking until the early hours. 'She never told me she loved me. Her whole life she's been ... not exactly miserable but a little disappointed. She was always on guard. And everything had a downside.'

Caroline had rolled onto her back and stared up at the sari she had draped across the room to hide the watermarks on the ceiling.

'It was all planned and controlled. I never knew her do anything out of the blue, not even agree to stay half an hour longer somewhere.'

'Did you ever gang up on her, you and your dad? Take charge?' Gail had asked, passing Caroline the joint.

'God, no. I think she'd have imploded.' Caroline had laughed, then choked on the smoke and had to get up to fetch a drink. 'What if I turn out like her?' she'd asked Gail, leaning on the doorjamb.

'Not possible,' Gail had said. 'You'll be an old hippie, or a New Ager. You'll live in a tepee and your kids will run wild.'

That prediction had never come true but Caroline had been tactile with the kids, made sure to tell them how much she loved them. Though whenever they accused her of bossing them about she felt a twinge of panic, that maybe she was too controlling as well.

The train passed by a village church, squat and dark, St George's flag flying from the square tower, a graveyard beside it watched over by large, dark-green yew trees. Friesian cows were grazing in the next fields, the soil black mud where they'd churned it up.

Is it awful to want her dead? Caroline thought. Because, if I'm honest, I do. Partly for selfish reasons, because I don't want another fifteen or twenty years of this, of more and more problems, of care homes and feeding cups and incontinence pads. And partly because this lack of control, this loss of authority, of agency must cut her to the quick. All her life she's been in charge, run everything just so, and now she simply can't.

The GP had diagnosed Phyllis with depression

last year and she was on medication, but Caroline couldn't see that it had helped much. Her mother's life was an endless cycle of fretting and dislocation, fear, confusion and anger. Would that change as the disease progressed? As more and more lesions ate away her brain? Might that loss of cognition bring with it contentment or at least an absence of negative emotion? That would be a blessing. Caroline couldn't remember the last time she'd seen her mother laugh, not that she'd ever been big on laughter. Couldn't even remember her smiling in recent months. And what sort of life was that for anyone?

Naz

'Thank you, sir.'

Naz swung his bag round to the other side. 'Thank you, miss.'

There was a problem with the toilet in coach A. He'd told the train manager, who'd given him an out-of-order notice and he'd stuck that on. Bit of a stink all round but they didn't give him anything he could use. No Febreze or Airwick or whatever.

He moved into coach B. 'Empties, please. Any rubbish?'

He knew there was a dog about halfway down. Naz hadn't got anything against dogs, he liked the idea of a dog, but he'd been bitten once, on his calf – the scars were still there. Man, it had hurt. He'd had to go to A and E, stitches, the works, innit. A pit-bull type had got loose in the park. Naz and his mates were having a kickabout and the dog had gone for him. Taken three of them to pull the beast off. Kicking it in the head till it let go.

Since then, it was like he was a marked man, like the dogs could smell the scars, wouldn't leave him alone.

Maybe when he was rich he'd get his own dog and break the jinx. Something smart, a Dalmatian or an Afghan Hound. Then, if he smelt of dog, the other dogs would treat him better.

'Excuse me.' A lady sitting on her own stopped him. She pointed. 'That toilet isn't working.'

'That's right,' Naz said, 'I've just put a sign on it. There's another one at the far end of this coach.' Then he remembered to add, 'Sorry for the inconvenience.'

She rolled her eyes and gave him a smile. Reached out with a fistful of tissues and dropped them into his sack. 'You'd think they could get it sorted out,' the lady said. 'They can plan a mission to Mars but a working toilet's beyond them.'

Naz didn't think it was the same company. He wondered whether to point that out but decided it was easier just to agree.

He turned to check the other side; the young guy, Asian with a beard, university hoodie on, was pretending to be asleep. Naz could tell, the way he had his shoulders, the tilt of his head – too stiff. When people did fall asleep they lolled all over the place. You got snorers and people with their mouths hanging open and dribblers. It still made Naz laugh on the inside when they startled awake and looked round dead shifty, like they'd done something wrong. Or they'd try to cover up the fact they'd just woken up and act like they'd been reading or looking at the view all along.

You could show clips like that on YouTube, couldn't you? Set it to music, get loads of hits. You'd need a camera, though, and someone like Naz wouldn't be allowed to do it, invasion of privacy or something, even though there was CCTV on the train.

Maybe the guy was pretending to be asleep to stop the lady chatting to him. Some passengers, most of them probably, wanted to be left alone. Like, even though they were in public, on public transport, they pretended not to be. You got that even more in first class, all in their separate bubbles.

Naz moved down to the next seats, the family at the table. The lady had a load of rubbish and passed it to him. The baby was asleep in its chair thing. It was fat and pink with no hair and dressed in a bright pink onesie. Really ugly. Hopefully it'd grow hair and get better-looking.

'Thank you,' Naz said.

The girl to his left dropped her coffee-cup into his bag and smiled at him. 'Cheers.'

Someone like that, lovely smile, neat dresser, someone like that could be his maitre d'. Set the tone for his restaurant: modern, stylish, not snotty. Welcoming.

Naz looked for the dog. It was between the two old ladies. They didn't have any rubbish. A lady with the group opposite asked him how long the shop would be open.

'Most of the way,' Naz said. 'We reach Euston at twelve forty-three ... so we'll be closing around twelve thirty. There'll be an announcement.'

'Thank you.'

Naz waited a moment to see if she wanted to ask anything else but she didn't speak and he was aware of the dog only a few feet away. It made his skin tingle.

He moved on before calling out again, 'Any more rubbish, please?' He liked to see a clean carriage. People were helpful usually, glad to get shot of their empty coffee cups and old copies of *Metro*. The stag dos were the worst. And the hens, the same. Like their mission was to make as much mess as possible, and as much noise. And it wasn't just cans and bottles and food wrappers: there'd be Crazy Foam and glitter all over the place, silly string and grease-paint. And some of them, the real morons, had to find someone to pick on, a person to insult or make fun of. Naz got it sometimes or a passenger, the pissheads making comments like he was there for their entertainment. He hated that.

But he just had to put up with it because, unless they actually became properly abusive or got physical, the train manager couldn't act. Though one time this group of women made racist comments at him, and as Naz was trying to decide whether to report it or not, another passenger did. Already past Stoke they were and the train manager contacted British Transport Police and then he told the women that they'd be met at

Euston. The language they used was unbelievable. The manager told Naz he needn't do coach A, where they were all sitting, but Naz thought that wasn't fair on the rest of the passengers. So he carried on but he ignored their tables and the nasty, muttered comments: the legs that were trying to trip him up.

Naz had been bricking it in case he had to go to court. In the end they were just given a warning.

Why couldn't people behave? Be nice. He didn't get it. Like, you've one life, innit, one chance, why spend it acting like a dick?

Meg

The girl opposite, the younger blonde one, had exquisite bone structure, cheekbones high and round, a long straight nose, pointed jaw. As though someone had grabbed her face, dragged the raw clay down and scooped out those hollows. A face like that brought to mind ethereal, mythic forms. Meg could imagine a figure in bronze, androgynous, shaved head. Somewhere like the Yorkshire Sculpture Park.

Things had gone quiet on that front over the last few years. Berlin had been her last commission, 2008. The Germans loved her stuff. God bless the bloody Germans. There had been talk of a retrospective – her agent had been talking to the Hepworth – but the silence since had been brutal.

Everyone was still in thrall to conceptualism, for fuck's sake, goggle-eyed with new technology. Badly shot videos and loops of sound, empty boxes in empty rooms. Meg wasn't a Philistine: she knew there was more to art, to sculpture, than Rodin's *Kiss* or Da Vinci's *David*. But, these days, if it wasn't multi-platform or digitally transformed or didn't need a tedious essay to explain every sniff, scratch and fart of the creative process, stuffed with four-syllable words and ruminations on agency, praxis, relational aesthetic and semiology, it didn't get a look in.

'They're wilfully obtuse,' she'd complained to Diana once at the Tate, studying a brochure to accompany a sequence of lithographs and fluorescent light bulbs. 'The work should speak for itself. All these...' she had waved her arms about '...manifestos and dissertations, load of bollocks. Never apologize, never explain. It's desperate. People don't need to analyse, they need to experience – here.' She thumped herself in the solar plexus.

Diana had moved her hand up and down to quieten her, like she was batting a very soft ball, and darted her eyes to the side where a gallery attendant was looking discomfited and a woman was shepherding two children out of the gallery.

'Coffee?' Diana said now.

'Gin,' Meg said.

Diana's mouth tightened momentarily.

'Oh, come on – we're on holiday,' Meg said.

'Anything else?'

'Just the drink, and make it a double, sweetheart.'

'No ice,' Diana said.

'No ice.' The pain in her teeth was unbelievable.

Boss got to his feet as Diana launched herself upright.

'Sit, Boss,' Meg told him. He looked at her for half a second. She narrowed her stare and he slumped back down.

Meg watched Diana sway down the carriage. Her hair, pewter grey, was thinning at the crown. Friar Tuck in cords and fleece.

Where had it gone? All those decades? One minute you're a filly, long-limbed and skittish, running fast and free. Ten minutes later you're an old nag only a few steps from the knacker's yard. Would it have been different, would she feel different now, if she hadn't settled with Diana? If she'd taken up the artist's residency in Montréal? If she'd chosen a different woman or left Diana for one of her flings? If she'd stayed unattached, available?

'It's not about you,' Meg had tried to explain in one of their tiresome rows. 'It means nothing. It's a bit of fun. Vacuous.'

'So why bother?' Diana had demanded, face red and tear-stained. "If it means nothing to you and it breaks my heart, why do it?'

Because I can. Because I want to. Because they still want me. And I want that kick. That fizz in my veins, that heat, crackling, dangerous.

Out of the window, Meg watched a cormorant, long-necked, arrow straight, etch flight over a lake. The water ruffled slightly, flung lozenges of silver sunshine here and there. The beauty of it.

Of all of it.

She swallowed and hitched herself up, wanting more support at the base of her spine. Here came Diana now, clutching brown bags.

Boss whined in greeting, thumped his tail.

Diana sat down, set the bags on her tray table. Blew air over her face, riffling her fringe. 'It's warm,' she said. 'I got myself one, too.'

Meg smiled.

Diana opened the dinky bottles and miniature tin cans, poured them, mixing gin and tonic.

'Cheers.'

'Cheers.'

They tapped plastic glasses.

We should have come first class, Meg thought, paid the extra for free booze in proper glasses.

But what would Diana, who was the bread-winner, have said to that? 'If we spend less then we'll still have enough for another break later in the year.' And how could Meg possibly have answered that without spilling the beans and shattering everything?

Nick

Lisa had gone to the loo when Evie woke up, crying before her eyes had even opened. Both of the kids had done that, and Nick could never tell whether the cry itself woke them up or if they were awake already, then made the sound. Her face was screwed up and he knew the screams would only get louder until she was fed.

He got up and felt in the baby bag, by the side of her chair, for the bottle. Found nothing. He unclipped her harness and lifted her out. Her eyes fluttered open. Nick patted her on the back as he eased her onto his shoulder and the crying cut out. He knew she wouldn't stay like that for long.

One of the women at the table further down, the redhead, was facing his way and shot him a look of sympathy. He gave her a quick smile in return but she'd already turned away, leaning in to her companions opposite.

Evie began to cry again, a grating sound that would scour her throat.

Eddie stopped colouring and put his hands over his ears, pursed his mouth.

Where the hell was Lisa?

Nick lifted Evie round into his right arm, licked his finger and gave it to her to suck. She tugged at it for all of three seconds, then started howling.

He saw Lisa heading back, pulling a face at him.

'Why didn't you feed her?' Lisa said, taking Evie from him.

'What with? There's no bottle.'

'In the bag.'

'I've looked in the bag.'

'You put it in the bag?' Lisa said.

'What?'

Evie's screams got more strident. Eddie flung himself back against his seat, hands still over his ears.

'It was on the side,' Lisa said, 'and I asked you

77

to put it in the bag while I changed her.'

Nick shook his head. What was she on about?

'You said yes,' Lisa said, 'I heard you.' She handed the baby back to him then and started looking through the bag, as if she didn't believe him. 'Oh, hell.' She straightened up.

'You never said that,' Nick said.

'I did and you said yes.'

'Lisa...' He could feel the heat up his back, irritation tightening his skin at her stupidity and her attempt to blame him.

'You did.' Her face was pinched, miserable.

'Why haven't I done it, then? If I actually heard you and said yes, then I'd have put the bloody thing in.' He stopped talking, Evie's cries drilling into his teeth, his skull. 'Is there more formula?'

'In the big case,' she said.

'Right.'

He passed the baby back, went to the luggage station and dragged the case out from under the other bags. He pulled it to the end of the coach and into the corridor where there was a bit more space. He laid it flat and unzipped it, found the canister of baby-milk powder and the spare bottle, then packed the rest of the stuff back in.

He returned the case to the bay – he had to pull out all the other bags, lift theirs in then stack it all again.

'I'll get some water from the shop,' Lisa said, when he got back.

She gave him Evie and picked up the bottle and the formula.

Nick put the baby back over his shoulder and began to walk with her up and down the coach, rubbing her back. It didn't make any difference to her crying but it helped him deal with it.

He was aware of the other passengers, the Paki and the middle-aged woman on her own, the coloured girl and the geeky-looking lad, the red-head and her friends, the old biddies with the dog, all listening to Evie's cries.

The dog gave a muffled bark as he passed and one of the women shushed it.

Nick reached the end and wondered whether to keep going. It would take a while for the water to cool enough for them to give it to Evie and maybe he should share the pain a bit.

The rubbish collector, another Asian, with big sticky-out ears, monkey ears, was coming down the train. Nick went through into the vestibule to let him pass but the bloke stopped. 'Aw, someone's not happy.' He ducked round the back of Nick and spoke directly to the baby. 'Hello, you. What's up, then, eh? Hello.'

She stopped. The little minx stopped crying.

'How old?' the lad said, sounding like a broody old hen.

'Twelve weeks.'

'I've a niece that age, grabbing things she is, blowing bubbles too. Oh-oh,' he said, as Evie cranked up again. 'Usually they like the motion of the train, innit.'

Nick patted Evie harder, waiting for the lad to get back to work but when he showed no sign of shifting, Nick said, 'Come on, then,' to Evie and headed towards coach C. There was Lisa at the counter, the girl serving talking to her.

Lisa turned, hearing Evie's cry. As Nick got

79

closer her expression changed: she looked uncertain, a bit puzzled, then frowned, her eyebrows pulling together, mouth open, and she said, 'Where's Eddie? You've not left him on his own?' Horrified. As if the train was full of paedos just waiting to snatch up unaccompanied four-year-olds and chuck them out the window.

'He'll be fine–'

'You wait for this,' Lisa said. 'Here.' She held out her arms and took the baby. Tutted at Nick and hurried off.

The girl behind the counter gave him a look, an amused tilt of the eyeballs, pulled her mouth down. Sort of 'Women – what are they like?' Nick agreed but at the same time wanted nothing more than to deck her and wipe the smirk right off her face.

'Anything while you're waiting?' she said, nodding to the bottle of formula, its teat off, steam still rising.

'No,' Nick said, his eyes running over the stock on the shelves. Then he changed his mind. 'Actually I'll have a ham and cheese toastie and a Coke.'

The girl nodded, began totting it up on the till. He surveyed the confectionery and picked up a chocolate flapjack.

Lisa had definitely not asked him to pack that feed. No way. Trying to put the blame on him when it was her fault. And it wouldn't have happened if she'd just listened to him in the first place. Bloody cheek. She needed to keep on top of things with the kids: she wasn't out working five days a week to pay the mortgage. She should have put the bloody feed in the bag. And if she hadn't, she should own up to the facts and not make out it was his fault.

Nick picked up a bag of Doritos. 'And these,' he said, putting it on the counter with the flapjack. The girl scanned them and he opened the tortilla chips then and there. By the time he'd eaten them his toastie would be ready and by the time he'd finished that maybe the bottle would have cooled enough to take back.

Nick chewed the snack, opened the Coke and took a long swallow.

Roll on Monday, he thought. Roll on Monday when this whole ridiculous waste of time would be done and dusted and consigned to the dustbin of memory.

Rhona

The baby kept crying and Rhona moved in her seat, but she couldn't get away from the sound.

She bent over the brochure again, the text blurring.

The father patted the baby and moved a few steps down the carriage.

'It's only going to keep growing,' Felicity said.

For a second Rhona thought she meant the volume of crying, then realized it was nothing to do with that. She nodded, her mind scrambling to find a clue as to what the topic might be.

'As long as there's this level of unemployment,

and with flexible working patterns becoming more and more common,' Felicity said.

Part-time? Rhona wondered

'Some people just can't cut it,' Felicity went on, 'because they bear the cost of the failure, not the business.'

Commission-only! It must be. Rhona chanced it, fighting through the fog that the baby's wailing summoned in her brain: 'In a fluid market people need to be able to be responsive, to react quickly to a changing landscape, source new revenue streams. Commission-only gives companies that opportunity. And the best talent gets rewarded.'

Agata nodded. 'No expensive outlay for holiday or sick pay, complete adaptivity.'

The baby's screams got louder and Felicity rolled her eyes, gave a small shake of the head. Rhona could imagine her as a mother: rigid, controlling, punishing, exactly like she was at work when she put the boot in. Though when Felicity did refer to her family it was as though they were all best friends and her children had grown up to be wildly successful and perfectly formed individuals.

'I don't know how you do it.' Agata smiled at Rhona, nodded towards the pacing father. 'On your own as well.'

Rhona's stomach flipped over. 'She's older now,' she said. 'It was hard at the beginning but you cope – you have to. I started out on commission.' She dragged the chat back to business. 'Vacuum cleaners. House calls in Glasgow and Motherwell. Some weeks it was cold beans and cornflakes.' She laughed.

That had been the low point of her working life. She could do the patter, build that bond with the customer – they should have been called 'marks', really. The machines were expensive, all bells and whistles, and the customers, often as not, the elderly and housebound. One wee old granny told Rhona her life story, served her scones, would probably have invited her to move in if Rhona had let slip how grotty her bedsit was. As soon as Rhona finished the demonstration, the old lady agreed to the sale, the fourteen-day trial.

Rhona had asked if she could use the loo and took the phone in there to make the call to the office. The one they did when somebody was being awkward, saying flat out they couldn't afford it, or that it was outrageous, or they needed to ask their son/daughter/cousin for advice. The 'just let me talk to my manager' call.

Rhona went through the spiel as though the client was in the room. 'Alan, I've a customer here who is bowled over by the product but the finance is a bit beyond reach. I wonder if there's anything we can do to make it a bit easier? Lady's in her eighties, disabled and housebound.'

Alan said, 'Discount at ten, go down to twenty but no lower.'

Rhona thought for a moment about killing the sale. Telling the granny that it was a rip-off, that she didn't need a machine like this in her wee flat. Her old carpet-sweeper would do just fine and she should use the money to keep the place warm and treat herself instead. But Rhona's overdraft was at the agreed limit, the direct debit for her phone would send her over the edge and then she'd be paying daily charges plus interest. She hadn't made a sale all week. She couldn't afford to be soft.

She looked at the fluffy pink towels, the elegant ceramic soap dish, the clutter of medicines and skin creams on the shelf, the broderie-anglaise curtains. She washed her hands, went back in and said, 'You've come up trumps, sweetheart. I've been able to get you a twenty per cent discount so that'll only be fifteen ninety-nine a month.'

The granny had smiled and called her a 'guid wee hen', and Rhona had wanted to weep.

As soon as she could she'd moved into a telesales job that was basic plus commission. She learnt to separate herself from the voice at the other end of the phone: empathy was a loser's game. You needed a clear division. They were just a number and a surname. Rhona could inject warmth into her tone, give the impression of compassion and understanding, without feeling a thing. She stuck to the script, a shell protecting her from people threatening complaints, blethering on about nuisance calls and telephone preference systems, and from those yelling abuse.

'It was a way to gain experience,' Rhona said now, 'a stepping stone.'

The father disappeared with the baby and Rhona felt the relief as her skin relaxed.

'Thank God,' Felicity said.

'Will she miss you when you're away overnight?' Agata said.

Rhona felt her face freeze. Did Agata know Rhona planned to leave early? How could she

84

possibly? But why else was she zoning in on Maisie?

Rhona swallowed, her windpipe on fire, her guts dissolving. 'Yes,' she managed. 'I've not done it much.' *Ever. Not one night away in five years. And I won't tonight.*

'Excuse me.' She stood up.

In the toilet, she checked her watch. Almost midday. She wished the hours away. Wished she was back home now with Maisie, the grind of the day done.

Saheel

They were blind, all of them, blind and deaf to what was really happening. In the lab sometimes you needed to introduce a catalyst to speed up a reaction. Saheel, the brothers like him, were that catalyst, but unlike a chemical catalyst, which remains unchanged and can be recovered at the end of the process, Saheel would be consumed by it.

Energy is never created or destroyed, it's simply transformed or transferred, fossil fuel to green-house gas, wave power to electricity. The energy of his actions, of those like him, in Syria, in Yemen, in Kenya, that energy would accumulate and grow. Already thousands of young people had heard the call, had seen the light, *allahu Akbar*. Every day people were travelling to join the fight: schoolkids, families, students. Or were keeping the flame burning here. On a regular basis the news would be full of arrests or trials, people charged with preparation of a terrorist act. Those were the ones who got caught.

That was the beauty of acting alone: there was no web of communication between a group. No one was already flagged up for special interest and liable to draw unwelcome attention. Alone he was safer, more likely to complete his mission. His actions were unexpected, a random strike. Every war needed outriders, snipers, black-ops. Those who had the insight and the courage, the unflinching conviction to act alone. And his target, carefully chosen, would make spectacular news coverage.

After decades of oppression, with the West allowing Netanyahu to pursue his policies of genocide, of apartheid against the Palestinians, after the slaughter in Iraq and Afghanistan, the mighty Caliphate had risen, growing stronger every day. Let the US and their British lackeys pursue the war on terror. *We are ready, more than ready*. This was his day, his century. And the righteous would inherit.

He imagined the aftermath, the way his life would be dissected, the interviews with school friends and university tutors, the examination of his Internet history, the analysis of his radicalization, the vain attempts to find conspirators, a cell.

He wore his university sweatshirt, dark jeans, trainers. He had taken time to decide whether to shave. To add to the squeaky-clean student image. But decided against it. He was a holy man now. A holy warrior. His name would join the ranks of those who had come before: Hasib Hussain, Mohammed Sidique Khan, Germaine Lindsay, Shehzad Tanweer. He thought about the war memorial outside the library. The names of those 'who gave their lives'. One day perhaps there would be memorials to all the fallen of the jihad.

His mother and father had tried to talk to him when he started going to the mosque in Oldham. 'I hope you're not getting any stupid ideas, are you?' his mother said. 'I've heard bad things about that place.'

How would she know? Saheel had thought. Women weren't welcome there. As it should be.

He had felt himself getting angry: his mother called herself a Muslim and so did his father, but they never prayed. They'd lost their way. Seduced by material goods and an easy life. Shutting their eyes against the injustices that befell their fellow Muslims.

'We want a better world,' Saheel had said. 'We follow the true teachings.' The interpretation of the Qur'an, according to great scholars and imams, like Sayyid Qutb, who'd been a leader of the Muslim Brotherhood in the fifties and sixties. He advocated that the revolutionary vanguard should use both preaching and jihad to spread Islam through the whole world. Or Abul A'la Maududi, who saw the need to follow Sharia and to defend Islam against secularism and the so-called emancipation of women. Women were not equal to men, never would be. These sacred philosophies were inherited and disseminated by the great preachers of today, like Anjem

87

Choudary and Mizanur Rahman.

'There are different interpretations—' his father said.

'No,' Saheel cut him off. 'There is only one true path.'

'There's more than one way to change things,' his father said. 'Look, at the end of the day, whether it's Northern Ireland or South Africa or Bosnia, the fighting has to stop and a political solution has to be agreed.'

Saheel shook his head. What planet was he on? This was a global struggle now. Way beyond ballot boxes or nation states. This was only the beginning. The corrupt, the apostates, the venal, the traitors, the infidels, they would all fall.

'Just be careful,' his mother said. 'Use your brains. And talk to us, Saheel. We're your family, we care about you.' She reached up and held his head, pulled it down and kissed his hair.

She loved him, both his parents did, and he loved them, but he no longer had any respect for them. He thought of Kulsoom, who behaved like a boy and had no shame. He wouldn't think about them any more.

Anyway, he had another family now, growing day by day, united and loyal to the very end.

A rush of motion to his right, a sudden loud racket. Saheel started, nerves jangling. A train, that's all, a passing train. He almost laughed out loud. He breathed steadily while his heart settled. The last thing he wanted was to draw attention to himself.

He had walked a fine line in the last few weeks, careful not to attract any unwelcome scrutiny.

They all knew the mosque was under surveillance, that there were probably infiltrators at prayers, so Saheel had taken a back seat. Even missed some of the gatherings, claiming he had deadlines at uni. For his greatest fear, once the plan had formed, was that he would be caught and prevented from carrying out his mission. So he was cautious and clever, and took his time making sure everything was watertight.

He was nervous but only about being stopped. No one could possibly know, though – how could they? Here he was, a grade-A student, minding his own business, polite and well groomed. No one would have a clue. Even so, when they made the safety announcements over the PA, 'Please do not leave any items unattended on the railway and be aware of any suspicious items or behaviour. Report these to a member of staff or police', his back stiffened. It was important not to show any signs of anxiety. It needed only one person with Islamaphobia to see a Muslim with a backpack looking jittery and it could all go wrong.

He had never felt this before, this sense of perfect clarity, of total belonging, of righteousness, of power. He understood he was only an instrument, a foot soldier in a much greater endeavour, but beside this everything else became empty, shabby, meaningless. There was no greater purpose to his life than this.

The train tilted, the whistle blew high and clear and the speed increased. There was no going back now. Only forward, at speed, to his glorious destiny.

Holly

The wife came racing back with the baby, her face like thunder, but she relaxed once she saw the little boy kneeling up on the aisle seat.

Holly smiled at her. 'He's been showing me his picture.'

'A police car.' Eddie waved his paper at his mum, then bobbed his head from side to side. 'Nee-naw, nee-naw.'

She paced up and down, the baby bawling away.

'What else can you draw?' Holly said.

'Lots of things.'

'A train?'

'No,' he said. 'A tractor.'

'Cool,' she said.

'Cool,' he echoed.

His mum gave Holly a quick smile, turned and walked the other way, shushing the baby. The train speeded up and Eddie's felt pens rolled across the table. 'Whoah!' he said. Then the coach pitched the other way, and the pens tipped onto the floor.

Before Holly could retrieve them, the woman in front, the one whose phone kept ringing, got them and handed them to Eddie.

'What do you say?' his mum said.

'Thank you.'

'You're welcome,' the older woman said, and sat down again.

Holly checked London's weather forecast for the weekend. Sunny. High of 16. Excellent for April. Be cooler at home.

Jeff had stopped the thumb dance and it looked like he was reading something now.

Outside Holly could see a plane high up. She wondered where it was going. Could be Manchester. Her dad worked there, in the freight terminal. He brought home stories of surprise finds by Customs: crates of tortoises or tusks, fridge-freezers packed with cigarettes.

The train hurtled through a small station, the whole thing a blur. Holly couldn't read the signs. 'The thing about sitting backwards,' she said to Jeff, 'is it gives you a cricked neck.'

'Unless you look into the distance,' he said, pointing one hand straight, the direction they'd come from. 'Don't crane your head round.'

'Have you prepared any questions to ask them?' Holly said.

'Yes,' he said, but he looked a bit wary, like she was trying to catch him out.

'Not "How much money will I get?" or "What benefits will you offer me?"' she said.

'Gone over all that with my job coach,' he said.

'How long have you been signing on?' she said.

'Too long.'

He really didn't want to share.

'Whereabouts in Manchester are you?' She tried another tack.

'Whalley Range,' he said.

'I'm in Northenden. But my best mate lives in Whalley Range. Did you go to Manchester Academy?'

91

'Chorlton High,' he said.

'And sixth form?'

'Did a BTEC, information and creative technology at Manchester College,' he said.

So he must be at least eighteen.

He bit at his thumbnail and she winced. He noticed and blushed. She hadn't meant to embarrass him and ploughed on with the conversation, if you could call it a conversation. 'So, you back up tonight?'

'Yeah.'

'You should get it,' she said. 'They reckon there's a shortage of IT people, don't they? Like nationally. Not enough kids doing it in school. And if you don't get through, it's still good experience.'

'So they tell me,' Jeff said.

'Ooh, cynic,' she said. 'Where's the interview, what part of London?'

'Charlotte Street,' he said. He tapped his phone. 'Got it on the map. It's the Northern Line.' He showed her the map.

'You could walk. I'm going that way,' she said. 'You can walk it in about fifteen minutes. I could show you.'

He opened his mouth, like he was going to refuse, then closed it again.

'What?' Holly said. 'I don't mind. It's easy to get lost, even with your maps.'

'Whatever. Cool,' he said. He sounded tight, like it wasn't cool. Not. At. All. Hand clamped round his phone like he'd strangle it.

'You'd rather I didn't?' she said.

'No, it's fine,' he said, still off. He made a fist,

92

tapped his tray table.

'Look,' she said, 'I'm sorry if I've pissed on your chips. I don't know what I've done wrong but let's just forget it, eh?'

He flinched and his face tightened. Maybe she had been a bit sharp. She was about to say sorry but he turned to her at the same time, said, 'No, that'd be cool. Safe.' He nodded repeatedly. The tension seemed to drain out of his body. 'If you've time,' he added.

'The day is mine,' Holly said. 'Let's do this thing.' She put on an American accent and he smiled. She liked it when he smiled, a broad, warm smile, his eyes all lit up.

The train speeded up again and Holly felt the tilt. 'A hundred and twenty-five miles an hour – do you reckon we're that fast now?'

'Probably, but they reach two hundred miles an hour in France. They were the record holders until China got its act together. The Shanghai Maglev gets up to two hundred and sixty-eight miles an hour.'

'God, you're not a train-spotter, are you?'

'Didn't I say?' The faintest flicker in his eyes told Holly he was winding her up. 'Besides,' he said, 'who needs train-spotting when you've got PHP or SQL?'

'Officially lost me,' Holly said.

'Programming languages.'

He was a weird one, she thought, cynicism only skin-deep, a defence mechanism. What did he need to defend himself against? What was he protecting himself from?

'We could get a coffee,' he said quickly.

93

She just nodded to his cup.

'After my interview. I can't travel back till seven.'

That sort of coffee. Oh. My. God. Who'd have thought? 'Off peak,' Holly said.

'Yeah, so if you wanted ... I just thought ... but not...' he stuttered, like he was losing power, faith.

'Cool,' Holly said, a flutter inside. 'What's your number?'

He reeled it off and she texted him so he'd have hers: *hello x*

He smiled again. All the edge seemed to have melted away.

He pulled something up on his phone. 'Go on, then,' he said. And handed it to her. 'Sample questions, try me.'

Holly began to speak and the baby ratcheted up the screaming and the dog gave a bark. She tried again. 'Which fields in the IT industry most interest you and why?'

She crossed her legs and leant in towards him, watching those sapphire eyes, those lips, and trying to pay attention to what he was actually saying.

Kulsoom

Kulsoom opened Saheel's door carefully, half expecting him to jump out at her even though she'd seen him leave the house earlier.

His room was so bare. Once, he'd had posters

on the walls, like she did, except hers were Taylor Swift and MIA and one of Malala. Saheel's were Man United and some hip-hop guys, and he had Man U flags and scarves too. He used to play at school in the under-sixteen league and Dad said he was really good.

But all that had stopped. And the walls just had marks on now where the Blu-tack had been.

He'd been much more fun, the old Saheel. Well, duh! He'd played footie with Arfan and Kulsoom when she was little, and taken her on the back of his bike to get sweets.

She switched on his laptop and waited for it to load.

She could remember a game they'd played one time when she was really small – she must have been about five and Saheel twelve – and their cousins came over. They'd all had water guns. It was hot and they had Super Soakers and Kulsoom was on Saheel's team and he said she was the Water Queen and they did a victory parade round the garden with her up on his shoulders.

His desk was all tidy, too. Even the charger wire all wound up neat and a little tray for paper clips and pens and Sellotape.

Arfan wouldn't let Kulsoom into his room any more – he probably had drugs in there but she knew it was a mess because every couple of weeks Mum would say, 'It's a complete tip, Arfan. If you don't clear it up it's all going in the bin. You hear me?'

She'd said the same to Kulsoom, and Kulsoom had said she liked it like that, hers wasn't messy. She just had a lot of stuff and not enough space and she knew where everything was, and if her mum went and moved stuff it'd be her fault if Kulsoom got into trouble at school because her projects had been ruined.

'I don't think dirty T-shirts and mugs with mould growing in them has anything to do with school work,' her mum had said.

'What about Tracey Emin's bed?' Kulsoom replied. 'What if someone had made her clear that up? Her whole career would have been totally ruined.'

'Her bed?' Arfan sneered.

'It's a work of art, dumbo,' Kulsoom said.

'It's a disgrace,' her father said, 'showing dirty linen in public.'

Facepalm. 'That was the whole point,' Kulsoom said. Though it was a bit gross, too, some of the things she had there.

Then Mum had got really cross and forced her to tidy up, standing outside the room with a black bin liner, checking every five minutes and making her go on until she could hoover the carpet. 'When you have your own house you can live like an animal but not in mine.'

Kulsoom couldn't wait.

The laptop made its wake-up sound and Kulsoom put her memory stick in the USB port, navigated to the drive and opened it.

She was about to play the file when there was loud hammering on the front door. *Shit!* He was back! Her mouth went dry and her heart did this jumbly beat like falling downstairs. Quick as she could she pulled out the stick without doing the safely-remove-hardware thing and clicked shutdown. She closed the laptop and hurried down-stairs. Her phone! Her phone was still up there. *Shit!*

'Just a minute,' she called out, ran back upstairs and grabbed her phone from the bed.

Down at the front door, panting, she drew back the bolts and pulled it open, excuses at the ready.

'All right, love?'

It was the postman. She nearly collapsed. 'Hi.'

'Been running?'

'Working out,' Kulsoom said.

'I need a signature,' he said.

'OK.'

'Your name?'

'Kulsoom Iqbal.'

'Fine. Just here.'

Kulsoom signed her name on the screen with a little plastic pen thing. She'd been practising her signature but it still didn't come out always the same. You needed it to be identical once you were famous, so when you signed DVDs or whatever, it was always perfect. That was mainly actors but some directors, like Steven Spielberg or Nick Park, they'd get to sign things.

Kulsoom Iqbal was a bit long but maybe she could just go with her first name, like Rihanna or Adele did, or if she used her initial and surname then it was Kiqbal, which sounded good, like Kick Ass but not so rude.

The packet was for her mum, probably shoes. Her mum was shoe mad – she got them online. She'd buy shoes and then the clothes to go with them. Kulsoom wore trainers, except for school when she had to wear black shoes or be shot at dawn. When she grew up she'd just wear trainers. She'd get the best ones in all her favourite colours.

Kulsoom bolted the door and leant back against it. Her heartbeat was almost normal again. The fright had made her thirsty but she wanted to hurry up and check the titles before Saheel got back and then she could start filming the next bit.

She'd got the set all rigged up in her bedroom the night before: the interior, which was a living room in a cave. She was going to film all the interior scenes first, then change to the exterior set: the mountain. She'd used a colander and papier-mâché and green fake grass, and some fish-tank pebbles for the path. It wasn't to scale with her figures but when she told Miss Weston about it they agreed that might be part of the humour, the mismatch. 'Cause things that were mistakes in real life could be just part of the style when you were making something creative – they could be a feature.

Kulsoom took off her sweatshirt and lifted the hair off the back of her neck to cool herself down. Then she started the laptop again and ran the titles. They were OK. A bit jerky in the middle but pretty good, really. The jerky style could be a feature too. There's a penguin putting its head down a hole and each time it comes out with a little placard with a word on and sticks it in the sand (which was Plasticine covered with brown granulated sugar) until it reads *A Very Special Day* and then the penguin sits on the hole and lays an egg – a mini chocolate egg. The colour wasn't as bright as she'd thought but there wasn't time to fix that.

She had been going to use a flamingo but the Plasticine legs wouldn't work so she'd tried sticks, but getting something with long legs and a Plasticine body to balance was really hard. The penguin was better and she took care to make it totally different from Pingu and the penguin in *The Wrong Trousers* and she began to see why penguins were so popular with animators. Her penguin had a Mohican quiff and big earrings like ice cubes (made from Glacier Mints) and lipstick. She was a mosher/scene/vamp penguin.

Saheel hadn't even got wallpaper on his screen. Kulsoom had a photograph from *Game of Thrones*: Arya Stark with her sword. Kulsoom loved *Game of Thrones* but not the sex bits, they were gross, so she fast-forwarded them. She would never, ever, ever watch it with her parents. How could anyone do that? She didn't know what Arfan had for his screen saver – probably something disgusting.

Would Saheel be able to tell she'd used his machine?

She'd not launched the browser so there wouldn't be anything in his history. They'd done a session at school on safety in the digital age, saying things like 'Don't put it on Facebook if you wouldn't want it on an advertising hoarding at the end of your street,' and maybe sending nude pictures to your boyfriend wasn't a clever thing to do. OMG, it had been so embarrassing – Kulsoom couldn't wait for it to be over.

Kulsoom didn't do Facebook much any more.

People were so mean and horrible and, anyway, she didn't care how many likes she got or who had the skinniest bum.

Would her file show up on the recent-items tab if it was on an external drive?

She clicked on the tab and saw her file at the top of the list. She didn't know how she could get rid of it. The file below it was a video too. Probably some preachy thing. But the name had today's date *April 17 Mission Statement*. Could that be a uni thing? Aims for a project, like they had to do in science and technology at school?

Kulsoom went to click shutdown and hesitated. If he was at uni why wouldn't he answer her or text her back?

Her stomach hurt and there was a fizzy feeling at the back of her head.

He'd kill her if he knew she'd been snooping at his stuff. But each time she read the file name her chest felt tighter.

Too scared to open it, she launched the browser and went into his browsing history. Saheel had been on loads of sites in the last couple of days, mostly Islamic from the addresses, but he'd been on one more than any of the others. And he'd been on it early this morning. The words rang in her head, like blows. *Euston Station Bombing*. She clicked through to the site. There was just a banner headline and a photograph of Saheel, taken in this room. No links, no posts.

Shaking, rocking in the chair, she clicked back to the recent-items list, selected *April 17 Mission Statement* and pressed play.

CHAPTER THREE

Jeff

She'd said yes to coffee. He'd actually asked her and she'd said yes. He'd nearly blown it just before that, beginning to get anxious when she wanted him to change his plans, walk instead of getting the Tube. A rush of panic but he'd recovered, hidden it well enough. And asked her for coffee.

The train slowed and Jeff looked out of the window, trying to see if there was anything to show why. They weren't due to stop anywhere else: the train manager had already announced they'd be going straight through to Euston now.

He waited, expecting it to pick up power, and saw a stream snaking through the field, a silver thread. And further away a lake, the water a scummy brown-green colour. Some ducks there. Or geese, maybe.

The train continued to lose speed and eventually came to a complete stop in the middle of nowhere.

Jeff looked at Holly.

She shrugged. 'Maybe we're early.'

Would that matter? A big, busy station like Euston would have slots, like airports did, to make sure trains could get in and out of the correct platforms. And there'd be people employed to make sure that all ran smoothly, to switch platforms if need be, or prioritize incoming services.

'Now what?' the dad across the way said, as if there'd already been tons of stuff go wrong on the journey.

Then the notification chimes sounded and the voice came over the PA system: 'Ladies and gentlemen, your train manager speaking. I'm afraid we've been notified of a signalling problem up ahead of us in the Milton Keynes area. I can't tell you any more at the moment but as soon as I have an update I'll let you know. I'd like to apologize on behalf of Virgin Trains for the delay and any inconvenience this might cause.'

A groan and muttered comments went up from the passengers.

'What time's your interview?' Holly asked Jeff.

'One thirty.'

'As long as we're there for ten past, you should make it.'

His stomach dropped and with it his mood. He could see it now: they'd be delayed for ages and he'd give totally the wrong impression, being late and stressed. He should have known when he forgot his phone and missed the first bus that it would all go to shit. 'And what if we're here all afternoon?' he said.

'Look on the bright side, why don't you?' Holly said.

'You don't have to be anywhere,' he said.

'True. But it's not like the end of the world, is it? You're late, OK. But hey ... nobody dies.' She put on a stupid voice and he just looked at her.

He didn't see how she could be so flippant when this was his chance. Could be his only chance.

'OK.' She put her hands up, a surrender. 'If we're here more than fifteen minutes, you ring ahead, you explain the train's delayed, you still hope to be there on time and will call again if that changes. You have got the number?'

Had he? Jeff checked his phone, opening the file where he'd kept the details of the apprenticeship, then one of the emails he'd had from them. There was a number at the bottom. 'Yes.'

'Simples,' Holly said.

Jeff nodded. Outside he could see farmland stretching to the horizon. A house in the distance. The fields were divided up by hedges. Sheep in one of the fields, two horses, coats on, in another. He couldn't imagine ever living somewhere like this, he'd go mental ... well, more mental. No shops, no buses, no crowds, no late-night curries, no streetlights or banter at the chippy about the Reds and the Blues.

He tried to imagine it at night. How scary that would be. His mum sometimes talked about moving out of Manchester but she wouldn't last a week. No audience, no company, no one to keep her calm, turn her volume down. She always had people around, was forever arranging get-togethers. Couldn't bear to be on her own. To be quiet.

'I'd hate to live here,' Jeff said.

'You'd need a tent,' Holly said, 'unless you bought that place.' Meaning the house.

'Anywhere like this,' he said.

'Me, my top three locations: New York, London

and Paris,' Holly said.

'Paris?' The others he could see, but Paris? Jeff's only notion of Paris was of French people who hated the Brits, and the Eiffel Tower.

'It's beautiful,' Holly said. 'There's an amazing music scene, all these clubs, and there's the fashion, of course.'

'You speak French?'

'There is that.' She sucked her teeth. 'Where would you go?'

Jeff had never really thought of going anywhere, apart from the cheap package holidays they'd had, or maybe a trip to Thailand, like some of his mates had done after school. 'New York,' he agreed, 'that'd be cool. Tokyo.' Somewhere so different...

'Whoah!' Holly said.

He pictured himself in a room, high above the city, neon everywhere. He'd have some amazing job, coding games. Or writing games. But there was no one with him and the idea was suddenly cold and unwelcoming. City living, it was all luxury apartments and marble floors. That wasn't really his thing.

'I can't speak Japanese, though,' he said. 'Somewhere by the sea – that'd be cool, Brighton or Barcelona, a big old house on the beach. Lots of rooms.' Lots of kids. The twins could come and stay, too.

'You need to make your million first,' Holly said.

'There's always a catch,' Jeff said.

A crow – or was it a rook? – landed at the side of the tracks, stabbed at something on the ground.

'You been there?' Holly said.

'Brighton?' Jeff said.

'Or Barcelona?'

'No. Only Majorca,' he said.

'That's it?' Her eyes were bright with surprise.

'So far. Family holidays.'

'No school trips, then?'

'No,' Jeff said. He didn't elaborate, didn't want to get into all that – how they'd never had the money when he was younger. And the one time they could afford it he'd bottled out because his head was a mess, he wasn't sleeping, he was anxious all the time and just couldn't face it.

'We went to Germany,' Holly said, 'I can't remember the name of the place. It was pretty boring. And Washington DC. That was so cool. I've been to Italy and Greece and Morocco with my family.'

There was another announcement: 'Ladies and gentlemen, this is your train manager again. Work is now being carried out in an effort to repair the signalling in the area, which appears to have been damaged by vandals. As soon as I have any more information, I'll come back to you. I would like to apologize on behalf...'

Jeff checked the time.

'The knee thing,' Holly said.

Jiggling again. He sighed, moved in his seat. If he missed it, though.

He opened his phone and texted Nana. *Train delayed, signal failure. Fingers crossed we get going again soon x.*

Maybe he should ring the Charlotte Street place now, give them more notice, but then if he wasn't late...

Nana replied: *hops u mak*

And again: *jeff hop u make it let me no on bus xcc*

And again: *u cud ring 2 sat*

He texted back: *Ta. Will do x*

Holly was watching him. Nosy. She didn't say anything but he put her out of her misery. 'My grandmother. She likes to text.' Holly smiled.

'Maybe it's time for the sonic screwdriver,' Jeff said.

Holly laughed, the hooting sound that made him laugh in turn.

Just get the signal fixed, he prayed. Get it fixed and get the train moving. And things might still turn out OK.

Caroline

It didn't really make much difference to Caroline if they were delayed. She'd arranged to meet Gail late afternoon so unless they were stuck for hours she wouldn't be affected.

It did happen, sometimes, horror stories about passengers trapped overnight or all day long on trains. Usually in extreme weather conditions. Stories of people simmering in suffocating heat, breaking windows to leave the train or people huddling together to keep warm in snowstorms.

She remembered one Christmas when she and Trevor had taken the kids to visit his family in Pickering, North Yorkshire. Paddy had been five and Amelia four, and the car had broken down on the North York Moors in blizzard conditions, just after dark. Neither of them had owned a mobile phone back then, and they'd estimated it could be eight or nine miles to the nearest hamlet. So, rather than one of them setting off, ill equipped, they had spent the night in the car. Each of them holding a child like a live hot-water bottle, draped in coats and jumpers. A snowplough came through the next morning before dawn and went to fetch help. Caroline had watched the red sun rise over the snowfields, the sky turn to the brightest blue. They'd shared the last two bananas and snack packs of raisins for breakfast and she felt dizzy with happiness.

The children were delighted, making wee-holes in the snow a particular highlight, and for years after referred to it as the best Christmas ever.

Now Caroline wanted a cup of tea. It would be easier to leave her weekend bag on the seat, in spite of all the security announcements exhorting passengers not to leave luggage unattended.

'Excuse me,' she said, to the young Asian man, across the aisle. He was awake now, studying his phone.

He looked at her warily. Did he speak English? She'd assumed he did. He had a Salford University sweatshirt on.

'I wonder, could you watch my bag for a minute?' She pointed to it.

He said nothing, barely moved. Was he all right? She was about to repeat herself when he said, 'Yes, sure. No problem,' in a Mancunian accent.

'Thanks,' she said.

He looked back to his phone. Perhaps he was shy. Or she'd interrupted some important messaging.

She'd turned her own phone back on and it rang, in her handbag, on the way to the shop but she ignored it.

She bought tea and a packet of shortbread biscuits. The cup was the size of a small bucket and she asked the woman serving to fill it half full to save on the waste.

'No news?' Caroline said, while the woman got her change.

'I'm as much in the dark as you,' the woman said. 'I guess it depends on how bad the damage is.'

When she reached her seat again, Caroline said thanks to her neighbour.

The young man gave a nod. No smile.

She could hear other people making calls, warning they'd be late for appointments. Once she sat down, she checked her voicemail. The message began with silence, then rustling and she could hear her mum breathing. The click as she hung up. No plea for help. No traffic noise. No need to ring her back. The carers would be there any time with lunch. A sandwich or a cup of soup.

The land sloped up on this side of the tracks: fields gave way to a wood of fir trees and above them, on the top of the hill, stood a castle with ramparts and battlements. There were splashes of pink and white on the small trees to one side of its wall. Caroline wondered how long they'd been there. Had the people who lived in the castle planted cherry and hawthorn? Did those sort of trees live that long?

She loved this time of year, the first burst of spring with dusty catkins and primroses, and trees unfurling buds of acid green. The thought was followed by a wash of sadness. You're tired, she told herself. Ignore it. She would see Gail and enjoy herself. Problems parked at the door.

She and Trevor should start making plans: if they were to take advantage of the kids finally leaving the nest, it made sense to set the wheels in motion soon. At least talk about the general drift of things – what time of year to travel, where they'd like to go first. She'd probably have to look into respite care for her mother. Could you still get that or had it been cut?

The young man across the aisle kept picking up his phone, checking it, then putting it down again. Like a nervous tic. Probably looking for news of the delay on Twitter or something. People heard about things first on social media, these days, didn't they?

'The woman in the shop says they've no idea how long we'll be,' she said, raising her voice to reach him.

Again that peculiar hiatus, stillness. This time he didn't even respond, just looked back at his phone. She liked to think she could connect with young people (at least, those who weren't her blood relatives). She managed well enough at work. Treat them with respect, praise good effort, share your passion for your subject and they'd flourish. Not all of them, that's true, but most.

She ate one of the biscuits, crunchy and buttery, and watched a horse in a field at the bottom of the hill break into a canter. What had spooked it? Or was it just the season? That sense of new life, of renewal.

The young man was sweating, really sweating, beads of moisture rolling down his face, and his lips kept working, twitching. It was very warm in the carriage. Caroline had taken off her cardigan and she was still hot. So why was he still wearing his sweatshirt? She braced her cheek on one hand, elbow on the armrest, hoping to conceal her face, then swivelled her eyes to the left so she could see him without it being obvious.

He swung to his feet, picked up his rucksack and made his way towards the shop. I could have looked after your bag, she thought. Was he making a point, snubbing her for some reason?

Something felt wrong. Something about him. Was she being paranoid? What did she have to go on, apart from a sensation, an instinct? Trust your instincts: she'd taught the kids that. There were times when they were all you could rely on. If something feels weird or frightening, leave the situation even if you can't explain why.

Was she being racist? She tried to imagine a white man in that seat, with a backpack, fidgeting, sweating. Would she react in the same way? It was an impossible question. She tried to think logically. Had the young man done anything threatening? No. Had he said anything threatening? No. His edgy behaviour might just be how he was. Or he could have an important meeting to get to. Perhaps he had mental-health issues.

She took the first sip of tea, scalding her tongue. *Report any suspicious behaviour to a member of staff or the police.*

Should she hang fire, see if he settled down once they were on their way again? Give him the benefit of the doubt.

There'd been all that business in the press about the grooming scandals lately. How the authorities had failed to act because the perpetrators were Pakistani (and the victims were girls with troubled lives) and those in power feared accusations of racism.

What would she say, if she did report her concerns to anyone? *My guts tell me there's something off about this young man, that he's up to no good. But I've nothing to support it, except he's sweaty and stand-offish.*

They'd write her off as a hysterical, menopausal woman. And if she was right to feel anxious and said nothing? Did nothing? Then what? They were still miles from anywhere. From help.

Oh, God, what should I do?

Naz

Naz had almost filled his bag when the guy collared him, the student with the beard, rucksack over one shoulder.

'When are we moving?'

'No word yet,' Naz said. 'They'll announce it as soon as they know.'

'How long does it usually take?'

'Hard to say.'

'What's this signalling trouble?' The sun was coming in the windows and his face was shiny. Hot and bothered, he was.

'It's probably theft,' Naz said. 'They steal the copper from the cable. So the engineers need to repair that, innit. Can take a while.'

'What's a while?'

'Sorry, mate.' Naz shrugged. He wasn't a fortune-teller. 'If you are delayed and it affects your plans, you can claim compensation.'

The bloke laughed, but he wasn't smiling.

'Better than nothing.' Naz added, 'You can get a form from the train manager. He's in coach C near the shop, or you can get them at Euston. Or online.'

'We are going to Euston?'

'Yeah, eventually,' Naz said.

The guy kept swallowing, the lump in his throat bobbing up and down, so maybe he wasn't well, felt sick. That could be why he was sweating.

'You all right?' Naz said. 'Is there anything I can get you? It's quite warm in here, I know.'

The man just looked at him, suspicious, as though Naz had said something out of order. He didn't even answer the question, just said, 'They won't divert us?'

Naz thought about it for a moment. 'We will still go through to Euston even if they end up with rail-replacement buses but I don't think they'll do that. They usually fix the signals. The buses – that's usually more for scheduled engineering works.'

The guy gave a nod and turned away. Not even a thank-you. Acting like he was the only person who had an important journey to make. The train would be full of them. Even those travelling for pleasure not business. They'd be fed up but most people understood. You always got one or two tearing their hair out and getting nasty with the staff.

Naz moved through coach B.

The mum at the table, the one with the baby, stopped him. The little boy had spilt blackcurrant juice all over the table. Naz went and got his cleaning kit and began to mop it up.

The little kid was wailing because his pictures were all soggy and had to be chucked.

'Could you do me another one?' Naz said.

'The paper's all wet,' the boy cried, strings of spit in his mouth and his nose snotty.

Naz wiped the felt pens too because those would be sticky.

'Stop it,' the dad said. 'Stop it right now.'

'I'll go see if I can get you some paper,' Naz said. 'How about that?'

The kid had his mouth clamped shut, trying to stop crying but his shoulders were jumping up and down, his face red with the effort.

'Anyone got any spare paper?' Naz asked, walking down the carriage. 'A couple of sheets of spare paper, anyone? Budding artist in need.'

Some of the passengers smiled – they liked it when staff went off script, went that bit further to help the passengers. And Naz liked doing it, helping people.

He stopped by the student. 'Any paper? File paper?' The dog across the way seemed to be asleep. Naz hoped it would stay that way.

'No,' the student said.

Naz had needed loads of paper when he was at school, and at college doing his HNC. But some people did everything on their tablets and that, these days. Then someone called from the table further down, the three ladies. The one with the red hair had a notebook, one with wire coils down the side.

'The pages aren't very big,' she said. She tore a bunch out and Naz thanked her. So did the mother.

'What you going to draw, then?' Naz said, giving them to the little boy.

'He does a wicked tractor,' the girl, the fit-looking one he'd picked for his maître d', said.

'A fire engine,' the little boy said.

'Cool,' Naz said.

'Thank you,' the mum said again.

'No worries,' Naz said.

There was a queue for the shop and another by the train manager's office. People wanting complaint forms, probably, or help with planning alternative journeys out from Euston now they'd missed their connections. And people always bought more food when there was a delay. Maybe it was some sort of reflex, like an instinct thing, Naz thought, the not knowing where the next meal was coming from and how long they'd be stranded. It meant he'd be busier but that was OK.

The catering manager called out to him: she needed the rubbish emptying already.

'Right,' Naz said. 'I'll just...' He held up the bag he'd filled from the coaches.

'Two hands, Naz,' she said. 'Push the envelope.'

'What?'

'Take this with you now,' she said. 'No need to make two trips.'

'Oh, right.'

Naz took the shop bag as well and carried them both to the back of the train where he sealed them up for disposal at Euston.

He was getting warmer: the air con was off now they were stationary. Maybe he'd take his jacket off. Should he? He was still trying to decide when the train manager requested him to go to coach H, first class. He'd keep his jacket on for now. He pulled on a new pair of latex gloves.

He'd like linen for his restaurant, linen and silver. But a lot of places nowadays were using simpler tableware. Black slate platters or bamboo mats and that. Could he do both? Could do what he liked, he decided. It was his business, after all, innit. Fusion on the tables as well as in the menu. Sorted.

Meg

Meg was watching the women on the other side of the carriage. The physical form never ceased to amaze her. The thousands of variations of features that made each face, each body, unique. She couldn't hear much of their conversation, another consequence of her increasing decrepitude, but the way they moved, the way they inhabited the space around the table, told her more than the words they were spouting could.

Most communication was non-verbal. Body language was seminal.

The triangle the women formed was unequal, lopsided. The strength lay with the two who sat side by side, that blonde with her stark beauty and the older one, the brunette whose mannerisms reflected her status as top dog or bitch in the same way that her choice of seats did. She sat well back, her movements measured, controlled, economical. She used few, if any, displacement techniques, fiddling with her hair, say, or with her necklace. Queen Bee. The girl beside her angled her body towards Queen Bee, reflecting her pose. She nodded frequently, laughed.

The redhead, on the other hand, was subservient. And knew it. She couldn't keep still, she kept leaning in to the others, her back bowed slightly. When she spoke, her hands were all over the place, and she repeatedly touched her earrings, or messed with the folder in front of her, or with her handbag. She kept checking her phone, the time perhaps, every minute or so, crossing and re-crossing her legs. Whether it was the company, her status in the pecking order, or the interruption to the journey that was making her so restless, Meg had no idea.

Meg liked to imagine people as animals, not just in her work, in capturing the essence of their physicality, but in situations like this. The older woman was a tiger, the blonde a heron, the redhead a rodent, a squirrel or gerbil, nervous and quick.

116

We are all just meat, Meg thought, so much bone and offal and nerve endings and blood and shit.

And we are magnificent.

On the floor, Boss's legs skittered; perhaps he was dreaming.

Meg drained her glass. The drink had taken the edge off nicely but she'd be wanting another before long to keep the momentum going. Diana had half of hers left. 'Are you going to finish that?' Meg nudged her.

Diana didn't reply. Her head was propped on her hand and Meg wondered if she'd nodded off.

'Diana?'

'I don't feel very well.'

'Oh, Christ, why?'

Diana looked at her, face pasty, frown deep. 'I need some air.'

Diana was never ill. Only with head colds and the like. She was a good traveller. So what was going on? *I'm the one who's ill, for Christ's sake.*

Diana got up and Boss scrambled to his feet.

'Sit!' Meg said.

Diana stumbled as she stood and Meg went after her.

The table of women looked up with concern.

'Just wait there.' Meg made sure Diana had hold of the seat, then ducked back to get the end of Boss's lead. She turned to the family at the table. 'Would you mind looking after the dog? My friend's not feeling very well.'

'Of course,' the woman said. 'He'll be all right with the children?'

No, he's a track record of savaging babies and

mutilating toddlers. That's why I picked you. 'Good as gold,' Meg said.

The man held out his hand and Meg passed him the lead. The little boy clambered up and stood on the seat leaning over.

'He's called Boss,' Meg said, as she moved away. 'He'll shake hands, if you ask nicely.'

Diana looked dreadful, whey-faced.

'Come on.' Meg touched her shoulder as they moved up the coach. 'Do you want the loo?'

'No. I just want some fresh air.'

'Well, we're not going to be able to open a window,' Meg said. 'It's all air conditioning.' That was the constant roar from before, like being on a plane. 'But maybe we can find out if there's a cooler spot.'

The vestibule was a possibility but it was warm there and it stank. Diana said, 'I'm not standing by the toilet, Meg.' With her eyes closed. Peeved.

'Would water help? A drink of water?' Meg said. 'From the shop.'

'Yes,' Diana said. 'I'll keep walking, see if there's anywhere cooler, like you say.'

Is that wise? Meg wondered. What if Diana keeled over, fainted or something? She did look bloody dreadful.

Meg joined the queue for the shop.

It couldn't be something Diana had eaten, could it? She'd had toast and eggs for breakfast, same as always, nothing since.

The queue moved up. Outside Meg could see clouds high and white chasing their shadows over the farmland. It must be windy. She wondered if the crew had any way to open the doors. She was pretty sure there'd be some regulation to forbid that other than at a scheduled stop. But there must be ways to open the exits in an emergency. Did anyone ever read those notices, those diagrams, ever remember them? Anyhow, she didn't think a pensioner having a funny turn counted as an emergency. That was all it was, surely, a funny turn.

Meg paid for the water and went in search of Diana.

She found her in the quiet coach. The temperature was much lower there for some reason. Diana was sitting at an empty table, head in her hands.

'I've got your water.' Meg sat opposite her, twisted the cap off the bottle.

Diana took it, drank some.

Meg reached over, touched Diana's forehead. 'You're clammy.'

Diana didn't reply.

'Do you need a doctor?' Meg said.

'No,' Diana said. 'I just need to sit here for a bit.'

'What's wrong?' Meg said. 'Are you in any pain?'

'Meg, please.' Diana closed her eyes and braced her temples with one hand. 'Just a bit of peace. I'll be fine.'

She was a fine one to talk, Meg thought, chattering away like a magpie, day in day out. Nosing into people's business, gossiping and wittering on about this, that and the other. Always prattling. And now she wanted Meg to hold her tongue. Bloody liberty.

There was a different view from this side of the train, pine and birch woods rising up the slopes towards an old castle.

They'd stayed in a castle, twice. Once over in Spain, where a castle had been converted into a *parador* on the pilgrimage route, and another time on a trip to Scotland. Grey granite, forbidding in aspect. Terrific material, granite. Bloody hard going, though – have to use diamond tools. They'd had a four-poster bed and a roaring log fire, a wonderful trip. The early days when they couldn't keep their hands off each other.

Diana opened her eyes and took another drink. She had more colour now, a blush of delicate pink in her cheeks. The ghastly paper-white had gone. Thank God.

I should have got myself another G-and-T, Meg thought. Time yet.

She smiled at Diana, squeezed her hand, then sat back, watching the trees in the wind and following the flight of a wood pigeon, rosy-breasted in the spring sunshine. Like Diana, her wood pigeon.

Nick

Nick had fancied a dog but they'd put it off. The expense, the commitment, a step too far when they'd got Eddie and then Evie to deal with. Even if you got a rescue dog there were still vet's bills, insurance and kennels if you wanted to go away.

Eddie wanted to pet the animal but he couldn't reach so Nick let him out in the aisle and showed him how to stroke the fur backwards, not ruffle it the wrong way.

They'd always had a dog when Nick was growing up. A Retriever, then a Labrador. Better than a burglar alarm, his dad said.

It was Nick's job to walk the dog and when he'd got a paper round, the dog had gone with him. He'd liked that. People wouldn't mess with you if you had a dog: they'd no way of knowing how vicious it might be.

When Rex, the old dog, died and before they'd got Trigger, Nick's bike had been stolen. Three lads, one shoving him, his face really mean, the others name-calling. He couldn't do anything, three against one. He'd had to wait months, until his birthday, for a new bike. His mother had wanted to report it to the police but his father said there was no point and they'd bigger things to be doing than looking for kids' bikes. Nick got a feeling that his father was disappointed he'd let the lads get away with it. Not that he'd ever said it outright. And what could Nick have done? Three against one.

After that Nick had taken up jujitsu. Got very good at it. Still could make the moves if he had to.

The spaniel yawned, then licked Eddie, who squealed, 'He licked me!'

'That's because he likes you,' Lisa said.

She was feeding Evie, the bottle almost empty, the baby's eyes closed as she sucked, tiny blue veins on her eyelids.

121

'Can he shake hands?' Eddie said, kneeling, facing the dog.

'Let's try,' Nick said. He bent over, extended a hand and said, 'Shake a paw.'

The dog looked at him.

'Shake a paw,' Nick said, and waved his hand up and down.

The dog lifted his paw and plonked it on Nick's open palm. Nick grasped it.

'He did it!' Eddie said.

'He's very clever,' the coloured girl butted in.

'You try,' Nick said to Eddie.

'Shake a paw,' Eddie said.

The dog obliged.

'Shake a paw,' Eddie said again.

Nothing.

'He's had enough of that for now,' Nick said.

Maybe they should think again about a dog. It wasn't far to the meadows – they could walk it there. Nick wasn't doing overtime at the moment, so he was usually home by six thirty. Could they afford it, though? They owed money on the overdraft and this weekend would add a few hundred to that.

Couldn't even afford to go to the match, these days. Years he'd been in the crowds, a Red to the core, but now, if he was lucky, the closest he got to Old Trafford was the pub on a Sunday afternoon.

'It's not like they're doing very well,' Lisa had said, the last time he'd brought it up. Typical woman. No clue. It wasn't just about winning, it was about loyalty, about being in the tribe. Through thick and thin.

Of course they couldn't get a dog. The mortgage ate every spare pound that wasn't nailed down, and would do for the foreseeable future. That thought felt like a lead weight, cold in his belly. His boss had made it clear that they wouldn't be expecting a pay rise this year. The market was still jittery and all the uncertainty over the election and the European question didn't help.

What was needed was a referendum, Nick was convinced. Let the British people decide. When you were hobbled by the Human Rights Act into letting prisoners vote and allowing terrorists to sit pretty at home, when you couldn't change a light bulb without several EU directives, then the only thing to do was to stand up and stand firm. Take sovereign power back. Stop the influx of immigrants once and for all. They were sucking the country dry. The ban on benefits for immigrants was a start, sent a clear message. British jobs for British workers.

The coloured girl laughed at something, an ugly noise, and Nick felt a burn of irritation in his gullet. The dog barked and Eddie jumped up, clung to Nick's leg and began to whimper.

'Stop that,' Nick said. 'He's only barking.'

'I don't like it.' Eddie's lip trembled, his eyes pooled with tears.

For Christ's sake. 'Come on, soldier,' Nick said. 'Be brave. He won't hurt you – the lady said so. No crying now.'

He coaxed Eddie to touch the dog again, 'There, see? Friends,' Nick said.

Evie was asleep now and Nick saw Lisa was almost as well, she had put the bottle down and was leaning her head against the seat, eyes fluttering shut. Evie wasn't sleeping through yet – Lisa had probably been up in the night.

An announcement came over the Tannoy: 'Ladies and gentlemen, your train manager here again. Our engineers are attending to the problem but I'm afraid I'm not able to give you an estimate yet as to when the repairs will be completed. Once again Virgin Trains apologizes for the delay and inconvenience this will cause.'

'Can we get a dog?' Eddie said. 'To keep at our house all the time?'

'No,' Nick said.

'Why?' Eddie said.

'Because. Now get back in your seat. He'll probably settle down and sleep.'

'It's not bedtime,' Eddie said.

'Come on.'

Eddie did as he was told and the dog lay at Nick's feet.

Trigger had lived until he was nineteen, greeting Nick with love and affection every time he came home as a student and once he'd moved to Urmston and started working. Nick had been visiting the day that Trigger started choking and whining. He was already blind and half deaf by then. Nick had taken him to the vet and had him put down. Miserable, it had been. That was the thing with pets, with dogs: they were so much trouble. Best not to bother.

Rhona

The sun glanced off the rails, dazzling. Beyond them grew weeds and what looked like bluebells, the green spikes, the flowers not open yet. 'In and Out the Dusty Bluebells' – Scottish country dance class. Rhona's mother had made elastic garters for her white socks. They'd worn pleated tartan skirts, white blouses and green sweaters. One year they'd won a prize.

Her phone went, a private number. She stood up to take it, moving towards the vestibule between carriages. 'Hello?'

The signal dropped and the connection was lost.

The handset vibrated again.

'Hello?' Rhona answered.

'Miss Gillespie, this is Jennifer Ball from St Philip's.' The school secretary.

'Yes?'

'I'm afraid Maisie had a serious asthma attack during lunch and she's been taken to the Royal Manchester Children's Hospital, the paediatric emergency department.'

Oh, God. Oh, God, no. 'Oh, God.'

Sweat prickled Rhona's scalp, slicked her neck. She felt it trickle down her sides, making her itch. She should never have left her. Never made her go to school. What was she thinking? What *the hell* was she thinking?

'I can give you their number.'

'Yes, please.'

Rhona fished her pen from her handbag, with the brochure. She scribbled down the number and rang the hospital immediately.

The person she spoke to confirmed that Maisie been admitted as an emergency and was currently being assessed for treatment.

'How is she? Are they giving her any medication? What about oxygen?'

'I'm sorry, I don't have any more information but if you can come in and speak to the doctors yourself–'

'I will, as soon as I can. I'm on a train to London. I'll get there as soon as I can. But she's all right, isn't she? She is all right?'

'All I can tell you is that she's being assessed at the moment.'

Not good. Not good at all. 'Thank you. Yes.'

Her head light, teeth clamped, cheeks fixed, gulping, she found the nearest toilet. *It'll be fine, she'll be fine.* She retched thin, foamy bile into the bowl while the jaunty announcement played: 'Please do not flush nappies, sanitary towels, old mobile phones, unpaid bills, your ex's jumper, hopes, dreams or goldfish down the toilet.'

She had to get off the train. Now. Get back to Manchester. She went in search of a member of staff.

A queue of people, half a dozen or so, were waiting to see the manager at the little office in coach C. God knows how long that would take. Rhona saw the laddie who was clearing rubbish, the one who had helped mop up the table when the bairn had spilt his drink. He was heading away from her. With the train stationary, more people were moving about or standing in the aisles, stretching their legs and striking up conversations. Rhona had to jostle past them to catch up with him. She finally did in the vestibule at the end of coach D.

'I need to get off the train,' she said, the words spilling out. 'My wee girl's very sick. You've got to help me.'

He looked sympathetic, but said, 'I'm sorry, but we can't let people off until we reach Euston.'

'But we're not moving, are we?' Rhona said. 'We're going nowhere. We could be here all night.'

'I don't think–'

'I have to get off the train,' she said again. 'I have to get back to Manchester. She's been taken to hospital, she's no' well. I have to get there as soon as I can.' Rhona wiped at her face and sniffed.

'I'm really sorry,' the laddie said.

'Surely you can stop at the nearest station, any station. I could get a service from there.'

'Nothing is moving on this line.' He nodded towards the front of the train.

'We could go back then,' she said. 'Somewhere there's connecting services.'

'I don't think so.'

He was just a big wean, obviously, he'd no authority. 'Who's in charge?' she said.

'The train manager,' he said, 'in coach C.'

'There's a queue,' Rhona said. 'Please, could you ask? It's an emergency.'

'I don't think it will do any good,' he said.

127

'What if I was ill,' she said, 'if I had a heart attack?'

'We've a first-aider,' he said. 'And sometimes they ask if there's a doctor on board.'

'But you'd get them off the train,' she said.

'At a station,' he agreed. 'We're not at a station, miss.'

'You could open the doors,' she said. 'I can walk.'

'I couldn't, I'm sorry. You'd probably be better waiting, anyway. They are working on the signals. It could be fixed any time.'

'Ask the train manager,' she said again. 'Please? Please, just ask.'

He hesitated, looking pained, then gave a nod.

She followed him back through the coaches. Her stomach hurt, nagging cramps.

Maisie. Maisie.

The queue for assistance had grown, nine people now. At the head of it, by the tiny compartment that served as an office, an elderly man was saying something about the Victoria Line.

The laddie – his name badge, which he wore low on his jacket, said *Naz* – moved between the old man and the woman behind, saying, 'Excuse me, miss, I just need a quick word with the train manager.' Rhona clung close. The woman looked fed up but Rhona didn't give a toss. She had to speak to the man and impress upon him how serious the situation was. Persuade him to let her off the train.

The old guy shuffled off, tube tickets in hand, and Naz said, 'This lady has just had some bad news.'

128

'My wee girl has been taken ill. She has the asthma, really bad. It's an emergency. I have to get to her. She's gone to hospital. I have to get off the train.'

The manager's face told her no, the set of his mouth, cast of his eyes, even before he drew in a breath and said, 'I'm afraid I can't let you off unless we're at a designated station.'

'But the hospital said to come straight away.'

'Whatever the circumstances, I can't let you off the train. I do apologize. If we can assist in any other way...'

Shitting shit.

'Once we're under way,' the manager said, 'we'll do our very best to make up time and you'll be able to get straight back on a train to Manchester from Euston. It wouldn't be quicker on any other route. It's your best option.'

Rhona was crying openly now. She could feel the people around her responding with a mix of embarrassment, curiosity and concern.

Someone passed her a tissue.

She heard someone else mutter an explanation, 'Little girl's very ill.'

She nodded and staggered away. She had to get to the toilet. Pains in her belly and her bowels, like knives. She wove past people, to the end of the carriage, relieved to find the cubicle vacant. When she'd finished, she washed her hands. Her makeup was smudged but she didn't bother trying to tidy up.

Please, she prayed. Please. Please fix the train and get me home. Get me home to my babby.

Saheel

It was stifling, hard to breathe. Saheel was soaked in sweat. It was all falling apart.

No, he admonished himself. No. There is a way. Think calmly, find a way.

The nosy woman opposite kept looking at him. He pretended not to notice, hoped her phone would go again and distract her. Nosy, just like the cleaner, being all pally and asking for paper. Fool. A fool and a loser. Handling other people's trash, their waste. Running around after them.

Saheel felt his stomach drop. Had the boy wanted to trick him? To see inside his backpack? He couldn't know, could he? Not an idiot like that. He couldn't possibly know.

A fresh wave of sweat broke across him. His T-shirt was drenched. He lifted his hoodie away from his chest, trying to let some cooler air in but couldn't feel the difference.

Think. Think. OK, at the moment he was stuck, his timing ruined. Options? A: Abort the mission and rearrange for next week. B: Reschedule for later today.

The cleaner had said they would definitely be going into Euston, so if Saheel was patient and waited, he could still make it work. He'd need to log into his website and change the scheduled time for the post to be published, the video of him, but that would be easy enough to do.

Yes. The realization settled him. The pulse jumping under his skin eased off a little. No need to change the plan. It could still work. Maybe an hour or two later but that was a relatively minor adjustment to make.

Across the way the woman had picked up a newspaper and was waving it in front of her face.

No one knows a thing, Saheel told himself. Just because I'd asked about how long they'd be delayed. He wasn't the only passenger to request help or advice.

'We're so proud of you.' His mother's voice was so clear that he looked around to see who'd spoken. *And after today?* He didn't want her in his head now. Personal matters were irrelevant to him: he was beyond, above, all that.

Recalibrate the plan. Once they were moving again he'd be able to calculate the arrival time at Euston. They'd probably announce it, wouldn't they? *Now expected to arrive at whatever* and then he could alter his website to publish five minutes after that time.

Thieves, the cleaner had said, stealing copper. Saheel wasn't going to let a bunch of thieves derail his day of glory. With the decision came certainty, relief. He closed his eyes and said a prayer of thanks.

In a just world, thieves would lose their hands. There was no justice here: the UK was steeped in depravity – abominations like allowing perverts to marry each other, something that had always been forbidden, unnatural.

And women, his mother and sister included, who called themselves Muslims but dressed immodestly. He'd told Kulsoom she should wear the hijab and she'd rolled her eyes, like the insolent brat she was. She had even put up a poster of Malala, that agent of the West, a puppet for the CIA.

When Saheel had spoken to his father, inviting him to the mosque, his father said he was happy as he was, that he said his prayers at home, that he didn't need to go to a mosque. 'Islam is a beautiful faith,' his father said, patting the arm of the chair for emphasis. 'It is light, it is tolerance. Beware of people trying to twist it, to make it narrow and full of persecution. We are in the twenty-first century, Saheel. We are not stuck on some God-forsaken mountain bound by the short-sighted teachings of some third-rate mullah.'

Saheel had wanted to strike him for the way he disrespected the tradition.

'We all adhere to the five pillars,' his father said, 'but we must be strong enough as a community to embrace different ways of being a good Muslim, to open our hearts not close our fists, to preach love not hatred.'

'People stray from the true faith,' Saheel had said. 'They weaken it, forget the tradition. They are not devout. They have forgotten what it means. Radical Islam is the holy way, the one true way.'

'Where is the joy? Where is the beauty and love in radical Islam? It's choked, poisoned. Life is sacred. Islam, our tradition, has been one of civilization, of tolerance, and now those who whip up hatred make us all savages,' his father said.

132

'Palestine,' Saheel had said. 'Bosnia. We are being slaughtered.'

'And slaughter is wrong,' his father responded. 'I agree. So are suicide bombings and attacking schools.'

'It's a holy war,' Saheel had said. 'Should we do nothing, let the oppressors destroy us all?'

'I won't have it, Saheel. You are an intelligent boy, bright, gifted. You wish to study Islam, all well and good, but find yourself a good teacher, a learned man. Not some ranter on a soapbox who can barely speak English, and can only obsess about world domination and waging a senseless bloody war.'

'Drone strikes, every day,' Saheel said. 'They didn't even count the casualties in Iraq. We didn't count. That's a senseless bloody war.'

'Who is dying in this jihad?' his father said. 'Children, women, Muslims many of them.'

There will be casualties, Saheel thought, but he didn't say it aloud. He'd probably said too much already. It was before he'd decided to act but even then he'd known he had to take some care not to alarm his family, who were so comfortable in their lazy, decadent lives, who swallowed all the propaganda and lies the BBC shovelled at them. He had to take care not to sound too radical in case they tried to interfere and prevent him from following his chosen path.

It had become harder and harder to stomach university life. The lectures were OK – there weren't many women in his chemistry classes – and there were other brothers at uni, a handful, who shared the same truth. Would understand, even envy, Saheel's mission. But everywhere on campus women took delight in flaunting themselves. Screeching about equality and identity and demeaning themselves, showing their flesh, like so many whores. And men, homosexuals, taking delight with wanton public displays of sexual perversion. Others were drunk, even in daylight. It was Sodom and Gomorrah, like the people of Lot in the Qur'an who were destroyed for their sinfulness.

Destruction was needed to cleanse, to renew, to wipe out corruption. Fire and flood, to scour the places clean. That was what the jihad would do. He and his brothers, the ones who had gone before him, the ones fighting and dying today in Iraq and Syria would be united in Heaven. Those who had taken up the sword, following the Prophet, those who had sworn to strike down the Jew, the homosexual, the impure woman, the Christian. A mighty army of mujahideen.

And then the great Caliphate would rule the world. A global force of purity and grace.

Holly

'Excuse me?' Holly said to the dad (Nick, his wife had called him). 'Please could I charge my phone?'

There was a moment, dead quick, a speck of time when she could tell he wanted to say no. Then basic manners or whatever won out and he took her charger and handset, and reached past Eddie to plug it in.

Was he a racist? Or just a miserable git? Imagine a life like that, everything a hassle, a pain in the arse. If she ever got that moody, she'd sort it out, get some therapy, try some medicine, anything rather than wallow in it. Of course, if the guy was depressed, proper depression, she knew there was no magic wand, but even then people could improve, find a way to cope with it, periods of being well. It wasn't like a fixed thing. A life sentence.

'I'm going to ring them,' Jeff said.

'OK. What's the time?'

'Twelve o'clock.'

He pulled up the number. Then he hesitated. His knee bounced up and down.

'Just tell them your train is delayed, you may be a bit late, you'll ring when you know more,' she said.

He nodded. Swiped the number, turned away from her a little. When he spoke it was fast and his voice sounded deeper, as if he was trying to make it more forceful. 'Hi, my name is Jeff and I'm coming in for an interview this afternoon. I'm on my way down from Manchester by train and we've run into signal problems so we're going to be late.' Whoever was on the other end said something, then Jeff said, 'It was one thirty.'

A pause. Then he said, 'Yes. I can ring you again when I know how late.' Then, 'OK. Cool. Thanks.' He turned to Holly. 'I don't need to ring again, just turn up.'

Without her phone, Holly hadn't anything to

135

do – she'd read most of her magazine. She'd noticed a copy of *Metro*, the free paper, on the table behind when she'd gone to the shop, and no one had been reading it. Now she asked the blonde woman there if she could take it.

Holly sat down and flipped through it. 'I love that picture.' She showed Jeff: a shot of the prime minister boring some little primary-school girl to death. David Cameron reading a book, the girl face down, her forehead on the desk.

'We've another three weeks of it,' Holly said. 'Have you registered?'

'What?' Jeff said.

'Have you registered to vote?'

'Nah. Makes me feel like she does.' He nodded to the picture.

'Come on. You don't vote, that lot could get in again.'

'They're all the same, politicians,' Jeff said.

'That's not true,' Holly said.

'A load of public-schoolboys,' Jeff said.

'I'll give you that,' Holly said. 'But you have to consider the policies.'

'It's all for old people,' Jeff said, 'or hard-working families.' He made quote marks.

'Have you been listening to Russell Brand?'

'I don't need some celebrity to tell me not to vote. I figured that out for myself,' Jeff said.

'That is so wrong,' she said. 'Of course nothing changes if we don't bother. It's compulsory in Australia.'

Jeff shrugged.

'So you just sit and moan? You must have an opinion on things. Like the bedroom tax.'

'Wrong.'

'Tuition fees?'

'Wrong. And that just goes to show you can't trust them. They'll tell a pack of lies, then do what they like anyway. They don't care what people like us think. It's all about London and the south, and the banks,' he said.

'But if we all voted, they'd have to take notice. If they get in again it will be ten times worse and they'll break up the NHS and make it like in America–'

Jeff yawned. *Cheeky sod.*

'You did not just do that!' she said. 'You did not just yawn at me.'

He went pink, then said, 'It's the lack of oxygen, automatic reflex.' A twinkle in his eyes again.

'Well, if that lot get in I shall know who to blame,' she said.

'They need to put the air con back on or we'll all suffocate. And then we'll starve and have to pick off the weakest for dinner.'

'I thought we'd suffocated already,' Holly said. 'You know, they blame everything that's wrong on benefits and immigrants.' Out of the corner of her eye, she saw movement, indistinct, but heard a snorting sound too. Nick. At her? Was he earwigging? She looked at him directly and he acted all interested in Eddie's drawing so Holly could tell she'd caught him out. So he was a Tory, then, maybe a Ukipper. Or he'd just got a downer on those worse off than him – claimants, immigrants. Lots of people had.

Drove. Her. Mental.

Jeff was texting, his nana maybe. Sweet. Holly

returned to the newspaper. Skimmed pages. Read a recipe for salmon with sesame seeds, soy sauce, ginger and coriander, which sounded tasty, and studied the fashion page. Maxi dresses were in, very like the one she wanted to look for in London. A lot had ethnic prints, throw-backs reworking the seventies, some psychedelic, others with tribal influences.

Holly fancied something in black, orange and gold. She'd already got some strappy gold sandals she could wear with it. She missed her phone but at least she wouldn't run out of juice halfway through the afternoon when Jeff would be getting in touch to arrange meeting her for coffee.

She folded the newspaper, got out her magazine and found the horoscopes.

Once Jeff had stopped texting, she said, 'What's your star sign?'

He pulled a face. 'Hades,' he said.

'Behave.'

'You don't believe in all that,' he said.

'Course not but it doesn't do any harm. So...'

'Virgo,' he said.

She lifted the magazine so he couldn't see it, angled her body towards him. 'It's been a long time coming but things are finally going your way. Today is a red-letter day with both money and romance on the horizon.'

'Give it here.' He snatched it from her and Holly began to laugh.

'You muppet,' he said. '"Virgo,"' he read out. '"Every cloud has a silver lining so don't lose hope. A letter will bring the chance of a big

138

change but look before you leap.'" He scoffed, 'Cliché Central.'

'My version was better,' Holly said.

'What are you?' Jeff said.

'Guess.'

'Loco,' Jeff said.

'You're funny,' Holly said. 'Leo.'

Jeff cleared his throat. '"Be careful with money this month. Not everything that glitters is gold. A chance encounter may bring turbulent times but follow your heart."'

She grinned at him and he grinned back.

'Seriously?' she said.

He shook his head, and said, 'Load of rubbish.' He shoved the magazine back at her. Still grinning. She checked the horoscope – he hadn't made it up.

She put the magazine away, settled herself into her seat, smiled at him.

'What?' he said.

'We shall see,' she told him. 'If it comes true. We shall just have to wait and see.'

Kulsoom

'My name is Saheel Iqbal. Today I brought jihad to Euston station. Punishment for the West, for this country that persecutes true believers, that slaughters the children of Islam around the world.'

Kulsoom, watching the video, froze. Shock, ice-

139

cold, swept through her.

'Today's bombing, which killed so many infidels, is done in the name of Allah. Allah is good, Allah is great, and I am a soldier of the Caliphate, a martyr of the holy jihad.'

Kulsoom felt blood pounding thick in her head, as though someone was strangling her, and an awful clutching in her belly as he sat there and spoke about death and Allah, jihad and victory. He was calm, he didn't shout or anything, but he was intense. The look in his eyes was scary. A bit mad.

'I go proudly to my death in the name of Islam. *Allahu Akbar.*' He placed his palms together. He smiled – he actually smiled – and closed his eyes.

This was insane.

The video ended and she sat there for a moment, thoughts wild in her head. Could she be wrong? Was it some weird trick like one of those programmes on the telly? But Saheel didn't play tricks any more. Everything was deadly serious.

Deadly.

Oh, my God. She stood up so quickly that the chair fell over.

He couldn't do that.

He mustn't do that.

All those people. All the people.

Her eyes stung as she pulled out her phone and speed-dialled her mother. She tried rehearsing what to say but it was all jumbled, a mish-mash of words all tangled. 'Mummy, Mummy,' she muttered, listening to the ring tone.

Her stomach dropped as the voicemail kicked

in. What should she say? Mum would check her phone on her lunch break but what could Kulsoom say? The tone sounded and Kulsoom felt panic run through her. She hung up.

Oh, Saheel. Oh, Mummy. Help.

She rang her mum's number again. This time she said, 'Mummy, ring me, straight away. It's really important. Please. Just ring. You need to come home. Something's... Just come home.'

Kulsoom shut the laptop. She wanted to get out of the room, away from it. She felt sick.

She sat at the top of the stairs and rang her dad. He was even less likely to answer. He kept his phone off most of the time, or forgot to charge it. Loads of times they would leave messages and he'd never get them. The family ganged up on him about it and he'd promise to keep it charged and check it but it never lasted very long. It drove them all crazy.

'I needed a lift.'

'I wanted you to pick up some flour.'

'Arfan's come off his bike. We're at A and E.'

It started to ring at his end. *Please let today be different.* Her dad would know what to do. But, oh, God, when he heard what Saheel was doing, it would break his heart.

Kulsoom waited, the phone ringing and ringing.

She heard them arguing sometimes, Saheel being mean and Dad trying to stay calm and reasonable, explaining where he was wrong, what the right thing was to do.

He was brilliant, her dad, but this... What if he had a heart attack or something?

The phone rang on and on, then switched to voicemail.

'Daddy, can you ring me?' Her voice was all wobbly – she sounded like a little kid. She wished for a moment that she *was* a little kid and she'd never needed to use Saheel's laptop or seen the stupid website and the horrible video. 'Something bad's happened. Please come home.' She left her message.

'I hate you, Saheel,' she said out loud. 'I hate you.' She hit her knees hard, once, twice.

Well, she wasn't a little kid so she would just have to work out what to do, wouldn't she? Because there were all those people at the station and Saheel there wanting to kill them. Babies and old people, people who worked at the station and people going to their jobs, visitors... And they all had families and friends and they were just ordinary. How horrible was that? Like the beheadings. Ordinary people. One of them had been from Salford, Alan Henning, and he'd taken aid to refugees in Syria, and they'd done it to him. He was a good man, doing good things, and they had killed him.

Kulsoom had had a nightmare about them doing it to her, and her family watching and not doing anything.

Should she ring Arfan? She wasn't sure that he'd know what to do.

Remembering how she'd called and texted Saheel earlier made her skin go cold. Of course he wouldn't answer her. What if she was too late?

She went downstairs and switched on BBC News while she rang Arfan.

142

He didn't answer. 'What is it with this stupid family?' she shouted. 'Arfan,' she said, 'you need to come home now. There's an emergency.'

Saheel couldn't do this! How could he do this to them?

There were people going out to Syria, like the schoolgirls, but that was different. There was a war going on there and people thought it was a just cause. Kulsoom had decided she was a pacifist, and even if she wasn't, she would never go out to be a jihadi bride. Some warrior's third or fourth wife. No, thanks very much. The only way she'd ever go, if she wasn't a pacifist, was if she was the same as the men, fighting alongside them. Islamic State were just like the Taliban: they wanted to put women back into the dark ages.

But Saheel's mission, that was just murder. Anyone with half a brain knew that.

She went up to her room and got a tissue. Looked at the picture of Arya Stark. She made herself stop crying and she dialled 999.

'Emergency. Which service do you require?'

'Police.' She said it twice because her voice was so weedy. 'Police.' And she bit at her fist and stared at the mountain she'd made and the penguin with ice-cube earrings, and her heart was like a trapped bird, beating at a window. It was like a bad dream, the worst sort, when you tell yourself to wake up and you'll be safe. You'll be safe if you just wake up. He was going to kill himself too. Her mum: she loved them all, but she loved Saheel in a special way. Kulsoom didn't know if it was because he was the first child or because he was the eldest son or because her mum worried about him in a different way from worrying about Arfan. Man, was she right to worry.

'I hate you, Saheel,' Kulsoom yelled. Her cry was swallowed up in the silence of the house.

It would never, ever be the same again, she realized, even if she got them to catch Saheel in time. Everything would change. And not in a good way. She had to be brave. She had to be brave and strong. Even though she wanted to just run away or hide. *She had to be brave and strong.* And then the voice on the phone said, 'Can I take your name, caller?'

'Kulsoom Iqbal,' she said, getting to her feet.

Kulsoom Iqbal, and my brother is a suicide bomber.

CHAPTER FOUR

Jeff

His nana texted, *how around*
  Jeff waited.
  how about looms
  What looms? he replied.
  4 twins
  Jeff had an image of Faye and Violet crawling under clattering machines, dressed in mob caps and pinafores and clogs, pale and half starved.
  Weaving looms? he typed.
  banks
  Jeff gave up and rang her. 'Nana, what looms?'

144

'The bands, like rubber bands.'

For birthday presents! 'Oh, got yer. They had some at Christmas but they still play with them. You could get them some more.' The house was littered with the Day-glo coloured straps that the twins wove into bracelets and necklaces and little toys.

He couldn't hear what she said next as the train suddenly shuddered into life and the announcement came, too loud, over the PA. 'Ladies and gentlemen, we've now got the go-ahead to resume our journey, with repairs to signals successfully completed. Thank you for your patience and once again we apologize for any inconvenience this may have caused. Our estimated time of arrival into Euston is now thirteen oh-eight.'

'We're moving,' Jeff said, into the phone.

'Will you be on time?'

'Should be.'

'Good luck, then. I think I'll get these loom bands.'

'OK. Bye.'

He wished she'd ask his mum about this sort of thing but his mum and his nana worked best with a bit of distance between them, like a no-go zone, and Jeff was the messenger running between them.

'My kid sisters,' he said to Holly. 'It's their birthday soon, and my gran's looking for presents.'

'How old?' Holly said.

'Seven – they will be. Twins.'

He thought for a millisecond about showing her a photo but decided that might be a bit pathetic. Then she said, 'You got any pictures?'

145

He pulled one up – they were in elf outfits from the Christmas show.

'Sweet!' Holly said. 'They look totally identical. Can you tell them apart?'

'Yeah, just tiny things.'

'They're like little versions of you,' she said.

'Nah. They take after our mum. The eyes, the nose. We've got different dads.'

'What are they called?' Holly said.

'Faye and Violet. You got any brothers and sisters?'

'One brother, Oliver. Older. He works in a bank.' She mimed a yawn. 'But he's happy. Married, mortgage, baby on the way. I'll be an auntie. They know it's going to be a boy and they're calling it Rodney.' She curled her lip.

Rodney. Jeff thought of the old sitcom *Only Fools and Horses,* the dim younger brother. 'You're not keen?' he said.

'Rodney? Seriously?'

Her eyes were so bright, the way they sparkled. Jeff wondered if she did anything, had special drops or something that made them gleam like that. 'Roddy's not bad,' he said.

'Not good either. I'd want to meet the baby first, decide what suited it.'

Jeff typed *Rodney* into his browser. He felt his cheeks glow and he stifled a laugh as he read the first result, in the Urban Dictionary. 'Referring to someone with an unusually large penis'.

'They might want to check this out.' He showed Holly the screen.

'Epic!' She laughed and passed the phone back. He caught a whiff of her perfume again. 'Thing

146

is, it's her dad's name – the baby's mother,' she said. 'She might not appreciate the heads-up.'

Jeff glanced at the other links. The name meant 'famous', and had something to do with a place called Hroda's Island.

'What's Jeff mean?' Holly said.

'"God's peace",' he said, 'or "traveller".' He preferred 'traveller'.

'Today at least,' she said.

'And Holly?'

'Apart from prickly? That was bare rude,' she said.

'Called it as I saw it,' Jeff said. He liked the banter.

'I'm a shrub,' she said, 'nothing deeper. It's all old-fashioned names coming round again now, like Oscar and Felix and Phoebe. When I have kids, I'll go for simple, ordinary names like Sam or Amy.'

'You want kids?' Jeff said.

'Think so. Some day. Not until I've established myself, done something career-wise. Not till my thirties, I reckon. You?'

Jeff hadn't expected her to ask but he didn't have to think twice.

'Yes,' he said, sounding more intense than he'd meant to.

She narrowed one eye, looked at him. 'Not that you're sure or anything. Got the names picked out?'

'No–'

But she laughed and put her hand on his arm. 'I'm joshing.'

Jeff found it hard to concentrate but he muttered, 'Nothing too naff about covers it.'

She took her hand back and he wanted to tell her to leave it there. She liked him. He'd no idea why but she definitely liked him. She'd agreed to coffee. OK, maybe that would be it, a coffee and goodbye, never meet again, but why agree to coffee if that was all you wanted?

He hadn't been out with anyone for more than two years. Not even close. Jeff wondered at what point you told an inconvenient truth to someone you were interested in. At what stage did you come clean? How many dates in? Before the first sex? After? It must depend on how quickly things developed, he thought. Exactly when did you say, 'Oh, by the way, I've been treated for anxiety and depression, and I'm fine now but there's no guarantee it won't come back'?

Not much of an ice-breaker, more a wrecking ball.

Not today, he decided. Today was turning out to be better than he'd expected. Now they were moving again. He would just sit back and go with the flow, smile and hope it wouldn't be too long before Holly touched him again.

Caroline

The student hadn't come back and Caroline couldn't stop wondering about him. She felt as though her teeth would shatter, her jaw was so tight. And the tension sent pain lancing into the

148

back of her eyes. She tried rolling her head from side to side, dipping her chin and stretching her neck, but everything stayed locked tight.

They passed a small village clustered round a church with a slender spire, a granary close by, then more farmland. She saw a blasted tree, black limbs jagged against the sky. And as the train canted left she glimpsed more canal boats and then a row of poplars, like feathers, ranked along the edge of a field.

She had an image of the children building sandcastles, scouring the beach for feathers and shells. The largest feather always had pride of place stuck in the highest tower. They picked up feathers on walks too. Paddy had kept a collection, stuck in little blobs of Plasticine and labelled: *crow, pigeon, magpie*. Amelia had worn hers in her hair.

Where was Amelia now? Drunk or high with friends? Having sex? Window-shopping? Shoplifting?

The cleaner came through the carriage and Caroline made her decision. She felt a swoop in her belly and a wave of dizziness as she got to her feet to follow him. She didn't want to risk being overheard by anyone else.

'Excuse me?' Her mouth was dry.

The cleaner turned.

They were just beyond the toilet, near the doors into coach A, the back of the train.

'Miss?' His face was open, pleasant and friendly.

'Naz, isn't it?' Caroline said.

He glanced down at his name badge as if he

149

was checking. 'That's right,' he said.

'It's probably nothing,' she began, 'but I ... well...' The words ran away from her.

He smiled, a little uneasily she thought, picking up on her fears, perhaps.

God, she was an idiot. She was making a complete fool of herself. But she couldn't back down.

'The man in my coach, across the aisle from me, the Asian one with the university top on... Well, I could be way out of line here but you're supposed to report any suspicious behaviour. I think he's behaving suspiciously.'

'Right...' Naz said. 'Well...' He licked his lips, looked around, as though he might enlist help from somewhere else.

'He's really nervous,' Caroline said, 'on edge. And he's sweating, pouring with sweat, but he's kept his sweatshirt on.'

'OK.' He nodded slowly, and kept nodding, but his look was unfocused and he was frowning. Thinking, maybe.

'When I tried to talk to him he was ... well, he ... he cut me dead. He's got a rucksack and he could have asked me to watch it – I'd already asked him to keep an eye on my bag...' She was aware that she was talking too quickly, keen to dredge up everything she could to support her concern.

The train gave a jolt and Caroline lost her balance, fell towards the curved wall of the toilet cubicle. She stuck her hand out to save herself and jarred her wrist.

'Are you OK?' Naz said.

'Yes.'

He stroked the back of his head with one hand, blowing air out through his mouth. She could see he hadn't a clue what to do. This was way out of his league.

'There must be some sort of protocol,' she said to him.

He pulled a face. He was so very young, maybe eighteen, seventeen.

What if it was all a ghastly mistake? she thought. What if the student was neurotic or he'd had some bad news that had made him jittery? What if he was arrested and held under the Terrorism Act, when he was just going about his ordinary business? She'd have ruined his life. *Oh, God.* She had an impulse to backtrack and say, 'Maybe I'm imagining things.'

She flexed her wrist, felt the tug of pain. 'There's someone you can tell?' she asked. 'Get some advice?'

'Yes,' Naz said, 'I'll talk to the train manager. He can contact the Transport Police.' He looked ashen. 'Do you know where he is now? The passenger?'

'He went towards the shop,' Caroline said.

'OK.'

'I hope I'm wrong,' Caroline said.

She felt close to tears. She shouldn't even be on this train. If only she'd caught the one she was booked on. This wasn't real. It wasn't happening. How could she be standing here, talking in a lowered voice about– Her mind shied away from the thought. *Coward.* A bomb, then. A bomb or a grenade. Some way to hurt people, kill people. How had she got to that from someone sweating in an overheated train and not wanting to chat?

She was sweating herself, a hot flush. Bloody great timing. She felt her cheeks burn, her arms and thighs, everything. Knew she'd look red as a tomato. The dizziness persisted, and the high, keen fear that thrummed in her veins.

Then she saw him – the student – coming back.

'He's there.' She felt guilty, exposed. 'I'll, erm...' She pointed to her seat.

Naz twisted his mouth, hesitated.

Maybe she should move, sit elsewhere, Caroline thought. That would be the sensible thing to do, wouldn't it? But what if it alerted the student? Freaked him out and prompted him to start shooting or whatever?

Caroline had felt this level of fear just once before in her forty-nine years. It was different from the fears she'd had at times for the children when they were ill or hurt, even when Paddy, at the age of nine, was knocked down and concussed and there had been hours of not knowing if there was any brain damage. Different because this was terror, not fear. She had last felt it one evening, as she walked home alone after drinks with her colleagues. She had been stopped by two men with a knife. A horrible, savage-looking thing. A hunting knife. They'd stolen her bag, screaming at her all the time.

The terror had made it impossible to think, to talk coherently. Dread had flooded her system and her animal instincts had taken over. Shivering uncontrollably, she had handed over her bag, averting her gaze. She'd expected them to cut her, to kill her, the earth had opened beneath her feet.

She was shaking now.

'I just ... OK.' Naz moved away slowly.

Her phone rang.

She drew it out, the display juddering in her hand, but she could make out it was Amelia calling. She swiped at the screen twice before she managed to answer it.

'Amelia?'

'Mum–'

Caroline watched as the student reached his seat, his shoulders rounded as though he were shielding the rucksack in his arms. His eyes flickered around the carriage. His look settled briefly on her, still in the vestibule, and darted away so quickly. Too quickly.

She knew.

She was right.

'I love you, Amelia,' Caroline said. 'Whatever happens, I love you and Paddy and your dad. You know that? I love you so much.'

'Mum, what's wrong?'

The connection failed.

Caroline stared at the phone for a moment. She tried to call Trevor. No signal.

The train clattered on and she watched the greenery swallow them up as they dived into a deep embankment, choked in ivy and brambles.

Unsteadily she moved back to her seat, swallowing the bile at the back of her throat.

She tucked her hands under her armpits to hide the shaking.

And waited, stiff with fear.

Meg

Diana finished her water. She looked fine now, the pallor gone.

'Better?' Meg said.

'Yes.'

'What was it?' Meg said.

'I don't know. Probably my blood pressure. It was low last time they checked. I made an appointment yesterday for the end of the month.'

'So it's not the first time?' Meg was shocked. 'You never said anything.'

Diana looked at her, steadily.

'I should fetch Boss – if you want to stay here,' Meg said, an itchy feeling across her skin. 'And the bags–' Could she manage them on her own?

'Neither did you. You never said a word,' Diana said.

'Oh, let's not,' Meg said, trying to shut her up but Diana ploughed on, 'Did you think I hadn't noticed? You're skin and bone. You barely eat.'

'I was always skinny.'

'Why is it so hard?' Diana said. 'Why can't you share?'

'I didn't want to worry you,' Meg said. *And I didn't want to deal with you going on and on about it.*

'This is worse,' Diana said, banging the plastic bottle on the table. 'Lying to me, shutting me out. After everything–'

154

Oh, please, God, not another lecture about loyalty and cheating.

But Diana said, 'I can't believe you thought I wouldn't know, wouldn't see.'

'Can we do this later?' Meg said. 'Just enjoy the holiday and then ... face facts later.'

'What are the facts?' Diana said.

Meg shook her head.

Diana's mouth tightened and tears filled her eyes. 'It can be treated?' she asked. Begging.

'They could buy me a little time,' Meg said.

'And you said no?'

'Diana–'

'Of course you did. I know you.' She rubbed her brow. 'Where is it?'

'Everywhere. Bones, lungs, liver, brain.'

'You were going to tell me? Or were you going to make some bloody grand gesture and just disappear, jump off some cliff?'

Meg reached out to touch her but Diana jerked her hand away.

'I don't know what I was going to do,' Meg said. 'But now you know.' There was a pause, leaden, between them. 'There's always a hospice,' Meg said.

'Is that what you want?' Diana looked incredulous.

Meg couldn't reply. She covered her eyes, forced her tongue against the roof of her mouth. Of course she didn't want that. She didn't want any of it. She didn't want to be dying, she didn't want to stop. To stop work, to stop waking up every morning eager to get into the studio. To stop shaping and moulding and discovering form

155

and feeling. To stop breathing.

She didn't want to think about any of it.

'I want you to be at home,' Diana said, 'if that's what you'd like. I want to look after you.'

Meg turned her head, stared out of the window. They were passing rows of houses, tiny windows, ugly proportions. Then a playing field, goalposts set up, seagulls in a line on the crossbar. Pylons on the horizon and concrete towers, an electricity plant.

They rode through a copse, the sun's rays interrupted by the tree trunks, a strobe effect. Come the summer it would all be thick with leaves, a wall of green. And at home the cow parsley would be up to her shoulders and the hedgerows would be thick with dog rose and honeysuckle, the first hazelnuts. The swifts would be back. The kitchen full of flies.

Meg sometimes slept in her studio in the summer when the weather was fine, the Milky Way visible through the large Velux windows. Waking to the wash of red as the sun rose.

They had slept there together once, the two of them, had a christening for the space, when the last of the building conversion had been done, the smell of raw wood and fresh plaster and putty strong in the air.

Diana had served steak and chips and salad with blue cheese sauce, then strawberries and cream from the farm shop, all laid out in style on a trestle table covered with their best tablecloth. They'd drunk champagne, then a plummy rioja followed by cognac.

Diana had got sunburn on her shoulders that

weekend and yelped every so often when they were making love, then dissolved into fits of giggles.

Meg had spent the rest of that summer equipping her studio, dragging in her gear from the old outhouse, then begun to design the cast for a large bronze – one of her first big site-specific commissions.

Thirty years ago, that was. Gone so fast. So very fast. Water sinking through sand.

She turned back from the window. 'It won't be easy,' she said to Diana.

'It never has been,' Diana said. 'But if you think I'm bailing out on you now you've got another think coming.'

Meg nodded once. Her chest tight. She swallowed.

'Should we cancel?' Diana said. 'Go home?'

'No. It'll be fine. I want to see the sea,' Meg said. And she did, a powerful longing, made even stronger because it would be the last time.

'But the walks,' Diana said.

'You can carry me,' Meg said.

Diana gave a rueful smile.

'We'll take it easy. Call a cab when we need,' Meg said.

Diana took her hand. Diana's was plump, pretty, the nails trimmed and shiny with the pale pink polish she wore. By contrast Meg's hand was a claw, scrawny, blotched with liver spots and riddled with rope-like veins.

'Let's rescue the dog,' Diana said. Practical again but a tinge of sadness in her eyes.

Back at their seats, Meg took Boss from the

157

family. The dog wriggled and whined, as if they'd been gone for days. She staved off any interest in Diana's well-being saying, 'She's fine, thanks – she got a little dizzy with the heat.'

'The air con's back on,' the father said.

'Boss shook hands,' the little boy said. 'But he barked too.'

'That's him saying hello,' Meg told him.

She sat back in the window seat and Diana beside her. Diana leant in and touched her cheek. And Meg, her throat aching and the pressure in her chest like a fist, turned and held Diana's face to kiss her full on the lips.

She drew back and Diana beamed at her, face pink, eyes full of mischief. 'I might need a lie-down when we get there.'

Meg burst out laughing. 'Me too,' she said. 'A nice long lie-down.'

Nick

They were lesbians! For fuck's sake. It turned his stomach. Swapping tongues in public. Disgusting. People like that shouldn't be allowed to keep animals. Or have children. That was one thing the Muslims got right: no homos. He'd never have looked after the dog if he'd realized. He didn't think Eddie had noticed – he was still bent over his drawings. It was a perversion, a sin. That was what the Bible said. In fact, he was pretty sure that all the major religions were against it.

Of course, the Church of England had been watered down so much, trying to be trendy, trying to stay in business – they'd got women bishops and gay vicars, the lot.

And it spread, that sort of free-for-all, like a disease, with all the equal-opportunities crap, where you couldn't call a spade a spade or a queer a queer, until people couldn't tell right from wrong any more.

If either of his kids... Just the thought made him want to thump something. And tomorrow the wedding, the best man – he was a shirt-lifter. Lisa had told him.

'I don't want you making any nasty comments,' she had said. 'He's a nice bloke. So live and let live, yeah?'

He'd grunted some sort of agreement even though he thought she was wrong. Live and let live was really a form of apathy, laziness. Everything deteriorated, standards and that. Values, morals, tradition went out of the window. Take St George's Day, next week: it should be a public holiday. They should celebrate it at Eddie's school, our patron saint, but no – it was an afterthought, if that.

'Can we have a cat, then, Dad?' Eddie said.

'What?'

'You said we can't have a dog so can we have a cat?'

'No.'

Eddie wrinkled his nose. 'A fish?'

'Maybe,' Nick said.

'A shark?'

'Don't be stupid.'

'I'll draw a shark,' Eddie said. 'I'll draw a shark eating you.' He eyed Nick, his mouth set, mutinous.

'Yeah?' Nick said.

'With lots of blood and your leg hanging off.' He picked up a red pen, found a clean piece of paper.

'That's not very nice,' Nick said.

'You're not very nice,' Eddie said. 'I hate you, you're so mean.'

'Oi, that's enough.' He checked his watch. It was ten past twelve and their new arrival time was 13.08. An hour, near enough.

The coloured girl's phone, still charging, trilled with another alert.

He got out his own phone, looked up the odds on the Manchester derby. The signal was patchy and he couldn't connect. At least they'd be back home in time: kick-off was at four o'clock, Sunday. United would win it, he just knew they would. They were already doing way better than the previous year – which had been an unmitigated disaster. Moyes couldn't run a bath, let alone a Premiership football team. He'd cocked up the transfer window, trying to buy three of the world's best players and failing every time. Then he'd stuck in his old pal Fellaini, who played like a girl. United hadn't even made it into the Champions League. But Van Gaal had got the team back on form. And Fellaini, like the rest of them, was playing a decent game again. Strong management was crucial. Nick would watch the game on the big screen at the Chadwick. A few pints, couple of chasers, wash away the taste of

160

this weekend and set him up for the week ahead.

A wail went up from Eddie, waking Lisa and making Evie flail in her sleep.

'Jesus Christ! What?' Nick said.

Eddie's mouth was a hole. He jabbed his pen down on the drawing. 'It's broken.'

He'd put so much red on the page that the paper was torn.

'Stop that noise,' Nick said.

'Never mind,' Lisa chipped in.

Eddie wailed on.

'Don't be a cry-baby,' Nick said. 'You can draw it again. Come on, you big cissy.'

That prompted another howl and a 'Nick!' from Lisa.

'Here.' He pulled a piece of paper from the small pile and grabbed a blue pen. 'Noughts and crosses.'

He sketched the grid. 'You can go first.' He handed Eddie the pen. *Just shut the fuck up.*

Eddie sobbed a couple of times, then scrawled a cross in the centre square.

'Good move,' Nick said, acting like Eddie didn't always start there.

There was a whooping sound, someone pressing the emergency call button in the bog instead of the flush. Idiot. Like it wasn't labelled clearly enough.

The cleaner came past, bag in hand, but he didn't bother asking if anyone had any rubbish. Typical.

'Hey,' Nick called after him. He took the torn shark drawing and screwed it up.

The lad just stared at him, like he'd lost the

power of thought. 'Rubbish,' Nick said, holding up his hand.

'I just...' His words trailed off. What a prat. He never even took the picture but carried on walking.

Eddie began to cry again. 'My picture. You squashed my picture.'

'It was ruined anyway,' Nick said. A flash of rage sent heat across his shoulders. 'Here, have it!' He slammed it down, pulled it open, spread it out and pushed it over the table.

He heard Lisa breathe in sharply and glared at her. He could do without her sticking her oar in. She was too soft on him.

They were passing a village, a lake with someone fishing, a cricket pitch. Timeless. He imagined playing, a warm summer's day, cold lager in the pavilion. His mouth watered. He'd get one in a few minutes. No driving to do, so why not? Something to wet his whistle. And if there was any room to sit near the shop, he'd drink it there. Have a break from the kids.

Christ knows, he deserved it.

Kulsoom

The man at the other end of the line kept Kulsoom talking. He said officers were on their way to the address but meanwhile he asked her questions. *Was she alone in the house? Was anyone expected home? Could she confirm her date of birth?*

She'd already given it twice. *Where was her brother now?*

'I don't know. In London probably.'

When had she last seen him? Where did her parents work?

She was answering that when she heard the piercing sound of sirens getting louder and louder. Then they stopped dead. She looked out of the window. There were three police vans, cars, lots of cars, pulling up. Some blocking the road.

Men in black uniforms streamed out of the vans. They had big round helmets on, a bit like motorbike ones, and bulky clothes. There were others in normal police uniforms. Those ones began banging on the doors of all the houses along the street. It looked like they were evacuating people.

'The police are here,' she said to the man on the phone.

'Just do exactly what they tell you,' he said, 'and—'

There was hammering on the door and an amplified voice, loud and angry, called, 'This is the police! Open the door slowly and then wait. This is the police. Open the door slowly and wait for further instructions. Open the door now!'

Kulsoom went to the door. Her fingers slipped on the latch.

'Open the door!' the man yelled.

She pulled it open and stood there trembling.

A semicircle of figures in riot gear ringed their drive and the drives either side.

They had guns. They were pointing them at Kulsoom. Kulsoom's knees felt weak, like she was a puppet.

'Put the phone on the ground!' the man yelled at her. He had a megaphone.

Slowly, she bent to put it down on the mat just inside the door.

She tried not to cry.

'Put your hands on your head. Hands on your head, and step out of the house.'

They were going to arrest her. She was the one who'd told them but they'd arrest her and lock her up. They might not even tell her why. There were different rules if it was terrorism.

Kulsoom raised her hands, she put them on her head, she moved over the edge of the door and onto the front step.

'On your knees,' the man said.

She tried to talk: 'I've not done–'

'On your knees!' He was like a machine. Barking instructions.

She could see people running to the back of the house and hear the crackle of police radios or walkie-talkies.

She couldn't get down on her knees with her hands on her head, she'd lose her balance and fall over. She let her arms drop.

'Hands on your head! Hands on your head!'

Don't shout at me! She needed Mum and Dad here, she needed help.

She landed heavily on her knees. Put her hands back on her head.

She waited there until a man ran up and used a wand, shaped like a bat, to scan her front and back. He spoke into his walkie-talkie, then someone else came forward, a woman in plain clothes, and told Kulsoom she could get up.

Kulsoom went to pick up her phone but the woman said, 'Don't touch it. Come over here, and sit in the car.'

They hadn't handcuffed her but it still felt like they might take her away, as if she had done something wrong.

The woman didn't smile. No one did. Lots of them were staring at her. Some had their mouths hidden, the sun shining on the visors of their helmets, but the ones she could see, they were all so serious and some of them looked angry.

'I want my mum,' Kulsoom said.

'Your parents are on their way,' the woman said. She wore a headset, like people in call centres. A bit of it dangled down. 'Kulsoom, I need you to answer these questions and it's very important to answer carefully. If you don't know the answer then please just say so. Don't make anything up.'

Kulsoom nodded.

The men in the special clothes – well, they all looked like men but you couldn't really tell with the big black gear – they were filing into the house, shouting things to each other. They had a dog too, a big one.

'You found a video on your brother Saheel's laptop?'

'Yes.'

'Where is the laptop?'

'In his room,' Kulsoom said.

'Which is his room?'

'The one at the back, on the left, next to the bathroom.'

'Have you been in contact with him today?' the woman said.

'No.'

'So if we check your phone...' she said, like Kulsoom was lying.

'I tried to ring him,' Kulsoom said, 'but he never replied.'

'Why did you try to contact him?'

'To ask if I could borrow his laptop,' Kulsoom said.

'This was before you saw the video?'

Duh!

Kulsoom wanted to cry but she was cross, too, that the woman was treating her like some thick little kid or someone who had something to hide. 'Yes,' she said. She thought of Saheel in London and the video, and she said, all in a rush, 'You've got to stop him! He said he'll blow up the station and he'll die and–'

'We're tracing him now,' the woman said. 'Do you know when he left for London?'

'No. He was here last night.'

'How would he get there?'

'He hasn't got a car,' Kulsoom said. He had wanted one but the insurance was too high.

'So the train or a coach? A lift?' the woman said.

Another van arrived, plain white. People got out and began pulling on blue jumpsuits. The man with the dog came out of the house and talked to them.

Kulsoom could see the police had sealed off the road and that some of the neighbours were waiting by the tape. The man with the ponytail, who worked at Tesco Extra, had his phone held up: he was filming or taking photos.

They would know – the whole world would know. But if they could catch Saheel. If they could just stop him...

'Have you a photograph of him?' the woman said.

'On my phone,' Kulsoom said. 'And there's a picture in the living room.'

The woman picked up the hanging bit of her headset and spoke into it. Told someone about the picture.

'What is Saheel's date of birth?'

Kulsoom had to think for a minute: she knew it was 14 March but the year... He'd been twenty-one this time, so that meant it must be 1994. She told the woman.

'Does he just have the one mobile phone?'

'I think so. I don't know,' Kulsoom said.

'Does he work?'

'No, he's a student.'

The woman watched her all the time, leaning towards her, listening hard as if she might miss something.

'Where?'

'At Salford University.'

'And what is he studying?'

'Chemistry.'

A policeman appeared, holding the family photograph. It had been taken at Saheel's sixth-form awards ceremony, the five of them posed together outside the Bridgewater Hall. Saheel had won prizes.

The woman lowered the window and the

policeman passed in the photograph.

'This is Saheel?' The woman pointed.

Kulsoom's throat hurt when she looked at the photo. She nodded. 'But he's got a beard now,' she said.

The woman handed the photograph back to the policeman and shut the window, then spoke into her little microphone, talking about Saheel's beard and CCTV and Euston.

Someone else came out of the house with a plastic bag and what looked like Saheel's laptop inside it.

'The video's on there,' Kulsoom said, 'and the website.'

'Yes. Has your brother ever been in trouble before?'

'No,' Kulsoom said.

'Has he travelled abroad, to Afghanistan, Pakistan, Syria?'

Kulsoom thought of the trip to her grandfather's funeral. 'Only for a family thing in Pakistan.'

'He travelled with you?'

'Yes.'

'He didn't stay on?' the woman said.

'No,' Kulsoom said.

'Has he any friends who might be with him now?'

'No. I don't really know who his friends are. He never brings anyone home.' He used to before he got all strict and religious. He had a gang of mates back then. They'd pile in from school, with bags of sweets, and play video games for a couple of hours. But they all studied hard too. They were

168

going to be doctors and engineers and business-
men. 'Is Arfan all right?'

'We're not sure where Arfan is,' the woman said.

Were they together? Kulsoom's hands felt sticky.

'Could Arfan have gone with Saheel?' the
woman said.

'No. No, he wouldn't,' Kulsoom said. Saheel
hated Arfan even more than he hated Kulsoom.
All Arfan wanted to do was mess about and have
a good time. He'd never be into anything like
that. And how could Saheel do it? How could he
do this to them all?

Kulsoom thought of her mum again. She'd be
at work, thinking about what to make for tea,
wondering if her new shoes had arrived ... and
coming home to this.

A car pulled up then, an ordinary car, and
Kulsoom expected it would be more plain-
clothes police but she saw her dad get out of the
back seat. He was grey and wobbly. He gazed
about like he was lost. He looked awful.

Kulsoom moved to go to him but the woman
said, 'Stay here.'

'My dad,' she said.

'You can see him in a few minutes. We need to
talk to him first.'

Kulsoom felt like exploding, telling the woman
to stop being so mean. If it hadn't been for Kulsoom they wouldn't even know about Saheel so
they could at least show her some respect and
treat her nicely.

A man in a suit tapped on the window, and
when the woman opened it, he started asking
about telecoms. Quick as she could, Kulsoom

swung her door open and ran towards her dad. He had his back to her so he hadn't seen her.

'Daddy!' she cried. 'Daddy!'

He turned, his face all creased up, and opened his arms. She ran into his embrace, ignoring all the shouts and the blur of people moving towards them.

'My sweet girl.' He kissed her head. 'Oh, my sweet, sweet girl.'

Then she couldn't do anything, she couldn't say anything, she couldn't tell him anything because she was crying so hard.

Naz

Naz couldn't think straight. It was like his head was full of voices, telling him what to do, but they were shouting over each other and the words were mangled and didn't make sense.

He stopped in the vestibule. He felt breathless, like he'd been running.

He closed his eyes and tried to concentrate. He'd said to the lady that he'd tell the train manager. So maybe he should just do that. But there was this niggling in his head. What if he went to do that and while he was away the student did whatever he was planning? If the lady was right and he was a terrorist then all those people, they'd be hurt, killed even. So the thing is, should he leave them while he went for help, or should he get them out of the carriage and then get help?

And if Naz started moving people wouldn't the student get all stressed and blow everything up?

Naz could come up with a story maybe, like 'The electricity unit's failing so we want to move you to alternative seats', and leave the student to last. Pretend there was some problem finding spaces further up the train.

Or should he just see the train manager first? He would have been told what to do in this sort of situation, wouldn't he?

Naz couldn't decide. He was never good under pressure. He needed time to weigh things up, even sweating the small stuff, like which trainers to buy or what to have for tea when his mum offered a choice, cos you never knew if you were going to get it wrong. His mum would get in a state with him about it and that only made it harder to decide. He'd been the same at school, when they'd had to decide on which questions or topics to do in some subjects and Naz would spend far too long picking one, or he'd start one, have second thoughts and start another, then run out of time.

He hated it, hated the way it paralysed him. Like a useless idiot.

The lady could be wrong. There were a lot of false alarms: controlled explosions of somebody's groceries and raids on the wrong people. So maybe he'd look like a prat but at least he'd be a living, breathing prat.

What if he did a baggage inspection? Said there'd been an increase in security and he needed to do a routine check for suspicious items.

But if the student did have a bomb or a gun in his bag he'd hardly be happy to let Naz go nosing about. He'd be more likely to set it off. It couldn't be a sword – you wouldn't fit a sword in there, innit. It could be a vest! Naz's stomach flipped. The man wouldn't take his hoodie off. He was sweating. He could be hiding a suicide vest.

He must evacuate the passengers as quickly as possible, find a way to leave the student there then get help. He needed to be careful so he didn't start a panic and freak out the whole train. He could maybe use the emergency call button. The train manager would be able to talk to him over the call system. The only people who would hear Naz would be anyone close by. So if he cleared out coach B, told the student he'd find him a seat, then made the call from the other end of the coach, no one could listen in.

The train manager could arrange an emergency stop at the next station and they could get help from British Transport Police or the Anti-terrorism Squad or whatever it was.

He nodded to himself. He would start with this end: the old ladies and their dog, then the ladies on business and then the family. Work his way down the carriage.

If the lady was right and the student was a terrorist, Naz hoped he'd be caught and sent down for a very long time. People like him gave Islam a bad name, gave Muslims a bad name. The government and the news talked like all Muslims were to blame for a few nutters, said that the rest of them should be responsible, that it was their job to identify the radicals and stop them. They never said that when it was some Christian psycho killing people. Never blamed the bishops or the pope or all the people at church for it.

As far as Naz was concerned, it was all bad news, a waste of life, a waste of time. People should just get on together, like most people did, and if things were fair, there'd be no need for fighting and violence and that. Things just needed to be fair.

'Right,' he said aloud. He was scared, like shitting-himself scared, but there were all those passengers to think about. He straightened his jacket, picked up his rubbish bag, and pressed the button to go back into coach B. His favourite teacher, the one at college, she'd once said to him, 'You know what wool-gathering is?'

He'd shrugged. 'Some sort of recycling?'

'Daydreaming. And it's your default setting.'

'Yes, Miss,' he'd said.

'You need to apply yourself. You've a lot to offer, Naz, you could be amazing, but only if you apply yourself and stop the daydreaming. Decide what you want and do it.'

'Yes, Miss,' he said. 'I will, Miss.'

And now he would. Now he'd show them all.

Holly

On her way to get another drink Holly met the cleaner, Naz. He looked weird. He'd been cheerful and friendly before but now he was scowling. He looked worried.

173

Before she could ask him if he was OK, he said quietly, 'Please could you move up the train. We've a technical problem with this carriage.'

Oh, great. 'I need my phone.' She pointed her thumb back over her shoulder towards her seat.

'No,' he said quickly.

''Scuse me?'

'I need to evacuate the coach,' he said. 'People can come back for their belongings once the problem's been fixed.'

He was lying, she was sure. He couldn't look her in the eyes and he kept licking his lips. Why was he lying?

'What's going on?' Holly said.

'I can't–'

'What? What is it?' She didn't like the vibes coming off him.

'A security issue,' he said, 'so please–'

'What sort of issue?' she said.

His eyes flicked from side to side but she waited.

'Miss, please.'

'What sort of issue?'

'There's been a report of suspicious behaviour,' he said.

Oh, God. Holly felt adrenalin surge through her, a tingling in her wrists and a tightening of her skin. 'I'll get my friend,' she said, turning back.

He caught her elbow. 'We don't want to alarm anyone,' he said. 'It's just a technical fault.' He spoke firmly now, sounding older, more sure of himself

'Of course.'

This was the sort of thing they'd be covering in

174

her training course: safety for staff and clients, how to evacuate in case of fire or for a bomb scare, the role of first-aiders. She knew from her work so far that the priority was always to minimize the risk, to protect people, to remove them from potential danger and secure the assistance of the emergency services. Exactly what Naz was doing now.

'Got it,' Holly said, feeling sick.

'That was quick,' Jeff said, as Holly reached him but the smile died on his face when he saw her expression.

She bent close. 'We have to go into the next coach,' she said.

'Say again?'

'I'm not messing,' she said. She nodded towards Naz. 'The staff want us to move.'

'I've got a reservation,' he said jokily.

'It's nothing to do with reservations. It's important,' Holly said.

'What can be–'

'Keep your voice down.'

Naz was talking to the older women, the ones with the dog.

'Holly?' Jeff said.

'Will you just move?' she said, through gritted teeth.

He glared at her. 'If you tell me what this is all about, then maybe I will.'

Stubborn sod. But she saw he meant it.

She whispered in his ear, 'Someone's behaving suspiciously. They want people out of harm's way.'

He looked at her like he didn't believe it.

'Swear down,' she said.

'*Fuck,*' he mouthed.

'So let's move it, shall we?' She was surprised she could still string words together, only the faintest tremor in her voice, when inside she was quaking. It all felt unreal, like she was split in two. Watching herself, hearing herself from above. Part of her up there floating and seeing herself walk and talk like a robot while the real her was howling with fear and wanting to run as far and as fast as she could.

She'd gone several steps before she realized Jeff wasn't with her but standing by their seats. She gestured to him to hurry but he shook his head.

Holly hurried back. 'What the fuck?'

'Who is it?' Jeff said, his voice low.

'The Asian guy, I guess. I don't know.'

'Ask him.' Jeff nodded at Naz.

'Why? If you're so bloody interested, you ask him.'

'Holly, I can warn people this end but I need to know who to avoid.'

She felt a ripple of fear for him. 'Jeff, no. Just come.'

'You go.'

She hated him.

Stupid bloody hero.

She reached Naz, who had turned his attention to the three businesswomen, only two of them at the table – the redhead must have gone to the shop or the loo.

Holly looked back to Jeff. She touched Naz's shoulder. 'Is it the Asian guy?' she said, as quietly as she could. 'The one with the beard?'

176

Naz gave a nod, small but clear.

'OK,' Holly said.

'If you can just move,' Naz said to her.

'It's all right,' she said, 'we will. But it'll be quicker if you have some help.'

Naz looked surprised, then gave a quick grin.

Seriously? She needed a brain transplant. *Just. Walk. Away.*

But she went back to Jeff, whispered in his ear, then bent over to speak to the family, to Nick. 'Can I have my phone?' she said.

He passed it to her and she stuck it into her pocket, dropped the charger on her seat.

She turned back to the family. 'We've been asked to move further up the train, a technical fault, they say.'

'Oh, for Pete's sake.' Nick flung up his arms.

'You can leave your stuff here,' Holly said. 'They're going to sort the fault out at the next station so–'

'Well, we might as well stay here until then,' Nick said. 'What a bloody show.'

The mum, Lisa, was dozing and Holly shook her shoulder. 'Excuse me, you need to move up the train, into one of the other carriages. Take the children. There's a technical problem.'

The woman nodded sleepily and turned to pick up the baby.

'Stay there, Lisa. We're going nowhere,' Nick said.

'This is not a drill,' Holly said clearly, her eyes locked on his, her face close. 'Stay calm and leave the carriage.' And if he didn't do as she said, she'd pull him from his seat and kick him down

177

the aisle, the lardarse knobhead.

His expression changed, uncertainty slackening his muscles.

Naz joined her and leant over. 'Sir, you need to go now. Your luggage will remain here. Your co-operation is appreciated.' He gave a tight smile.

Nick opened his mouth to speak, closed it again and rolled his eyes but got to his feet: he must have picked up on the atmosphere. His wife moved too.

Holly scanned the carriage, the queue of passengers filling the aisle. Why was it taking so long? They were sleepwalkers.

She wanted to shout, to hurry them up, but knew that might be the worst possible thing to do. It was like there was a clock ticking in her head. The noise getting louder all the time. The danger drawing closer. She could feel her heart in her throat, choking her.

She looked to Jeff, who gave a nod, his eyes calm and steady. She'd expected him to be a puddle on the floor after all the knee-jiggling and the nerves about the interview.

'Nearly done,' he said.

'You two go now,' Naz said.

Yes. Holly wanted to run – to run and shove the people taking their own sweet time out of the way.

Jeff said, 'No, you're all right, mate. See the job done.'

'Jeff,' Holly said, appalled.

He gave her a smile, apologetic. 'You go.' Jeff tipped his head in that direction.

And leave you?

Naz walked on to the seats where the student

178

sat across the aisle from the middle-aged woman with streaked blonde hair. Holly's stomach fell.

Holly caught Jeff's hand and squeezed, she touched her head to his briefly, then put one foot in front of the other as they walked after Naz.

Jeff

Holly was squeezing Jeff's hand so hard he thought she'd cut off his blood supply.

He watched Naz speak to the woman sitting across the way from the Asian lad first, telling her there was a seat in coach D, the next but one coach, if she'd make her way there. She didn't need telling twice but got up and passed Jeff and Holly, joining the line filtering from the carriage.

'If you'll wait here, sir,' Naz said to the student, 'I'll check out how we are for space. We need to fix a technical issue in this coach.'

The rucksack was there on the seat. Jeff forced himself not to stare at it.

'So we're going to stop again?' the student said.

'Hopefully not for long,' Naz said. 'I'll be back in a moment, sir.'

The bloke looked from Naz to Jeff then glanced at Holly.

Jeff shrugged. 'It's all we need, more delay.' Keeping up the pretence, trying to sound natural.

The guy looked pissed off, hot and bothered, but so normal. Just like someone Jeff might have known at college. Maybe he was normal. Maybe all he had in the bag was his packed lunch and a change of underwear. Maybe this was one huge mistake and they'd all laugh about it later. He felt like laughing now, crazy, falling-apart laughter. Rolling on the floor laughing. ROFL. His nana had once asked him about that – said someone called Rolf must have hacked into his phone and was sending her messages.

Holly tugged at Jeff's hand and he wriggled his fingers. They could go now. It was done. He was giddy, light-headed. 'Come on, then,' he said to her. He wanted to hug her, kiss her, lift her up and carry her through the train. But she'd probably thump him if he tried.

A bang and a great roaring filled his ears. Darkness black outside. Jeff nearly collapsed until he realized it was a tunnel, that was all. The train lost speed, as if it was coming to a station. Slower and slower but still they hadn't reached the other end of the tunnel. The train creaked and rattled.

Then stopped.

Pitch black outside.

Naz looked round, his face confused, sickly in the artificial light. Taut with alarm.

Someone started shouting from the other end of the carriage where the logjam of people was. A woman with a Scottish accent. 'Why have we stopped? What's going on?'

Naz began to answer, 'It's probably a technical–'

Then the dog started barking and the Scottish woman kept shouting about having to get to hospital.

Jeff saw the student, on his feet now, behind Naz, the rucksack in his arms.

'It's all right, mate,' Jeff said. 'It's just the signals again.'

'How do you know?' the student said.

'He's right,' Naz said. 'I'll check with the manager and let you know. Just take your seat.' He raised his voice. 'If you please continue to vacate the carriage, ladies and gentlemen.'

The dog was barking on and on and the baby started to cry.

The student undid the flap covering the top of his bag, he was mumbling, muttering, a foreign language that Jeff couldn't understand.

'Sir,' Naz said, 'please don't do anything silly.'

'Let's talk,' Jeff said. 'Let's sit down and talk about it.'

Sweat was dripping down the student's face, little streams. 'You can't stop me.' He pulled open the drawstring.

'Mate,' Jeff said, one arm outstretched, palm facing him. *Stop. Don't.* 'Put the bag down.' His spine was jelly, hot, melting.

Someone else was screaming now.

'No, no, please,' Holly said. 'Don't be daft. Don't do this. There's little kids here.'

'Mate, please, we can work this out,' Jeff said.

'*Allahu Akbar,*' the man said, his eyes unsteady, his head shaking from side to side, his lips drawn back in a rictus grin.

Jeff tried to free his hand from Holly's but she clung tighter. She was pulling at him, trying to pull him back. He tried to push her off.

'Allah doesn't want this,' Naz said. 'We can

181

walk away from this.'

'*Allahu Akbar,*' he said, like a chant. He had his hand in the bag.

'Stop, bro, stop!' called Naz. 'Bro, stop!'

'Come on, please,' Jeff said. 'Put the bag down. It doesn't have to be like this. Think of your family.'

They were all talking at once, Naz and Holly and Jeff. Pleading.

'*Allahu Akbar!*' The man threw back his head and roared.

And then the air roared.

And then there was nothing.

CHAPTER FIVE

Holly

Holly was hurled through the air. Her body slammed into something hard and her arm was wrenched back. She fell in a shower of glass, shards of plastic and metal, landing heavily, the breath knocked out of her.

When she opened her eyes she saw suns, big black suns against a glaring white sky. She blinked and the suns flashed. That was all she could see.

The air was full of smoke and gritty dust, and a scorched smell coated her tongue, making her cough. Coughing hurt. Christ, it hurt. Her arm hurt and her hip and her back where she'd been flung through the carriage. There was a rushing noise in her ears, like a rainstorm, or a river. She liked the thought of water. Of bobbing in the waves, of a smooth dive into a clear cold blue pool. But she'd gone too deep: she was drowning, no air. With a gasp, she sucked in a breath and coughed, each spasm intensifying the pain in her arm and down her back. *Fuck!*

Jeff?

Was Jeff still there?

Under the swooshing sound she could hear voices, and a cry, indistinct. She twisted herself over, her teeth set against the pain, whining through her nose.

Prone, she lifted her head. The suns were fading, shrinking. She waited but she could see little. It was black, almost completely dark.

The pain became stronger, forcing her to squeeze her eyes shut and whimper again. The train seemed to sway. Then she thought perhaps the swaying was in her head. A fairground ride she couldn't get off. Spinning faster and faster, the loop stretching and distorting.

She must have blacked out. Waking to the dark, the sooty air and the savage pain, she heard crying and someone screaming, 'Help me! Help me!'

I'm not dead, she thought. Not yet. *Move.*

Her limbs, her muscles screeched in protest. She couldn't use her right hand but she struggled to her knees and then to her feet. Her shoes were gone. How come her shoes were gone?

She edged forward, her good arm held out in front of her, feeling for obstacles, her feet tripping over the rubbish, lumpy and uneven, that littered the floor.

She got her phone out of her pocket. The screen was smashed – she could feel the crazed spider web.

She tried to lift her bad hand to swipe the screen but there was no strength there. One-handed, she turned it on. It lit up. With her thumb she pressed the flashlight icon. Nothing happened but she tried again, harder, and the beam of blue-white light illuminated the space in front of her. The floor was strewn with lumps of plastic, shredded clothes, fragments of luggage, metal fittings, chunks of foam all scattered with a gravel of glass. And everywhere red, pieces of red. Like meat. *Oh, God.*

She tilted the phone to shine on her bad arm: her sleeve had been torn off. She saw all the blood, much more blood than on her good hand, which was flecked with cuts. And bone sticking out of her forearm. Ice water shot up her spine. She looked away, felt the lurch under her feet and her head swam.

She directed the flashlight ahead. To where she had been standing when the bomb went off. Something bulky had fallen across the coach, blocking the far end. It was a bank of seats, ripped out and flung down at a ninety-degree angle, creating a wall across the compartment, a narrow gap above.

The four of them had been on the other side of that when the bomb had gone off.

Jeff?

Could she climb it? Was there anything to step up on? Could she get over the top?

'Jeff?' It came out as a whisper. She couldn't clear her throat, and each breath coated her mouth with the thick grime in the air.

She tried again. 'Jeff? Jeff?'

'Hello?' A faint voice.

Was that him? 'Can you tell me your name?' Holly said.

A pause. Then, 'Rodney.'

She laughed, half choking, which hurt like hell. Stupid muppet.

Jeff

'There's stuff blocking the way,' Holly called. 'Can you get out your side?'

'Not at the moment,' he said. He was crushed, something wedged over his legs. And a weight across his chest. He couldn't see anything – his eyes were stinging. There was a high, chemical stink – burnt hair and melted plastic.

'Are you OK?' Holly said.

Was he? Maybe. 'Been better,' he said.

'Is Naz there?' Holly said.

He didn't know.

'Jeff?'

He wanted to rest, just sleep for a bit. Pain was gnawing at his legs, making him feel sick.

'Jeff? Is Naz there?'

'I don't know. It's dark.'

'Look,' she said. 'Try now. I'll shine my torch up.'

He wiped his eyes. They were gummy and gritty. He wiped them again and blinked. Saw a red wash. Then a cone of light, bouncing off the ceiling above, which was buckled and torn, illuminating the particles that trickled through the air, black snow. Jeff tried to focus on them but one eye wasn't working and the other ached.

The weight across his stomach was a person. Naz. He was lying across Jeff on his back, his head to Jeff's left and his legs to Jeff's right. Naz's jacket and shirt had been ripped off.

'He's here,' Jeff said. He couldn't see anyone else, couldn't see the bomber.

In the reflected torchlight he tried to focus on Naz's chest, to see any rise and fall. He thought he saw movement, but was that just Jeff's own breath lifting Naz a little too?

Jeff reached out his hand and touched Naz's neck, fearful of hurting him. He tried to find his pulse. It was a game he played with the twins. Him always the patient until he'd had enough of being prodded and bandaged and made to take his various medicines (Vimto and M&Ms).

He couldn't feel a pulse. He tried again.

'Jeff?' Holly called.

'He's in a bad way,' Jeff said.

Then Naz took a breath, a swift suck of air, and gave a faint groan.

'He's alive,' Jeff said.

'I can't get to you. I'm going to try and get help,' Holly said.

He didn't want her to go. He liked hearing her voice, knowing she was close by. 'Yes,' he said. He waited for her to say more.

'They'll probably be on their way by now,' she said.

'Are we still in the tunnel?' Jeff said.

'Yes,' she said.

Would there be any way out? He could imagine the whole thing had collapsed on them. That they'd have to be dug out, like trapped miners. 'Be careful,' he said.

'Of course.'

'I'd like to get out of here,' he said.

'Yes,' she said. 'Just hang on. It won't be long. Stay awake, promise me?'

'I will. Are you OK?'

'I'm fine,' she said. He heard a catch in her voice. 'I'd better go.'

'Yes. See you later.'

He watched the beam swing away and the darkness swoop back in again.

Naz made another sound, a moan in his throat. Jeff felt for his hand and gripped it. It was slack. Then Jeff felt Naz's fingers twitch and curl around his own.

'Naz,' Jeff said, 'Naz, it's me, Jeff. We're still on the train. But help's coming. You remember Holly? She's gone for help. Can you talk? Can you say something, mate?' Then he worried: maybe that wasn't the best thing to do. Should he get him to talk? Or not?

Jeff felt Naz's torso rise and fall as if he was taking a breath to speak but he didn't say anything. 'Help's coming,' Jeff said again. 'They'll get us out of here, yeah? Get us to the hospital. You just hang on and they'll sort us out and we'll be able to go home, yeah?'

Jeff's eyes stung again. With his free hand he wiped them, smelt the coppery blood. His head must be cut.

Another wave of tiredness rolled over him. It would be so easy to just sleep. But he'd promised Holly. The pain in his legs surged, like an electric shock in the marrow of his bones, and he howled.

Naz's fingers tightened.

'It's OK,' Jeff said. 'I'm going to stay here. They'll come and get us soon. They know what they're doing. You seen those documentaries? You watch them? *Traffic Cops* and the one about the fire service. They might have to cut us out.'

Jeff wondered how long the tunnel was and if they were near a town. Near a hospital.

He thought of himself walking into his home, back from his interview, where they'd accepted him then and there. He'd start his apprenticeship the following month. Back from coffee with Holly and a date to meet the following weekend in Manchester. Back from a kiss goodbye that went on for so long shoppers stopped and applauded. Back to the twins and his mum, Nana and Sean.

To celebrate.

He had to keep talking, to stay awake, to help Naz. He tried to think of something else to say but it was too difficult, so he said, 'It's going to be all right. Help's coming. We're going to get out of here. It's going to be all right,' repeating it over and over again in the dark, blood filling his eyes, and the smell of charred meat, chemical smoke and dead earth dense in the air.

Meg

Meg was choking, something thick in her throat. She retched and gulped in air but it was all smoke, oily and suffocating.

There had been a collision, a crash of some sort. Another train, perhaps. She choked again, tried rolling to one side. She was on the ground. That was good, wasn't it? With smoke. To be lower down.

She was by the tracks. Could just glimpse them in flickering orange light as the smoke billowed and moved. And the carriage above her, pitched to one side, the doors gone, some of the roof torn away.

She retched again, felt the contraction of her belly. Something wrong with her throat. She reached up and found a stake, hard and jagged, piercing her neck.

She tried to see Diana – she could make out some bodies on the ground but none she recognized.

There were chippings and dry dust against her cheek. She stretched out a hand, exploring. She didn't know what she was reaching for. She felt something soft and silky, a fabric remnant. She rolled it between her fingers. Her breath came in little snorts through her nose, but each one set her spluttering.

Meg closed her eyes. Thought of Boss. A pang

of worry. He'd be with Diana, looking after her. Yes, he would.

Someone started screaming, a horrible gibbering sound that made her heart clench. Then, just as suddenly, they stopped.

In the quiet that followed she heard a series of ticking, creaking sounds. She finally decided it must be metal cooling, resting. There was a fire, wasn't there? Dancing by the rails. There was smoke. The smell of bonfires. Of charcoal.

Perhaps she could whistle for Boss, whistle and he'd find her and bring Diana. She pursed her lips. Her whistle had always been clear and strong, carried a long way. But now her lips trembled and with the burbling in her throat she could make no sound.

Silly old bitch.

Her father had whistled beautiful tunes whenever he was busy drawing plans for his work. A civil engineer. 'Cyril the civil engineer,' he'd quip. 'Cyril by name, civil by nature.'

Daft old twerp. But she wished he were here now. He had made her her own drawing board, a smaller version of his, given her soft dark lead pencils and the biggest Meccano set on the market when he'd noticed how she coveted her cousin's.

When the schoolmistresses had talked about careers, about a shorthand-typing course or training to teach, it was her father who had brought home the prospectus for the Manchester School of Art. Who had built her a kiln in the garage. Who had taken her to the Tate Gallery and the Whitechapel Gallery in London, to the

British Museum. It was the sculptures, the marbles that had captivated her. And she had wanted to do that: to turn stone to something fluent, breathe life and movement into it, completing the circle.

Meg vomited, a gush of hot liquid that burnt her nose and mouth. The smell was foul. She inched herself over onto her other side and glimpsed Diana, a ray of harsh, white light sweeping across her. Her body was partially obscured by debris but her face and top half were visible. She looked to be asleep, her face blackened with grime, blood under her nose. Meg could almost touch her. She shuffled on her side until she was near enough to put a hand on Diana's arm. Meg felt the inertia, the lack of any resistance or the pulse of life she'd normally feel.

Oh, my love. Meg felt her own heart falter, the rhythm bucking in and out of time.

She closed her eyes. A wash of fluid filled her throat, bubbling inside.

There was a voice, a woman's voice, someone touching her shoulder. 'Hello, hello. Can you hear me? Please, stay with me. Stay with me.'

Why? Meg thought.

There was a fluttering in her chest. The wind was blowing hard through the tunnel, howling, and from up on the hills the sea was grey-green and white-capped. Shadows from the clouds raced over the grass slopes. The path went up, the hill was steep, but Diana was striding ahead. No sign of Boss – he'd be chasing rabbits – and Meg could hear her dad whistling and the gurgle of a stream somewhere, falling over the limestone rocks, creating caverns and crevices. She was carrying a rock. It was so heavy, too heavy, it was crushing her. So she set it down.

And flew up the hill into the sun.

Kulsoom

They were all in the living room, Kulsoom between her mum and dad on the couch, her mum holding her hand. Arfan on the chair. Every so often her dad leant over and touched him and Arfan let him.

Everyone was different, acting differently. Shocked and frightened.

The room was crowded with police, too: the woman who had spoken to Kulsoom, who was called Detective Inspector Kent, three men all in suits and then two more in uniforms.

Someone had made tea because that was what you did. Kulsoom didn't drink tea so they got her a Coke. Her mum never picked up her cup. She kept crying quietly and using lots of tissues. And her dad blew his nose a lot.

Kulsoom couldn't cry any more. She wished she could just stop everything and wind back time, or wake up and find it had all been a stupid nightmare and Saheel was just boring and bossy but not a jihadi.

Detective Kent had explained that they would all be taken to a police station so they could make statements and suggested the family stay somewhere else for a few days. 'There'll be a lot of press interest and disruption. We want to make sure you're somewhere safe.'

'People could come after us?' Arfan said.

'It's a possibility,' the woman said.

'Can't you guard the house?' Arfan said.

But Dad hushed him and said it would be much better to be somewhere else.

'Jane's,' Mum said. 'I'll ring Jane.'

Jane was her friend from work. She was a convert, married to Haroon, who taught at the university. They lived out in the countryside, in the biggest house Kulsoom had ever visited.

'It's in Marple,' Mum said.

Detective Kent said that sounded like a good idea and they would help make the arrangements.

'Do you know where he is?' Dad said. 'Have you found Saheel?'

'We don't have any information on that yet,' Detective Inspector Kent said.

'You've got to stop him,' Kulsoom said.

'Euston is being evacuated. No trains will be allowed entry, either Overground or Underground, and that section of the network is closed.'

Kulsoom felt a little better. She wondered if they'd find him in the station. How would they stop him? How could they arrest him? If they used a Taser or something it might set the bomb off. Maybe they could get someone to talk to him and persuade him to give himself up. But if he escaped, what would he do? Go somewhere else in London?

'There's been a newsflash,' one of the men said. He was quite small and thin and had googly eyes so he looked surprised all the time.

He put the TV on and went to the BBC News Channel and it was there scrolling across the bottom: *Security alert. Euston station is being evacuated and services suspended. Passengers are advised to avoid the area and make alternative plans.* Then the picture changed and the man put the sound up. They watched people coming out of the station and there were streams of police cars and ambulances on the roads nearby.

Kulsoom felt sick. It might be all right if they could just find him. Then he'd be sent to prison but at least he wouldn't get a chance to kill anyone.

Dad lit a cigarette, which was totally weird because he never smoked in the house. What was even weirder was Mum didn't say anything.

Kulsoom hated smoking but thought it might be good to have something to calm you down at a time like this.

Dad kept saying, 'We had no idea.' Every few minutes. Like it kept hitting him again and again and he had forgotten and had to explain.

'What about my exams? Can I still do them?' Arfan said. And Kulsoom nearly laughed because he'd never seemed to care about his exams before and he was always arguing about them with Mum and Dad. Then she felt sorry for him because how could you do any exams or even think about revising at a time like this?

'Don't worry,' Dad said. 'We'll figure something out.'

She hated Saheel. She hated him for this. The way her dad was shivering and little bits of ash were falling onto the carpet, and Mum so sad that it made Kulsoom's belly ache.

She knew she wouldn't be able to do her project either, even if she had a working computer. Everything was spoiled, trashed. She felt like breaking something. Going upstairs and squashing the penguin and jumping on the mountain and tearing up her storyboard. But someone would stop her. They'd probably handcuff her and decide she was an accomplice, if she didn't do exactly what they said.

So she sat and waited, and finally one of the men turned the television off and said, 'We leave in about twenty minutes. If you can pack an overnight bag with any essentials.'

Her mother started crying again and Kulsoom's nose burnt and Dad patted her knee.

She thought of Miss Weston in the art room finding out about Saheel, and all the other people at school, and she just wanted to die. To die and never have to see anything or anybody ever again.

Naz

The duvet must've fallen off because he was freezing. He should probably be getting up. He wasn't sure what day it was or what shift he was on but he could check his phone.

All that mess! He remembered he'd left a mess

but he knew he could clear it up if the other people would help him. And if he asked his family they would help too. Someone would have to stay at the shop but the others could come, and his sister when she got in from her job.

Perhaps the heating was broken. The boiler was newish but it kept conking out and his parents had argued about whether to get new radiators as well. If they'd only talk about it they could probably sort it out but they never did. They only argued. Like disagreeing was more important than getting the thing fixed.

'Put another layer on,' his mum said.

He would but he couldn't find his clothes. Or his bedroom.

He was so thirsty, like his tongue was a stone in his mouth. Water. A great cup of water. He'd chug it down and then... There was something he needed to do, something important. It darted away from him, like a fish, small and transparent and hard to see. He wished he'd kept his jacket on, and his shirt. He was cold as ice. He wasn't supposed to take his shirt off: it didn't look good. NSFW. Not good at all. Someone might complain.

'Mum?' he called out, but she didn't answer.

He'd just have to put it on again as soon as he found it. As soon as he woke up.

'Huddled masses,' the catering manager said.

Naz asked her for a drink and she handed him a cup but it was empty.

'I'll have to get off then,' Naz said, 'I really need a drink.'

'At the next station stop,' the train manager said.

The train stopped and Naz bent to pick up his bag but it wasn't his bag. Something was wrong. Really bad. He was falling.

'Mum?' he cried out. He was still falling.

Then someone was there, talking. He didn't understand what they were saying. It was muffled. They sounded nice, innit. Kind.

He should be up soon. He needed to find his jacket and get to work. And get a drink.

There was a sharp prickling in his fingers. Probably Suki. Ever since she was a kitten she'd wake him by biting his toes or his fingers, yowling for some scran.

He could see gold, shining gold. It would be good for the sign at the restaurant but maybe not too shiny, like a matt version instead. Then he could invite some special people to the opening, as well as his family. Like Dynamo and Amir Khan and someone to do the music, maybe Bilal or even Jay Sean. Sweet. Get people to use WhatsApp and Facebook to spread the word.

Once he'd sorted the heating out. Nothing worse than a cold restaurant. Well, maybe a dirty one. But he'd never let that happen.

'Mum,' he called. 'I'm cold.'

She brought a blanket. He forgot to ask for a drink. His throat hurt. Like it was filled with glass. The nice voice kept murmuring close by and Naz listened but still couldn't understand. But he knew he wasn't all on his own.

'Stay together,' Naz said.

His sister smiled and asked him to pass the potatoes and his dad poured a glass of water, a huge glass – the water trickled over the sides and ran over the table but no one minded. His mother brought in a bowl of her best chicken and almonds, and she told all the other people from work and all the passengers to dig in and don't be shy.

Naz looked round the table and knew it would be fine, even without his shirt, because they were all together again. And, really, that was all that mattered.

Nick

The train had left the ground, then crashed back down with a great screaming sound of things being ripped and crumpled.

Nick remembered that. But nothing afterwards. He must have passed out.

He was on the ground, outside the train, near the doors. Where the doors had been. A pall of smoke hung in the air, smothering everything, a faint orange glow barely illuminating the space.

He managed to get onto his hands and knees, pushing his way out from under the debris that covered him, shaking off a layer of glass and dirt. His hands were wet, bleeding, but nothing appeared to be broken.

'Lisa!' he called. 'Lisa?' His ears were ringing and buzzing so his voice sounded as if it was coming from under water. No – underground. They were still in the tunnel. They were underground.

He looked about for her, for the kids.

His breath was coming too fast.

He saw an arm. Somebody's arm. On its own, like part of a dummy. Or something from a horror movie. Smeared with blood and soot.

The fire was nearby. He couldn't hear it, couldn't hear much of anything. He should get away from the fire. Find the others. Start here.

He tried to make sense of what he could see. Their coach was skewed diagonally across the tracks, the end close to the doors, where they had all been filing out, disappeared into a pile of rock and brick. The back end was crushed against the side of the tunnel. He couldn't see anything of the last coach.

Nick searched by the firelight outside the length of their carriage. He saw more bodies, body parts, but no sign of his family. The fire spat, leaping higher, licking at the wheels of the coach and the rockfall.

Check the carriage.

He heaved himself up into the train. There was a body there, at the other side. Torso inside the train, legs hanging down. No head, no arms. *Christ!* Nick jerked away but the image was seared into his mind.

He had to find Lisa – Lisa and the kids. *My family.* His chest tightened, his throat too, and he tried to breathe.

He got to his feet but stumbled immediately. It was like trying to stand on broken bricks. They were tilted to one side, the windows blown out. The luggage rack was gone and all the luggage, most of the seats.

He couldn't get into coach C: the roof had been stove in by the tunnel collapse, as though a giant hand had squashed it like an empty beer can.

He picked his way in the other direction, searching under the broken bits of carriage and seating for any trace of his family. There was a blockage part of the way down, impassable. The explosion had ripped through everything. Perhaps Lisa and the kids had got out in time, escaped the rockfall on coach C and gone even further up the train.

Outside to the right he thought he saw a flash of white light glancing over shapes on the ground.

Nick retraced his steps, checking one last time for any sign of them. He fell once, colliding with the remnants of a table and twisted metal.

He sat on the edge, where the doors had been, careful not to look at the corpse there. He saw by the dim firelight that his trousers were shredded, flaps of burnt cotton around his knees. Cuts and black grease smeared his legs. His socks had melted. They were stuck to his ankles.

He could feel panic at his back, waiting to claim him, but that wouldn't do anyone any good. He had to find his family and get them to safety. Focus only on that and nothing else. Never mind the way his socks had melted or the obscenity lying beside him or the way his guts were turned inside out.

Because of the angle of the carriage it was a drop of several feet down to the tracks. He moved onto his front, grunting as shards of debris pierced his chest, and gripped the ragged edge of the floor in his hands. He lowered himself until he felt the weight of his body taken by his arms and the bite of metal in his palms, then let go. He fell and rolled, agony flooding up his legs.

There was barely any light from the fire over this side but he saw a beam close to the ground: someone bending over another body. When the torchlight moved, sweeping over the area, he saw that the last coach, coach A, had also derailed and jack-knifed across the tracks the other way so the two carriages formed a V and made a large triangle with the tunnel wall.

The trackside was littered with detritus, scraps of fabric waving in the wind, flakes of something blowing about, people lying here and there. Everyone, everything coated black.

A peculiar calm settled in the centre of him. A sort of blankness. Because if he was calm – if he was calm and logical and didn't lose it – then it would all come right. He just had to concentrate on what was important: find Lisa and the kids.

Rhona

Rhona told the lassie everything. She couldn't get up herself, she'd fallen flat on her back, and though she tried to move, nothing worked properly. There was something wrong with her mouth, a numbness, like after a particularly awful visit to the dentist, but she made herself talk.

'Maisie, my daughter, she's five years old and she's no' well. She's in hospital, an emergency,

201

Manchester Children's Hospital. They're really good there but...' She felt the guilt hot in her chest. *I should have stayed at home with her. She said she was tired. She said her chest hurt.*

'Please can you get my ma, Maisie's granny? She's in Glasgow. Tell her Maisie's in hospital. My keys are in my bag. You'll have to find my bag. Get my ma to look after Maisie until I can come home.'

I should be there. I should be there with her. I don't know how she is. How bad she is. She didn't dare think the worst.

The lassie told Rhona everything would be all right and Rhona wanted so much to believe her. That Maisie would be OK, please God. Rhona gave her the address where they lived in Manchester and she gave her ma's phone number too. Rhona knew it off by heart. Always had. Her mother must be the only person on the planet who didn't have a mobile. Her ma could come and look after Maisie or Maisie could go there while Rhona recovered. She thought she might have broken something – she could be in plaster for a while.

The lassie nodded and put a hand on her arm. The kindness, the forgiveness, was almost too much to bear. She didnae deserve it.

Rhona thought of Maisie, her red curls and her creamy skin so soft. The way she babbled on as Rhona brought her home, though sometimes she cried, a desolate wail that went on and on, when she was miserable with tiredness. A bath usually calmed her down, something quick and easy to eat and a warm bath, and Maisie would fall asleep halfway through a story, her eyelids flickering shut, her mouth slackening.

At least now someone knew about Maisie and to fetch her ma. They had her ma's number.

There was a pain in Rhona's head. A pure awful pain rocking her to and fro. She would wait until it passed and then she might try to get up again.

Holly

The woman with the red hair, what was left of it, jerked once and went still, her eyes blank and unfocused.

Holly, kneeling beside her, sat back on her heels. With her head like that, all mashed in at one side, it was amazing she'd not died immediately. She had been trying to talk, a jumble of sounds that could have been anything.

At first Holly had thought for a second about leaving her and just carrying on to see if there was a way out of the tunnel. But that would have been wrong. No one should die alone.

Holly had never seen anyone die before today.

Or anyone dead.

Making up for it now.

Her breath skipped and stuttered and she wanted to cry but she leant forward and touched the woman's eyelids, closed them. Her eyelashes were gone. Her eyebrows too. There was nothing to cover her with, just scraps of fabric, some rippling in the wind that blew.

Holly blinked away tears. She clambered upright. Her head swam, a blackness flooding her vision. She froze, waiting for it to pass.

Which way? Which way now? To the right of her, their carriage was slewed diagonally across the rails, plunging into a wall of bricks and stone that swallowed the rest of the train. A rockfall. A barricade. To her left, the last coach, coach A, was at the opposite diagonal with its nose cone butting up against the tunnel, forming another barrier. She was trapped: there was no way to escape. Dread reared in her.

She noticed light inside coach A. Moving light, the red and yellow play of flames. There were cries for help, weak and sporadic, an occasional shriek, coming from that way. Holly walked to the side of the coach and looked up. She couldn't see anyone at the windows. She edged her way alongside the train towards the end, using her flashlight again to guide her around the wreckage and the bodies. She tried to keep her right arm still but with each step the pain rocketed through her making her mew, like a kitten.

When she reached the very end of the train, crushed against the tunnel wall, she saw that there was no gap between that and the brickwork. And the space underneath the end of the train was cluttered with debris.

Fuck!

She knew she couldn't climb over, not one-handed. Could she clear the space and wriggle underneath? A burst of pain caught her, forcing her to bend over, eyes tight shut.

She thought about waiting, about sitting down

and giving up, just waiting to be rescued. But she didn't want to wait there in the dark with the dead and the dying.

And Jeff... She'd promised Jeff.

Anger licked after the pain. She'd show that bastard, murdering, skanky toe-rag.

She must get out of the tunnel. She must get help.

She was not going to give up.

No. Fucking. Way.

Jeff

Jeff couldn't do much of anything any more. Was that a good thing or a bad thing? His legs had hurt like fuck at first and it was still hard to breathe, like on a really cold day when you run, like frostbite in his lungs. Having Naz lying across his belly probably didn't help with the breathing either. It was like when the twins jumped on him, winding him.

Naz was shaking now, hard spasms. Jeff could hear the chatter of his teeth and a rattling as he gasped for breath.

Jeff squeezed his hand and kept talking. Riffs on the same theme. 'Hang on in there, stay with me, think about all the people waiting for you, your family and that, your mates. Holly's gone for help. Getting people out like that, what you did, that was epic, yeah? You know that. You must have saved lives doing that.'

Jeff's head swam. So tired.

He'd just close his eyes.

'Promise me,' Holly had said.

'I'm staying here with you,' Jeff said. 'Help's coming. They won't be long now. They'll fix you up.'

His tongue was sticking to the roof of his mouth, tasting of diesel and burning chemicals.

Naz shuddered. He must be cold. Was that shock? They gave people blankets and sugary tea. Something to do with the blood going inwards to protect the organs, Jeff thought. No way to check that now, though, not without his phone.

I don't want to die. The thought came fast and frantic, and his heart turned over in his chest. He could feel anxiety pooling around him, like scavengers gathering around wounded prey. Like rats. He tried to control his breathing, which sometimes helped, but the best he could do was to take shallow sips of air, trying not to cough, because when he coughed he could feel something tearing inside and taste blood, like rust, in his mouth.

Naz shivered hard.

Jeff tried to raise his head, wondering if he could see anything. He made it an inch or two but was too weak to stay like that. It was all dark anyway. He reached out instead with his right hand, carefully touched Naz's chest, waiting to see if that hurt him.

There was no change to the rhythm of Naz's shaking so Jeff reckoned it wasn't causing him any more grief. He laid his arm across Naz's chest covering as much of the bare skin as he could, his palm flat over Naz's heart. He could feel his ribs and the violent trembling. He kept hold of Naz's hand.

'Soon be warm.' Jeff thought of his nana wrapping him in a towel at the beach after a dip in the sea. 'The doctors will sort you out. Help's on the way. You did good, you know. You did amazing. Legend.'

Naz shivered.

Then stopped.

Naz gave a sigh.

Then he was totally still.

Silent.

Jeff felt the weight of him grow heavier.

Jeff began to cry, just from one eye – the other was messed up – tears running into his ear.

Oh, mate. Oh, mate, no.

He squeezed his hand and kept hold of it. He left his arm across Naz's chest, still wanting to keep him warm, even though it made no difference any more.

Nick

Nick heard movement further down the tunnel, saw a flash of light and recoiled, expecting another explosion. But the light danced about, a cone shape. The torch that he'd seen before.

He made his way towards it. 'Hello?'

The light swung his way. He saw a figure, and as he clambered over the rubble he recognized the coloured girl.

'Hello,' she said. She sounded stuffy, like she'd been crying. 'It was a bomb.'

'I can't find my wife, the kids,' Nick said.

'I've not seen them.'

She staggered and the light, coming from her phone, wavered and he saw her arm. 'Jesus!' he said. A bone was protruding from it, jagged, covered with blood. Some of her fingers were missing.

'Shine the light,' Nick said.

She swung the torch around and Nick caught a glimpse of blond hair under the edge of the train, halfway along coach A.

'There!' he shouted.

Together they picked their way through the mess. The woman was on her front. But she was bigger than Lisa. The hair wasn't right.

He took hold of her shoulder and pulled her over. Her limbs were slack, her mouth open, eyes closed. 'She's dead,' he said.

'She was sat just near the bomber,' the girl said. 'I think she raised the alarm.'

'Give me the torch,' Nick said, straightening up.

She hesitated a moment, then handed it over.

He sent the light rippling over corpses and bits of luggage. Searched, on his hands and knees, some of the time, crawling over the mess, trying to avoid the dead. And the rest.

'They're not here,' he said at last.

He handed her back the phone.

Rubbed at his face.

Nick could hear sounds, people's voices, calls

for help, sobbing. They bounced off the vaulted roof and echoed round the space. Were they coming from coach A? The fire inside looked to be growing.

He coughed and spat. 'Does it hurt?' He nodded to her arm.

'Of course it fucking hurts!' she exploded. 'It hurts like fuck.' And then she gasped, as if to prove the point.

'You should strap it up,' he said, 'keep it immobile.'

'With what?' she said.

'Give me some light.'

She angled the torch towards him.

He tore strips from his trousers. The cotton was blackened and thick with grime, so not exactly sterile, but it would have to do. He knotted the lengths together then held up the makeshift bandage.

'Can you bend it?' he said.

'I think so. I don't know,' she said.

'Try bending it up across your front and we'll make a sling from your wrist round your neck.'

She did as he said, crying out, then panting, ragged and fast. Nick eased the middle of the sling under her wrist trying not to look at the shard of bone or the flayed stumps where her fingers had been. He took the ends up either side of her neck, then moved to knot it at the back.

It was hard to remember exactly where they'd been, Lisa and the kids, when the explosion happened. The last thing he clearly remembered was getting up to leave their seats. The cleaner and this girl telling them to leave all their bags and just go.

'Done,' Nick said.

'We might be able to climb under the end by the wall,' she said, 'if we can move some of the stuff. The other way is completely blocked.'

'Let's have a look, then.' He pointed to the back of the train.

She shone the light. The gap underneath the train was choked with broken stuff. Nick pulled at the debris. There was the sound of scraping and squealing as bits moved and caught against others. Then he lay down on his back and used his feet to push more away, groaning with the pain.

Gradually he created a gap wide enough to crawl through.

'I'll have to go through on my back,' she said.

She was right. He could crawl Indian-style, using his arms to pull himself along, but with her arm like that... She was slowing him down. She wasn't up to it.

'You could wait here,' he said.

'No,' she said. 'We've got to get help. If you could pull me when you get through, pull my legs.'

'I don't—'

'Please. I can't just sit here.'

'Could be a rough ride,' he said.

'I know.'

'Give me your phone, then.'

She handed it to him and he put it between his teeth, the light illuminating his way. He edged his head and shoulders under the carriage and used his elbows and knees to hump forwards.

There was a muffled thud, then a cracking sound like gunshot and orange flame from somewhere above him. The crackling grew louder and fresh smoke filled the air.

Nick hit his head on something hard under the carriage, a sickening blow.

Once he was through, he scrambled back onto his knees, flinching at the burning pain in his ankles.

'The fire!' she shouted. 'It's spreading! I should go back. My friend's trapped in there.'

'You going back isn't going to do any good, not unless you can get him out.'

Smoke reached him, making his eyes water.

'Do you want your phone, then?' he said. ''Cause I'd rather not hang about and die from the smoke.'

'Wait,' she called. 'I'm coming. Pull me.'

He peered under the carriage and shone the torch. He could see her feet, dirty in the glare of the light. He shuffled forward under the train, the handset clamped in his mouth, until he could grab her ankles and then he yanked. It was the only way to do it. She screamed, like a fox or rabbit, high-pitched yelps. He tugged her again and again. Each time she screamed.

He was coughing and sweating, and his hands slipped several times.

Finally he was out from under the train and got to his knees, still holding her ankles, and heaved until he had dragged her clear.

Her face was a mask of pain and she was quivering, but the sling had stayed in place. 'You'd better rest,' he said.

'No.'

She used her free hand and her knees to get into a sitting position then held the hand up to him.

Smoke thickened and ballooned about them. Smoke was a killer. They should put wet cloths over their faces but there was nothing to hand. He might be able to outrun it but not with her.

He hesitated.

'Don't you dare,' she said, eyes blazing and she jerked her hand at him again, snorting in pain.

Christ. He took it and pulled her upright.

'Phone?' she said.

He handed it to her.

'Come on.'

They began to walk through the detritus. She played the light ahead of them, the smoke already swallowing the view. There were people here and there, bodies. He thought he glimpsed someone ahead in the distance, walking.

Nick called out, 'Lisa? Eddie?' though he thought they'd probably be somewhere in the other direction.

Nick heard a whine, then a yapping sound and she must have, too, because she waved the flashlight and Nick saw the dog, just sitting there. He bent to stroke him and the dog licked his hand. 'Come on, Boss,' he said. No sign of injury, apart from some burns on his fur.

The dog didn't budge.

'Come on.'

'Quickly,' the girl said.

Nick scooped up the dog. If it couldn't walk he'd carry it.

They staggered on. The girl leading the way and Nick following her. The smoke robbing his breath.

Then her torch went out.

Holly

The walking was a little easier now that there was less rubble. The smell of smoke still clung to her hair and now there was another smell, mushroomy, dank.

Looking back there was no sign of the fire any more. Just gloom. Perhaps it had burnt itself out.

She thought of Jeff, trapped. Had the fire reached their coach? If he...

Holly stared at the column of light ahead. She couldn't understand what she was seeing. A pencil of light in the middle of the tunnel. Dazzling in the darkness.

Beam me up, Scotty.

Like a searchlight beam. Perhaps that was what it was, people looking for them. But looking from the sky above?

She remembered the scene from the old sci-fi movie *Close Encounters of the Third Kind,* the rays of light from the aliens' spaceship.

Maybe I'm dead, she thought, or dying, and this is the bright light people talk about, going up to Heaven or whatever comes next.

'See that?' Nick said.

So she wasn't imagining it, unless they were

both dead and sharing some sort of dead transfer together. Two for the price of one. No single-person supplement.

'Ventilation shaft.'

They walked on and the light grew to be a huge pillar of bright sunshine. The shaft was lined with brick, like an enormous well, perfectly round. Holly guessed it was fifty feet wide at least. Motes of dust wheeled in the sunbeams and Holly could see up above a grid of some sort, then the blue sky and birds circling round the top of the shaft. Calling as they flew.

She closed her eyes. The sun was warm on her face and she longed to lie down and rest.

A rumbling started, thudding vibrations that she felt in her belly. An earthquake? Another explosion? The light darkened and the noise grew. An avalanche?

Her heart banged in her chest.

'Helicopter,' Nick said. And she saw the shadow, like a giant stinging insect blocking out the sun.

'They must know,' she said. *Oh, thank God.*

'Do you want to wait here?' Nick said.

She almost accepted. It would be so easy. Just to stop. 'No.' She was aware that she was bent over, her shoulders rounded, her head rocking, a way of trying to ride the pain that throbbed up and down her arm.

He stared at her, dubious. 'It's just maybe—'

'No,' she said, more firmly. 'We're wasting time. Let's crack on, eh?'

He shook his head, lifted the dog higher in his arms and walked away from the light. She followed.

The ground was silt and cinder but her feet were numb now, swollen and shiny. Occasionally she felt a sting from a particularly sharp piece of stone and welcomed it as a distraction from the agony in her arm. There was a whistle with each breath she took, no matter how shallow. Like someone who had smoked forty fags a day.

They trudged on. And on.

She imagined a drink waiting for her after all this. Ice-cold vodka or a large spritzer, white wine with cranberry juice. She wasn't hungry, only terribly thirsty. She wondered what Jeff drank. If he drank. If he liked real ale, or spirits or...

If he was OK. He had to be, didn't he?

She wouldn't have left him if...

Wind blew through the tunnel. She felt it in her face but couldn't tell if it was warm or cold. Couldn't tell if she was warm or cold. Like a fever. And this was her fever dream. Only her arm – her arm was on fire.

She tripped and fell hard, skinning her good hand and her knees. Jarring her broken arm. She vomited from the pain.

'Nick,' she called.

He was up ahead. He looked back. 'I'll fetch help,' he said. 'You can't do this. It'll take for ever. You wait here. It'll be quicker if I go on my own.'

'I want to come.'

He didn't answer.

She heard the crunch of his footsteps growing fainter.

Prat.

Holly rocked onto her back, then used her feet

215

and bum to shuffle through the dust and grit till she reached the tunnel wall. There, she would have something to lever herself upright against.

It took her three tries and she swore constantly, a stream of *fucking fucks* until she could stand.

She passed three further ventilation shafts, much smaller ones, where poles of light broke the gloom. Beacons in the dark.

After the last one the tunnel grew darker again but she could see a ball of light in the distance. She called to Nick, somewhere up ahead of her, 'Can you see that? At the end?'

Light at the end of the tunnel. She wanted to laugh. Why was it funny? It wasn't funny.

No answer.

It was harder to walk. Like the ground was spongy or her legs were. But slowly the archway of light grew bigger and she could still see Nick, just, his silhouette blurring and dividing. Double vision. Tunnel vision.

She was about a hundred yards from the entrance when she heard new sounds, saw more silhouettes approaching, resolving into figures in uniforms.

Then they were on her. Someone putting a space blanket round her, asking her to keep walking.

'There are people trapped,' she said. 'In the second carriage. Coach B. Two lads. My friend and ... my friends. You have to get them out of there.'

One man nodded. 'Got it,' he said.

They turned away from her and set off, jogging in a group.

Holly limped along to the end and emerged

into the glare of full daylight.

The place was awash with dozens of people. Police and fire-fighters, paramedics, other survivors, sitting with blackened faces, some in bandages. No one she recognized.

A woman came up to her. 'Come over here, love,' she said. 'Let's take a look at you.'

Holly's eyes burnt. 'It was a bomb,' she said.

The woman nodded. 'Yes, love. Awful thing.' Her blue eyes were sad and full of sympathy. 'I don't know...'

Me neither, thought Holly.

She heard the chopping noise of the helicopter again and watched it sway above, then peel off over the hill. The green hill.

'Can you tell me your name?' the woman said.

Holly smiled. *Oh, Jeff.* 'Holly Jukes.'

'Date of birth?'

Holly told her.

'We tried to stop him,' Holly said, 'the bomber. My friends.'

The woman's eyes sharpened. 'You were close to the site of the explosion?'

'Yes.'

The woman called to another paramedic to come over. 'Holly has an open fracture of the radius and traumatic amputation of three fingers. But the priority is to check for primary internal blast-induced injury. Get her to hospital now.'

'How come? Walking wounded, me,' Holly tried to joke.

'That's the adrenalin, love.'

The helicopter sound grew louder again and Holly felt the air pressure grow, the blades whirl-

ing in her head and the vibration in her blood-
stream.

Then the sky was falling and the ground rose to
take her.

Kulsoom

There was a flurry of activity in the house, several
people's phones going off and the woman in
charge getting a call over her headset and telling
whoever it was to wait a moment. She went
outside. Kulsoom strained to hear what she was
saying but it seemed to be mainly questions,
when, where, do we know?

One of the men swore under his breath. Then
Detective Kent came in again. 'So, we shall go to
the station,' she said. Her hands were clasped
together, a weird gesture. Kulsoom realized she
was hiding something.

All the police people were shooting glances at
each other but nobody was saying anything. It
was like at school when Katy Slater collapsed and
died on the netball court and the teachers all
knew but they had to keep quiet because the
family had to be informed first.

'What happened?' Kulsoom said.

'I'm afraid I can't discuss–' the woman began.

'Have you caught Saheel? Have you found
him?' She prayed that was it. That he was in
handcuffs in a van on its way to a police station.
Please, she thought, please, please, please.

'Have you?' Arfan said, getting up.

'Sit down, please,' one of the men said.

'Tell us,' Kulsoom said. She couldn't bear it. Her scalp prickled.

'Sit down,' the woman said.

'Arfan,' Dad said.

Arfan sat, throwing himself into the chair. Dad went to hold his hand but Arfan snatched it away.

'We've a right to know,' Kulsoom said, her voice was shaky. 'If you found him we've a right to know.'

Mum started crying again.

'There has been an incident,' the woman said.

Kulsoom couldn't breathe.

'We're waiting for further details so—'

'What incident?' Dad said.

Her mum looked up, her face wet with tears, mascara in big black rings under her eyes. Panda eyes.

'Possibly an explosion, in Northamptonshire.'

'That's not Euston,' Kulsoom said. Was it?

'Apparently involving a train travelling from Manchester to Euston.'

'Saheel?' her mother said.

'We can't confirm anything at the moment. We don't know at this stage if Saheel was involved or not. Emergency services are attending and we'll be kept fully informed.'

He was dead. He must be. There'd been an explosion. And perhaps other people were dead too. Kulsoom hugged her mother, who was sobbing and sobbing.

It was supposed to be Euston.

Kulsoom let go of her mum and turned to the

219

woman. 'It could be someone else, this one, couldn't it? Saheel said he'd blow up Euston station so perhaps there's more than one of them.'

'We don't know as yet,' the woman said.

Or maybe something had gone wrong with the bomb, Kulsoom thought, the timer going off too soon. Or he might have changed his mind, decided not to sacrifice himself. Got off the train somewhere but left the bomb behind. 'Is anyone hurt?' she asked.

'We don't have that information,' the woman said.

Dad put his hand to his head, eyes closed. Kulsoom saw his shoulders shake. Then he pulled his hand down over his mouth and chin.

'I don't believe it,' her mother said in the silence. 'Not my son. Not Saheel. There must be a mistake.'

But she was wrong. Kulsoom had seen the video, and heard him boast about killing infidels, about the martyrdom that would follow. She was so angry with him. And with the police. It exploded through her. 'Why didn't you stop him?' she shouted. 'I told you! I rang you and told you so you could stop him. And you let it happen – you just let it happen!'

Her dad tried to calm her but she got up, still shouting. 'Now he's dead and there'll be loads of people dead because you didn't stop him! And you should have! Why didn't you stop him? Why?'

Her yells echoed in the house and no one said anything.

'Why? Why?'

Her nose was running and she wiped it on the

back of her hand. Her mother was bowed low, hiding her eyes. Her father was staring at his shoes.

Kulsoom turned to Arfan. He looked straight at her, tears in his eyes, and he shook his head just once. In defeat or despair.

Jeff

They kept shouting. Too much shouting. Jeff wished they would just shut up. Die quietly.

He slept again. Vibrations rocking the wrecked carriage woke him and there was more shouting. The air was thick with oily smoke, the high stink of burning rubber. No air.

More shouting.

Someone touched him, touched his neck. Asked him to look at them. Asked him his name.

He couldn't speak, he couldn't see. He thought about trying but it was too hard. There was too much weight, like he was underwater or on a different planet with more gravity. Everything squashed, compacted under pressure.

Someone prised his hand away from Naz's. He didn't like that but there was no way to resist: he had no strength.

The pain had gone but he was choking and then someone covered his nose and mouth and there was air, cool as silk, air not smoke.

Someone steadied his head. The carriage kept rocking and there seemed to be several people clambering about. He had the feeling that something had gone wrong, that he shouldn't be there but it was impossible to grasp. To remember.

A prick, a scratch on his arm. Then there was a terrible sound, a metallic screaming and banging. Hard vibrations close by, shaking the whole of his body. Waking the pain in his legs.

More shouting.

He drifted off, down a long, slow slide but something yanked him back. Someone patting his face, like his nana did when she thought he was being cheeky.

There was a change in the air pressure, shifting the colour behind his eyelids. He felt himself swaying, still horizontal, bumping along. Like a baby in a pram.

He didn't think he was a baby. Though he wasn't totally sure.

The pain leapt into life, like a fire, sweeping up his legs, every nerve ending screaming. He couldn't cry out, he couldn't move, he couldn't stop it. There was nothing else, only the pain. Acid in every cell.

The pain swallowed him and he slid down the tunnel, in the heat and the dark, down and down until the pain was gone and he was free.

CHAPTER SIX

Nick

Nick had been treated at the nearest hospital burns unit where they had removed the remnants of his socks and the skin that was fused to them. Both his ankles were encased in special dressings. The cuts to his hands and face were cleaned and he was given a leaflet about the management of second-degree burns and a week's supply of paracetamol.

They had provided him with trainers, a pair of jogging pants and a sweatshirt, both pale grey, and handed him his own clothes and shoes in a bag.

'You'll need to give these to the police,' the nurse discharging him said. His confusion must have shown on his face because she added, 'It's standard procedure, any major incident, RTA, possible crime... It helps them with the forensics.'

He nodded.

'You'll want to go to the relief centre. I've put you down for transport, though it could be a while.'

'There's no news?' he asked.

She shook her head. 'I'm sorry.'

Nick sat with the bag on his knee in the discharge lounge. He kept drifting off, his mind meandering, like it was drunk, or he was drunk, then lurching back to reality with a thump. Thinking, Lisa, Eddie, Evie...

The relief centre was in a community hall, part library, part advice centre. Nick was shown to a desk where he had to give his name and date of birth, then sent through to see a police officer.

It was a large room, full of tables, people sitting and talking, screens too, like somewhere you went to give blood or parents' evening at school. But here some people wore bandages and some were still streaked with soot, grime and blood. The smell of burning hung in the air.

'My family are missing,' he said, before the policeman opposite could speak. 'My wife, two children.'

'I'm sorry to hear that.'

Nick gave their names, ages.

The man typed something into a laptop, waited a moment, then said, 'Yes, they're listed as missing, at present. We'll take any other details you can give us and get that all onto the system and circulated.'

Nick watched him take it down, dates of birth, where they had been sitting on the train, where they had been when the bomb went off. Nick's voice kept failing, fading. He coughed each time, sipped from the cup of water on the desk.

He couldn't remember what Lisa had been wearing. He was sure Evie had had a yellow sleep-suit on and Eddie was in navy trousers and a red T-shirt with some logo on the front. But Lisa? He thought of the wedding clothes they'd taken in the cases, of the months beforehand when Lisa had always been Skyping her sister to talk about outfits and colour schemes, then the fitting for her dress, all the business of finding something formal for Eddie. A little suit. A red velvet bow-tie.

'I just can't remember what she had on,' Nick said.

'That's fine,' the policeman said.

'I did look,' Nick said. 'I looked everywhere. I couldn't find them. It's like they've...' He rubbed his head.

'It would be very helpful if you could provide us with a DNA sample,' the man said.

The prospect brought Nick to his feet. *Fucking vultures. Giving up hope just like that.*

'It may not be necessary but it can help us with identification,' the man said gently.

Nick shook his head. His calves were burning. His head buzzing.

'If you change your mind...'

There was a pause. The man kept looking at him... With what? Pity? Sorrow?

Nick felt the rage drain away. 'OK,' he said, sitting down. 'I'll do it.' Whatever it took. It didn't mean... It didn't mean there wasn't hope.

'And the details of the family dentist? I'm sorry, I realize this is very, very difficult.'

Nick didn't want his sympathy. He reeled off the name of the dentist. 'And you want these, my clothes?' Nick held up the bag.

'Yes, please.'

'There's a list of what's in there,' Nick said. 'They made it at the hospital.'

The man took the bag and put it on the floor

beside his chair. 'We also need to take a witness statement but we can do that later, if you need some time.'

Time? What did he need time for?

'Now,' Nick said.

The man said he'd make some notes but also take an audio recording. 'It means I won't miss anything.'

'The train stopped in the tunnel,' Nick said. 'We hadn't been there long and we were told to move.' He continued: he couldn't remember the explosion itself, just the train lifting off the ground and crashing down. He didn't know how long he'd been unconscious but he described coming round and his search for Lisa and the children, his effort to find help with the coloured girl, taking the dog with him.

The man thanked him, then said if he went through to the next room he could get some help from the social workers there.

What? 'I don't need a social worker.'

'It's the practical things, really,' the policeman said. 'Money, accommodation, bank cards, house keys, letting family know. They're trained for situations like this.'

Nick was expecting some hippie type, all bangles and scarves in clashing colours, but the woman he met was quite normal, really, dowdy, maternal. She called him 'duck', which he reckoned was a regional thing. She talked to him for a while about Lisa and the kids, and he said, 'Someone must know where they are. All the police could say is that they're missing.'

'They're still clearing the tunnel,' she said. 'There was a substantial rockfall and they say it could take a while yet. There are still people being brought out.'

He didn't dare ask if they were alive or not.

'Have you spoken to the family yet? Yours, Lisa's?'

'No one left on my side. Hers...' The wedding. *Oh, Christ.* 'They'll all be at the hotel, in London. It's her sister's wedding tomorrow. That's where we were—'

'You give me her name and we'll get in touch.'

No melodrama, which Nick appreciated.

'I'll call them now, then sort you out with some emergency funds and the like.' He had nothing. Not a penny. No keys, nothing.

'I can't go home,' Nick said.

'Of course not. You'll want to be nearby. We'll put you in a hotel in town.'

She took his sister-in-law's name and the name of the hotel, then dialled the number. While she was waiting for an answer, she said to Nick, 'If you want to talk directly?'

He shook his head.

'I understand.'

He sat there and listened as the woman was put through to Cleo and spoke calmly and slowly. He heard the words 'serious incident', 'explosion', 'missing'. Heard her apologize for bringing such dreadful news, then repeating something in response to questions.

'Can I take a mobile number?' the social worker said. 'Nick's obviously in some distress... No, just minor injuries... I am sorry. I understand you

227

were supposed to be getting married tomorrow.'

Cleo must have asked again to speak to Nick but the social worker said, 'I'll ask him to call you as soon as he's able to.'

The social worker gave him a comfort pack, toothbrush and paste, comb and soap, a small towel.

At the hotel he didn't sleep. He sat in the armchair with the television on. The scenes of the aftermath of the bombing played over and over. A clot of emergency vehicles at either end of the tunnel, the smoke pouring from the ventilation shaft caught on amateur footage, interviews with people who lived near the tunnel and with some passengers. No one he recognized. A spokesperson for the police said they believed the explosion was caused deliberately rather than being any sort of technical malfunction. She couldn't comment at this stage as to whether there was any link with the evacuation of Euston station, the train's final destination.

As the night went on, they changed the script. The bombing was now an isolated incident and initial enquiries suggested the suspect was a home-grown terrorist acting alone. Eight were confirmed dead and twenty-three with serious injuries but many were unaccounted for and fatalities were expected to be significantly higher. The location of the train and the collapse of part of the tunnel's roof made the rescue operation particularly challenging.

A terrorist. A fucking Muslim terrorist.

At times Nick shut his eyes. Then he'd get a

glimpse of Lisa, sour-faced at him for forgetting the bottle. He'd hear Evie crying, and Eddie saying, loud and clear, 'I hate you, you're so mean.'

Jeff

The light was way too bright and Jeff closed his eyes again.

His legs hurt. He was aware of someone talking, of movement close by and someone saying his name. Then he slept.

The next time he woke, his vision was blurred but he knew he was in the hospital. He could make out all the equipment, the bland moulded-plastic furnishings. The notices. There was a tube going into the back of his hand. He could smell smoke, bitter in his nostrils.

'Jeff?'

Nana was there, at his side.

He tried to move to see her but that only created a sickening pain in his head.

'Stay still,' she said. He heard the scrape of a chair.

She leant over him, touched his cheek. 'How are you feeling?' She looked weird. He couldn't read her expression. Sad? Hurt? Nervous?

'Not great,' he said. 'My legs hurt.' He was hoarse, his voice cracking and breaking, his throat raw.

'I'll fetch the doctor,' she said. 'Tell them you're awake...'

'Jeff?'

He must have dozed off and she was back now, a doctor with her. The doctor asked him how he felt and shone a light into his eye, then looked at a chart hanging on the end of the bed. Jeff worked out that one of his eyes was covered up.

They'd put something in the bed, like a box or a cage, to raise the bedding off his legs. But they still hurt.

His head ached and he lifted his hands up to press at his temples. His hair was gone, just stubble there. That smell of burning.

'You remember being on the train?' the doctor said.

Oh, mate.

'Yes,' Jeff said. 'There was a bomb.'

'Can you tell me what year it is?'

'Twenty fifteen.'

'Can you tell me your date of birth?'

Jeff did.

'You were brought here with serious injuries, crush wounds to both legs.'

Jeff looked at Nana, hovering by the doctor. She blinked.

The doctor went on, 'I'm very sorry to tell you this, Jeff, but there was extensive trauma to both your legs and our only hope of preventing further complications, such as blood poisoning, was to amputate. Do you understand?'

Nana had her hand balled up, pressed to her mouth.

Jeff felt ice burning his skin. He nodded.

'This is obviously a life-changing injury and it will take time to adjust, to come to terms with it.

230

We were able to save the knee joints and that means the options for prosthetic limbs in the future are much greater. We'll talk later in the week about what happens next, about rehabilitation, but now you need to rest and recover. You've had major surgery with a general anaesthetic so you're going to be quite uncomfortable for some time.'

Jeff's eyes stung.

'Is there anything you want to ask?'

'I can't see properly.'

'Your left eye sustained some damage from the pressure. We'll be referring you to the ophthalmologist in due course.'

'They going to take that as well, are they?'

Nana gasped.

'I think that's very unlikely,' the doctor said. 'How's the pain?'

'Bad,' Jeff said.

His legs. *Both* his legs. *And* his feet.

'We can top you up. You're on strong pain relief and you may feel drowsy, possibly a little nauseous when it kicks in. We'll sort that out now.'

This was mental. He could feel his legs, his feet, the gnawing pain in them.

'I want to see,' Jeff said.

'See?' the doctor said.

Jeff nodded at the rectangular shape in the bed. 'My legs.'

'Jeff,' Nana said. Almost a cry.

'That's fine,' the doctor said. 'It's very hard to take in. I can understand.' He drew back the cellular blanket and the sheet beneath. Jeff was in a hospital gown, white, patterned with little blue diamonds. The diamonds quivered and danced because his eye was wonky.

The doctor pulled up the hem of the gown. Two stumps. Bandaged. White. Obscene.

Jeff shut his eyes. 'OK,' he said.

The doctor covered him up again. 'It's a great loss. And healing will take time, both physical and psychological. It may be hard to believe now but people can live happy, productive, successful lives after losing limbs.'

In what fucking universe?

'Now let's get you that pain relief.'

After the doctor had dosed him up and gone, Nana moved the chair so she could hold his hand. She told him it was Sunday and that his mother had visited yesterday and was coming again tomorrow. That the twins sent their love.

How could he not be able to walk or even stand? How could he have no legs, no feet? He had an image of his Converse and his Docs and his Vans, the pile of them under his bed.

He felt giddy now, like he was on a very slow roundabout. The pain was still there but muffled.

Nana said he'd be all right, not to worry.

His head felt buzzy. It was getting harder to concentrate, to talk. 'Nana, there was someone on the train. I was sitting with her. Holly. Is she all right?'

'I don't know.'

'Can you find out?'

'I'll try. A lot of people died, love. A lot of people.'

'Yes.'

Oh, mate.

Nick

The waiting was like torture. But he knew that, as long as there was no news, there was a chance.

Lisa's parents, her sister Cleo and Cleo's fiancé had driven up and were staying overnight in another hotel. They'd had a bizarre reunion yesterday afternoon in the bar there. No one knew what they were supposed to be doing, if they were in mourning.

He was forced to go over the bare bones of what had happened. He made stunted apologies about the disruption to the wedding. He drank too many pints which, along with the lack of sleep, made him almost catatonic. When he went to piss he caught sight of himself, glassy-eyed, unshaven, still in the cheap clothing he'd been given at the hospital.

Who gives a fuck?

Desperate to have a focus, something other than the smothering circle of her family, he suggested they visit hospitals in the region. He knew the relief operation had details of all admissions related to the attack, that if Lisa or the kids were in hospital they would know, but then again mistakes happen... Paperwork got lost, electronic records incorrectly logged.

'We could ring round,' the fiancé said.

Nick felt hemmed in. 'Better go in person. They'd have to pay more attention.'

Cleo leapt at the idea. Her fiancé drove them.

The pointless odyssey took the whole of the day and then they dropped Nick off.

He'd not been back in his room more than ten minutes when the phone rang.

'Mr Winters, it's Sally from the vet's here. It's about Boss. He's doing really well. There's no reason why you can't take him home as soon as you want. I won't be here tomorrow, I only work weekends, but you can talk to anyone at the surger–'

Nick felt a moment's pleasure, followed by a swirl of outrage strong enough to make his head spin. The bloody dog had survived unscathed – but Nick's wife, his little boy, his baby?

'No,' he said. 'He's not my dog.'

'Oh, I'm so sorry. I thought–'

Before she could finish, he hung up, trembling, sweat itchy across his scalp.

He fell back onto the mattress, gazed at the blank ceiling, and the smoke alarm winking its red light, tension singing in every cell.

When he closed his eyes unwelcome memories threatened. He made himself think instead of their wedding, his and Lisa's. Two years of fussing and interminable conversations about floral arrangements and the colour of stationery, bridesmaids' dresses and hot or cold starters. He'd put his foot down at cold tomato soup. Gazpacho, my arse. The whole shebang had driven him half insane, but the day itself had been pretty close to perfect. The service in a little seventeenth-century chapel, then a four-star hotel for the rest. His mates had behaved themselves, and the best man's speech was funny without being filthy. An extra day booked in the hotel to recover, then the honeymoon on Ibiza. He'd coped well enough that day with her family, who always talked over each other and argued and didn't listen and were on the phone every five minutes and even went on holidays together.

He had teased Lisa about that: if you bring any of them on honeymoon, the wedding's off.

When had that stopped? The teasing? When had it all got so hard, become such an effort?

Perhaps they'd had kids too soon. Too late to censor the thought, he groaned and raised himself up.

He'd shower. As soon as he'd seen what the latest news was.

He was reaching for the remote when there was a knock on the door.

Was it Cleo back?

Excuses at the ready, he answered it.

The policeman was there, the one he'd spoken to at the relief centre.

'Mr Winters, may I come in?'

Nick knew straight away.

'I was just...' he began, wanting to fend him off, but then he let his arms drop, stepped back and let him in.

Kulsoom

It was like a prison, cooped up in Jane and Haroon's house. Not allowed to go anywhere, do anything. Well, hardly anything. Dad had taken them to the supermarket yesterday to get some groceries, Kulsoom and Arfan. Mum had stayed at the house. She was either crying or asleep.

Jane and Haroon went to work as normal, leaving them there. The police said they'd let them fetch some of their own things but not yet.

Kulsoom watched the news when she could. Not when Mum was around but Jane and Haroon had three TVs, one in the kitchen, one in the sitting room and one in the bedroom Kulsoom was using, which used to be Josh's. He had left home and was working in Hong Kong now.

Dad had bought a tablet at the supermarket and was using it to look at places they could rent.

'Won't we be going home?' Kulsoom said.

'I don't think so,' he told her. 'We'd be like a sideshow or, worse, a target.'

'But we didn't do anything.'

'I know, but feelings run high. People lose their heads.'

Arfan was still asleep.

It was like they were hibernating.

Kulsoom was hungry. Hungry all the time.

She went upstairs and waited for the headlines

236

at the top of the hour. The bombing was the main story. Thirty-eight dead, it said yesterday, and over sixty injured, some still missing. They hadn't cleared all the wreckage yet. The tunnel location had created extra problems for the emergency services.

Now a picture of Saheel filled the screen. *Police name Kilsby Tunnel bomber.*

'Dad!' Kulsoom yelled. She hit pause on the remote. She ran out, and down the open-plan staircase as quickly as she dared. It had planks buried in the wall and no handrail on the outside so if you slipped you might just fall into the room.

Dad came out of the kitchen.

'The news,' Kulsoom said, 'I paused it. Saheel.'

Her dad followed her back upstairs. He sat in the easy chair and she sat on the bed and pressed play.

'Police have confirmed that twenty-one-year-old Saheel Iqbal, a British national from Manchester, carried out Friday's suicide bomb attack in the Kilsby railway tunnel. Thirty-nine people have been confirmed dead, including the bomber, who detonated his device, contained in a rucksack, in coach B, close to the rear of the Pendolino train.'

'How can they tell us like this?' Her dad waved his hand at the TV screen. 'Just announce it in public that he is dead. Tell the world before his family?' His eyes were shiny with tears.

So he was definitely dead. The small hope she had hidden away, that he might have survived, that he maybe got off the train, withered away.

Maybe she should be glad he was dead. She hated him enough. It was hard to imagine she would never see him again, that he was just gone. For ever. What about me? she thought. They didn't say anything about me warning them.

'Mum?' Kulsoom said.

'I'll tell her.'

Dad went to wake Mum, and Kulsoom didn't want to see her so she hurried downstairs and out into the garden at the back where Jane had planted rose bushes and trellises. There were stone paths all leading to a circular patio with a sundial in the middle. The roses were bare and thorny now. The only flowers were tubs of tulips at the end of each path.

Kulsoom walked to the centre. Today was quite dull, a cloudy sky, but still bright enough to cast a shadow on the brass plate with roman numerals. She ran her fingers round the engraving, round and round. Pressing harder and harder until the edges of the metal pricked her fingertips as her mother's screams echoed from the house.

Holly

They were discharging her for further treatment at Wythenshawe Hospital in Manchester. The first days in hospital had been a blur. They had scanned her for internal injuries and found an intestinal bleed. That had required emergency surgery. She'd had a second operation to am-

238

putate her right arm. She was deaf in one ear – the eardrum had been ruptured – and her lungs had suffered from the blast pressure but she'd responded well to oxygen. The burns on her face would heal in time and then, depending on the scarring, she'd have to decide whether to have skin grafts.

She listened to what they said, agreed with everything. She wanted to go home, to be at home.

Holly had given her statement to a police officer. They'd met in a little office near the ward while her parents went for a coffee in the café downstairs. He'd come back later with a written copy, asked her to read it and check she agreed with what was there. She couldn't sign it, though. There was an option to leave a mark. She drew a cross with her left hand. They'd given her sheets of photographs, too, asked if she could see the man who had carried the bomb. He was there: she showed them. They videoed her saying it was him.

It was clear in her head. She'd been over it again and again, but she couldn't stop thinking about it, as if she had to preserve it, to get it right in her mind. To fix it in her memory.

First Naz's warning. Jeff insisting on helping. The student – the bomber – screaming. The way she was thrown through the air. Leaving Jeff and Naz. Trying to help the old woman lying with her friend. Seeing her die. Then the other woman, the one with red hair, the awful gurgling sound. Nick pulling her under the wreck, the agony with each jolt of her arm. The great column of light. Sometimes Holly missed a step, got a snapshot out of place and then she would have to start again right at the beginning. Naz's warning. Jeff insisting on helping...

She got irritated by anyone interrupting her train of thought. The sequence of events was more real than all of this, the blood-pressure tests, the medication, the revolting hospital food. When they asked her about dietary preferences she told them she was vegetarian. She couldn't imagine ever eating meat again.

For one night there'd been another victim in the same bay as she was, the Polish woman who had been in their carriage. Holly wanted to know how she'd got out, what she remembered, desperate to see how it fitted, wanting to put together a bigger picture.

'I was blown out of the doors,' Agata said. 'I climbed over the train.' And then she began to cry, and said, 'I'm sorry, I can't. I can't.'

And Holly reassured her. 'Of course – I shouldn't have asked.'

Then Agata was moved to another ward.

The numbers of the dead had been climbing every day and they had begun now to release the names, once the relatives had been informed. Holly had asked her parents to bring in a newspaper and she saw a photograph there of one of the women from the table behind hers – Felicity Doyle, she was called – and the woman who had worked in the onboard shop had died too.

Holly asked about Jeff. Everyone was tight-lipped, bound by confidentiality, but she wouldn't let it go. She tried the doctors and the nurses, the nursing assistants. They all said they didn't know.

Were they lying? Was he dead? Were they waiting until his family had all been notified? She wondered if she should pretend to be his sister (different dads) or his wife or something to get an answer.

She asked the tea boy, in the end, a jovial, grey-haired man with a Caribbean accent.

'My friend Jeff,' she said, 'we were travelling together. My age, he has a tattoo on his knuckles.'

'Yes, a young fella. Me think he's acute surgical.'

Alive then. Oh, thank you, God. Thank you!

'And Naz? An Asian lad?'

'I don't know. Some of them, they's gone to other hospitals.'

'Yes. Thanks.'

She would be travelling by ambulance transfer and her parents were driving back up. She had to be ready at two. Her mum packed her things, something else Holly couldn't do, along with dressing herself, using a knife and fork, writing...

'There's something I need to do first,' Holly said, getting to her feet.

'But if they come?' her mum said.

'I won't be long.'

'Holly.'

'Chill, Mum.' Her mother looked stung. It was almost like she needed Holly to be falling apart, shaken and pathetic. That just because she'd lost an arm she should roll over and give up. Well, that was the last thing she'd do.

She had to walk slowly because she still got breathless, but no one in hospital batted an eyelid

241

at someone shuffling along.

Her arm, what was left of it, was dressed and strapped across her chest, immobilized. She had a very loose white shirt on, one of her mother's, and the empty sleeve was pinned to the hem so it didn't flap about.

She found the men's acute surgical ward and followed a porter wheeling an empty trolley into the ward.

Jeff was in a room on his own. A white-haired woman sat reading a magazine at his bedside.

He was bald. Had a patch over one eye. He looked to be asleep. His hand lay, palm open, on the sheets so she couldn't check for the tattoo. Was it really him?

'Hello,' Holly said. 'I'm Holly.'

Jeff opened his eye. She saw the vivid blue.

'He's been asking for you. You can sit here.' The woman (Jeff's nana?) got to her feet.

'No, I can't stay,' Holly said.

'I'll be back in a minute.' She left the room.

'Hi,' Jeff said.

'Your hair.'

'At least that'll grow back,' he said.

It took her a moment to cotton on. She saw the contraption on the bed. 'Is it your foot?'

'Both legs, amputated below the knee.'

'Oh, God. Oh, Jeff, I'm–'

'Sorted out the jiggling, anyway,' he said.

She mustn't cry. Who was she to cry? 'I'm so sorry,' she said.

'You broke your arm?' he asked.

'Same as you, below the elbow.' A pause. 'Naz?' she said.

Jeff shook his head. 'No.'

Oh, God.

'Not long after you'd gone.'

'I'm sorry, I should have–'

'No, there was nothing–'

There was a silence and she didn't know what to say, how to fill it. It was such a mess. He was broken and she was. Everything was broken.

Jeff closed his eye.

Would it have made any difference if she had pulled him away when they first knew of the danger? He might be walking now. Maybe the three of them had been too much for the bomber. Perhaps if Naz had dealt with it on his own. Even as she had the thought she cut it off. She had walked away. When Jeff was trapped and scared, she had left him.

'They're moving me now,' she said. 'I've got to go.'

'Right,' Jeff said. He didn't open his eye. He probably hated her. She'd be a reminder, wouldn't she? Of the worst day of his life.

'Take care,' she managed, and she turned away and left before she started crying, her breath aching in her chest.

CHAPTER SEVEN

July 2015

Holly

Her mum came into the spare bedroom where Holly had set up a home office, and Holly held up her hand for silence while she continued dictating into the headset: 'So contact us here on the survivors' forum of the website, day or night. And remember, this is a private area and your posts will not be seen by anyone outside the forum.' The words appeared onscreen. She rolled the mouse up to the small microphone symbol and clicked to turn it off.

'It's on the table,' her mum said.

'I'm nearly done,' Holly said.

'Just take a break.'

'It's important.'

'It will still be there after you've eaten. You're doing too much.'

She could never do too much. This was her second chance. She'd abandoned Jeff. She'd survived, unlike Naz and the women she'd tried to comfort, whom she now knew to have been Meg and Rhona. A total of fifty-six had died and she'd made it out alive. So every moment, every second of every day, counted.

The website she'd set up was a place where

survivors and their relatives as well as the bereaved could access resources for practical help
and advice on support, counselling and compensation, with links to medical and legal information
and to other websites like the Tim Parry John-
athan Ball Foundation for Peace. There was a
memorial page where the pictures and biographies of the victims had been posted, and loved
ones could add testimonials or obituaries. There
was a summary of the events of the day and a
news section. They had a Twitter feed too.

The event had become known as the Kilsby
Tunnel Bombing.

Holly acted as moderator.

There was still so much to do.

There was talk of an anniversary memorial
service next April. The majority of those who had
died had come from Manchester so some people
wanted it to be held in the city. Others thought it
was too soon.

Many of those who had survived the bombing
remained silent, hadn't engaged with any of the
forums. Like Jeff. She still had his number in her
phone. And she had come close to deleting it a
few times. But she didn't have the courage. Just
like she hadn't had the courage to stay with him
when he was trapped.

She logged off and went through to the kitchen
table.

Her mother had made mushroom risotto – the
whole family was eating vegetarian now in a show
of solidarity. Sometimes it made Holly want to
laugh as her father munched his way through
vegetable casseroles, cheese pasta and salads.

Laugh or weep. She suspected he made up for it at work, eating pies, bacon butties and burgers there.

Holly had managed two mouthfuls when her phone sounded. An email from a journalist doing an article for the *Catholic Herald:* she wanted to write about both the Kilsby Tunnel attack and the recent mass shootings at Sousse in Tunisia. Was there anyone willing to be interviewed?

Holly ignored her mother's sigh. She tapped out a reply that she would circulate the request.

'We were thinking about a weekend away,' her mum said. 'Cornwall.'

Holly felt a flash of unease. 'You should go,' she said. 'But it might be hard to get somewhere this late.'

'With you,' her mum said, putting her fork down with a clatter that made Holly start. She resisted the cascade of reaction. A fork. *Just. A. Fork.*

She said, as normally as she could, 'Don't be daft, I'm not playing gooseberry.'

'You could do with a holiday.'

'I don't want a holiday. I've things to do.'

'Everyone needs a rest sometimes,' her dad joined in.

'Well, not me, not now. You go. I'll be fine. If I get stuck I can get Oliver round. He can practise his parenting skills.' Her brother's baby was due soon.

'I know you want to be independent—' her mum said.

'I am independent,' Holly knew she sounded harsh, wired. 'OK, I'm not earning and I can't

246

drive any more, but I don't need looking after. I'm sick of you babying me.'

Her phone started ringing.

'Holly–'

'I'd better take this.'

She escaped back to her room and killed the call from some spam PPI mis-selling company. A holiday, she thought. She couldn't imagine ever having a holiday again. She had so much to do. And time was so precious.

At the computer she found a new post awaiting moderation.

It was about Diana Moffat, one of the women who'd been travelling with the dog. Holly had a sudden dizzying memory – of Diana's partner, Meg, with the jagged fragment in her neck. The life bubbling from her. Holly groaned and shook her head, forced herself to concentrate.

Diana was my twin sister and I don't think the shock of losing her in such terrible way will ever leave me. I'm told Diana and Meg were found on the floor of the tunnel, beside each other and that another passenger rescued their dog and has kindly re-homed it.

Holly could see the dog now, Nick carrying him along the tunnel. Those rays of light that grew larger as they trudged forward. The clattering of the helicopter vibrating through her body. She waited a moment, then returned to the post.

Diana was the most generous person I knew, and she would be the first to forgive anyone any wrongdoing. It is not easy for me to copy her example but I believe

247

it's what she would want and, as a committed Christian, love and forgiveness are the foundation of my faith. So I am praying to find the humility and grace that will help me forgive the man who took my sister's life and those of so many others. Amen.

Holly bit the inside of her cheek. Forgiveness? She didn't know what she thought about that. She didn't like to think about it. All she needed to do was keep busy. *Just. Keep. Busy.*

Kulsoom

The new house was small and dark and smelt of damp. There were little black splodges inside the built-in wardrobe in Kulsoom's room. Mildew. Dad said to air it out, keep the windows open and put her clothes in the drawer for now.

Her room was too cramped and too smelly to do anything in so she spread her things out on the table in the kitchen-diner. Dad was at work and Arfan was out and Mum was useless. OK, it wasn't nice to call her that but it was true. She didn't even cook any more. Kulsoom did it, and sometimes Arfan helped but he moaned all the time and did things wrong on purpose, and sometimes they got a takeaway because it was easier. And totally nicer than anything Kulsoom made.

Dad said Mum needed time: that she would get better, that at least she had seen the GP and the medication helped her sleep.

Yes. Like twenty-four/seven.

Kulsoom carefully tore out the finished page from her sketchpad and put it on the pile of drawings. The next page would be a single frame. The image of Saheel in the laptop screen. She wasn't sure yet whether to draw a speech bubble there too, and have him saying something or whether to use a caption instead, like the address bar at the top of the webpage, giving the name of the website or the name of the video file.

It was all black and white, but on some pages she'd use some colour, like red when the bomb went off.

She sketched the outline of his head and shoulders and then his arms with his palms pressed together. Hands and fingers were especially hard to draw so this was easier.

Using a faint pencil she marked where she had to do the eyes, nose and mouth, then rubbed out the nose and tried again because it was too low down.

She drew the outline of the eyes, the little dimple in the line near the inner corner where the tear ducts were. Then she put in the eye socket. It didn't matter if it looked exactly like Saheel or not but so far it was pretty good.

There hadn't been any funeral for him or anything like that. He was just gone. Kulsoom couldn't imagine him in Heaven. The Qur'an said suicide was forbidden. Anyone who committed suicide would burn in Hell. And murder was forbidden and so was killing innocents.

There had been memorial services for some of the victims in Manchester. One man had lost all his family, his wife and two children. But there could be nothing like that for Saheel. People wanted to forget him, not remember.

One day, while they were still at Jane and Haroon's, Kulsoom had seen the headline in a newspaper, THE FACE OF EVIL, and Saheel's picture. She had got upset and Dad had been angry about it: he'd said that Saheel had had a whole life before the bombing but that didn't count any more. All he was now was a terrorist.

'He was not evil,' Dad said. 'What he did was evil. He was wrong, terribly, terribly wrong, misled, misguided, poisoned by lies and fantasies. But he was more than that. He was my son. He was your brother. For twenty-one years he was kind and diligent and happy.' And Dad told her some funny stories about Saheel and her when she was little.

Because Kulsoom and Arfan were under eighteen, none of the papers that printed all the things about Saheel could give their names. They'd had to change their surname anyway so no one would be able to make the connection. Now she was Kulsoom Khan, her grandma's family name. At least when she started her new school she wouldn't have people pointing or whispering or threatening her.

Kulsoom filled in Saheel's eyebrows with a soft pencil, thick and dark.

The eyes were still blank. She drew the pupils, solid black circles, then larger circles for the irises. There was a trick Miss Weston had taught them when they did portraits that the eyes reflected light so you left a little white square or a

250

dot or a comma when you filled in the irises and it brought the eyes to life.

She had a brilliant idea. She could make that little blob in the shape of an explosion, like a star or even a curved sword. Most people might not notice it. That was something artists did, put little symbols in their work. Not everyone knew they were there or what they meant. Not that anyone would ever see this story. Not unless she published it with another false name, and there didn't seem to be much point to that because no one would know it was her. Some artists hid their identity, like Banksy. But if Kulsoom ever showed her stuff in public she'd want people to know that she had made it and to respect her work. Anyway, this was private for now.

Saheel had disappeared and they had too. They were hiding. Dad still had his job but Mum was on long-term sick.

She went and got biscuits and chocolate milk. Ate and drank. She drew a few practice shapes on a spare piece of paper.

They said there was an excellent art department at the new school. She'd been to visit and it did look good but it depended so much on who you got as a teacher. She couldn't imagine anyone could be better than Miss Weston.

It wasn't fair.

She ate another biscuit. Dug out the bits that were stuck in her back teeth.

She bent close to copy the little daggers, scimitars, in the left of each iris and coloured in around them with fine lines radiating from the pupils, the spokes of a wheel. She went over the line where the iris met the white of the eye, making it a bit thicker.

She never heard Mum come in. She was just there, ripping the page from the sketchbook, snatching up the pile of drawings, shouting at her: 'How could you do this? Are you crazy? Are you insane?'

'No – it's just–'

She never gave Kulsoom a chance to explain but tore the pages in half and half again.

'You make me sick!' her mother shouted. 'What is wrong with you? You wallow in this abomination! In our tragedy.'

Kulsoom bit her lip.

'Put it all in the bin.' Mum held out the torn pages.

How dare she? 'No.'

'Put it in the bin,' her mum said more slowly, glaring at Kulsoom.

'No. Why should I? I haven't done anything wrong. It's just drawings, that's all it is, drawings for me.'

Her mother moved across the room and shoved the paper in the pedal bin.

I hate you so much, Kulsoom thought. It's not fair. It is so not fair. Tears stung her eyes.

'I'll keep these.' Her mother swept up the pencils. 'You can have them back when you come to your senses.'

Kulsoom ran from the room, slamming the door. *I hate you.* She got halfway up the stairs then ran back down and slammed it again, six times, the words I HATE YOU, I HATE YOU chanting in her head to the rhythm of the banging.

Jeff

'Jeff,' Nana called, 'it's after twelve.'

And? he thought.

'You need a hand?'

'No.'

It was her way of forcing him to get up. He'd been out of the hospital two weeks now. He was still going to physio and seeing the occupational therapists. He would be considered for prosthetics in due course, probably in several more months' time. The stumps had to be fully healed first.

There had been long discussions about his discharge plan, what might need to be put in place to enable him to manage at home. It was Jeff who'd suggested moving into his gran's: her bungalow was all on a level, and they could convert the bathroom into a wet room.

His mum wasn't totally happy but she saw it made sense. The twins moaned when they heard about it, but he told them to visit whenever they wanted.

'You've lost half the day already,' Nana shouted.

Yep, that was the plan. 'I'm coming,' he said.

Transferring himself from bed to chair or wheelchair was one of the first tasks he'd been taught. The bed in his room here was equipped with rails to give him purchase. Now he pulled himself upright. His dressing-gown was in reach, and he put it on. He wouldn't get dressed today – he didn't have to be anywhere. He swivelled round from the bed, then levered himself over and into the wheelchair. He was waiting for an electric one, which he'd be able to use to go out, but at the moment he couldn't think of anywhere he wanted to go.

Jeff wheeled himself into the hallway and to the kitchen, where his nana was reading the paper. She'd had the washing machine on, so the place smelt of soap powder, and a pile of laundry sat by the back door. It was still pissing down, not a scrap of blue in the sky.

Nana glanced at him, then back at her paper. She didn't say anything.

Jeff got a bowl from the cupboard and found a spoon. He poured cereal, put the bowl on his lap and wheeled to the table. The milk was already out. He began to eat.

'You do your exercises yesterday?' she said, still looking at the paper.

'No.'

'So you'd better do them today.'

'Yeah,' he said.

But that wasn't enough for her because she added, 'You know it's important.'

'Yes,' Jeff said. 'Just leave it.'

He wheeled back into the hall, got his baccy and papers out of his pocket and rolled a fag. The front door opened inwards so he had to wheel up to it, unlatch it, then edge back as he drew it open until there was enough space to roll outside. An overhanging porch gave him some shelter from the worst of the rain.

He lit up his smoke.

The houses in the close looked drab in the murky weather, some worse than others, with torn curtains and weeds growing on the paths or in the roof guttering.

It was bin day. Someone who didn't know the rules had left a black bag out instead of using a wheelie bin. The bag was torn and three magpies were after the contents, stabbing and diving at each other for access.

Once he was back inside, she called out, 'Are you having a shower?'

'No,' Jeff said.

'You might feel a bit brighter.'

'I feel fine.'

She came to the kitchen door. 'Good,' she said. 'So maybe you could have a look at some courses, then.'

He gave a snort, shook his head.

'What?' she said.

'Just what's the point? Even if they have disabled access, why rack up fifty grand in fees with no guarantee of a job at the end of it?'

'I'm not talking about university, Jeff. There's colleges too. Your mum said there's still apprenticeships.'

'I'm not bothered,' he said.

'Exactly. You're not doing your exercises, you're sleeping all the hours that God sends. It won't all come to you. You need to put some effort in. I know it's hard–'

'You don't know anything.' He felt the anger, like heat, consuming him. 'Stop telling me what to do because you don't understand.'

255

She set her mouth. 'I know what I see with my own two eyes and–'

'You weren't there, you *don't* know.' He saw the spit fly as he yelled. He was furious: he wanted to push her, run her over.

'Jeff, I'm sorry, but–' There were tears in her eyes.

'No!' he shouted.

'So talk to someone. Talk to the doctor. See a counsellor. Go on to the forum and talk to the others, to people who do understand.' Now she was shouting. 'But you do not sit here in my house and just give in and give up. You still have a life to lead. And I thank God every day that you do.'

He spun the chair round and went back into his room. He was shaking, the anger choking him. He banged his fists on the arms of the wheelchair until he could feel the bruising.

Then he sat, thinking of Naz's hand in his, the quick smile Naz had given when Jeff had made it plain he wanted to help clear the passengers, the way Naz had called the student 'sir', the weight of Naz's body on his own...

He could still feel the weight of him.

He wasn't sure how long he sat there but it was after three when he booted up his laptop.

Talk to the others, to people who do understand.

He had seen the website, had looked at it a couple of times, and even joined the survivors' forum but every time he started reading the accounts of people's experiences it just brought back the fear and the horror of that day. He never got more than a few sentences in.

And those photographs on the memorial page – of the children (the youngest victim was only twelve weeks old, the baby girl from their coach), of the two old women who were a couple, of Naz (who was only eighteen and had had a sister). All those biographies...

He had never dared click on Holly's posts. He had never posted anything either. Not so much as a comment, certainly not his memories.

He found his new glasses. He could see very little with his poor eye but they helped him with reading and the screen. His hand was shaking and it took him two goes to get them on properly.

He clicked on a photograph halfway down the gallery of victims, Felicity Doyle, one of the businesswomen who'd been sitting behind him and Holly. He watched the page load, read the brief biography, then went on to the post below it, written by her son. Jeff skimmed over the first bit about what a good mother she had been and why she was travelling that day, then read more carefully, his back stiff with tension.

We knew my mother was missing pretty much straight away but we were in limbo for a long time, waiting for news. It was like a waking nightmare. Finally after nine days they told us they had identified some of Mum's remains. Some were recovered from inside the train and others from outside. They used the words 'severely disrupted', and told us they might still recover what they called 'secondary remains'. Horrific.We had to decide if we wanted to wait till all the remains were identified, which could be several months, or go ahead and have her funeral anyway. That's what we did in the end. We couldn't stand it any more. We wanted it to be over. We needed to bury her.

Jeff felt fear crawling all over him. He couldn't do it – he couldn't face any of this. He went to close the laptop, then hesitated. Maybe posting something himself would be easier than reading other people's stories. He could just stick to the facts, lay it out plain and simple. He signed in and began to type: *I almost missed the train. My bus was late and I had to run to get to the platform on time...*

Nick

The dog barked again. Nick kicked out, but the dog had learnt not to get too close at this point in the day. He barked several times more, backing towards the bedroom door.

Nick climbed out of bed, muttering, 'You're a pain in the bloody arse. That's what you are.'

Nick opened the back door and Boss ran out to do his business.

The sun was rising, the garden misty, the sky an unbroken blue. It had rained for much of the summer. Weeds choked the flower-beds and the grass almost hid Eddie's slide and mini gym.

It took Nick a moment to remember what day it was: without work the days all blurred together. He had tried going back in early July. He'd sat at his desk and stared at his screen and felt like a

258

fraud. It was all so irrelevant. Eventually, Tom had come in and suggested Nick go home, take some more sick leave.

So he did.

Not like he had a mortgage to pay any more: the life insurance had cleared that and left him a lump sum in the bank.

Leaving the back door open, he collected the empties from around the place. He dropped the cans and bottles into the recycling bin with a satisfying clatter. That'd rouse anyone who wasn't already up and running.

He fried eggs and bacon, toasted bread. Washed it down with a mug of tea.

Boss came back in and lapped at his water bowl. He looked at Nick, ears cocked, tail thumping.

'Don't know what you're so bloody happy about,' Nick said.

Boss whined, looked at the door, back at Nick.

'Later,' Nick said. 'Now lie down. Or go out.'

Boss slumped down, made a huffing noise.

Nick remembered, with a lurch in his guts, that Cleo had rung again last night. And he'd answered the phone. Her saying that she'd be happy to come and help him sort out Lisa's things, and the children's, whenever he was ready.

'Not yet,' Nick said, trying to remain civil.

He couldn't imagine ever being ready to pack up the clothes and toys, Lisa's makeup and shoes, dismantle Evie's cot. The muscles on his back twitched at the thought of it. Why make the place any emptier than it already was?

The dog was whining again when Nick came back from the bathroom.

'I should have left you there,' Nick said. 'Left you in that tunnel... Or with the vet at any rate.'

He blamed the grief. He'd gone to the vet the morning after, numb from the news and exhausted from spending most of that night with Lisa's family, hashing and rehashing the bombing and the confirmation of their deaths. He couldn't go home alone. So he'd taken the dog, leaving his details in case anyone came forward to claim the animal.

They'd got a coach back to Manchester. Nick walked in, Boss sticking close, like a shadow, and there on the kitchen counter, a baby bottle full of milk. Like an accusation.

Nick walked the dog for hours every day, whatever the weather. He avoided the park where other dog-walkers wanted to natter and swap dog stories but went up to the meadows or along the river or the canals. They walked till he ached and then some more. He walked and brooded on the savagery of what had happened, his hatred for the bomber hot coals in his belly, for the bomber and all his kind.

He walked fast and hard and at his heels always came the thought, it should have been me.

Today he got the bus out to Wigan and came back on foot, fourteen miles along the Bridgewater Canal, now a cycle route, the sun getting hotter until it burnt his scalp where his hair was thinning and the back of his neck. He bought some sausages at the Co-op, a bottle of whisky and some cans at the cheap booze shop.

He scanned the Internet, looking for any news

of an inquiry. There had been debate about whether Iqbal should have been flagged up by the security services, given he was visiting jihadist websites. They should be banned, anything like that, hacked into and destroyed with viruses. Anyone using them should be slammed with a control order or put on a free flight out and dumped in Syria or Iraq to slaughter people there.

He visited the website, their three pictures side by side. Clicked through to Lisa's biography, which he knew off by heart. He felt his heart hammer as he saw that someone, Cleo, had published a post. What a fucking liberty. He fetched a whisky, gulped half of it down, then raced through the post.

Lisa Winters was my sister, Eddie and Evie my nephew and niece, and also my godchildren. April 11, the day after the bombing, was supposed to be my wedding day. That's why they were all on the train to Euston. We were at the hotel, getting things ready, when my fiancé Craig said that there'd been an explosion on the West Coast main line. We tried calling Lisa and Nick but there was no answer from either of them. I felt physically sick. I was pregnant so I was used to that, but this was worse. We hadn't told anyone I was expecting. We wanted to wait until I was past the danger period.

Then we heard from the survivor relief centre, Nick was there but Lisa, Eddie and Evie were missing. We spent that evening cancelling everything and getting in touch with all the guests.

I barely slept and kept imagining Lisa with Eddie and Evie, huddled together and keeping warm, wait-

ing to be found. I hated to think of them being trapped in the dark. Lisa was scared of the dark but I knew she'd put a brave face on it for the children. I thought of those earthquake victims, the ones who get pulled alive from the rubble after days. Like a miracle.

We met up with Nick in Rugby. He was in a dreadful state, you can imagine. The next day we drove to every hospital in a fifty-mile radius. No one could help us.

The police confirmed they were dead that evening, all of them. It was devastating.

It's so hard to try and live any sort of normal life now. I miscarried a week later and took time off work. I know I need to go back but I just burst into tears all the time, and I start shaking. It overwhelms me. I can't concentrate either. I thought having their funeral might make it easier to accept but nothing's changed. Lisa was my best friend as well as my sister. She was always there for me. Those precious children had their whole lives ahead of them.

My world is such a dark place now. I understand that 'life goes on' is the best response to an attack like this but I'm not there yet. Most people meeting me would probably think I'm doing OK but it's all an act. I can't see an end to it.

Nick shook his head, swore as he slammed the laptop shut. She should never have done it without telling him. Asking him.

He poured another whisky and fed the dog.

He put sausages on to fry and chips in the microwave.

Then he set the table. Three places and Evie's bouncing chair. Just as it should be.

262

Holly

So far Holly had only once had to ask someone to modify what they'd sent for the website, and that was because they had wanted people to donate to a memorial fund for their son, who had been a keen cyclist. The fund would help promote cycling among teenagers in their area.

Holly had had to explain that the site already directed people to the British Red Cross, who were managing a disaster appeal fund and had the experience to deal with that side of things. She suggested instead that the family set up a dedicated website for the cycling fund and include a link to that from their post here.

Now she instructed her voice-recognition system to open the first new post that had arrived. Her stomach turned over as she saw it was from Hashim Dawood, Naz's father. She closed her eyes momentarily, breathed in deeply and rubbed the back of her neck before she began to read.

My beloved son Nazir Dawood, who was always known as Naz, was standing next to Saheel Iqbal when he detonated his rucksack bomb. We were told that Naz had been trying to get passengers from coach B to safety. It is a terrible, terrible thing to lose a child. He was so young but he gave his life trying to save the people around him. Naz died from damage to his internal organs. We're not sure how long he lived after the attack but they told us he was most likely unconscious. He was trapped in the carriage with one of the other passengers.

Holly broke off. The pressure in her chest made her feel like she was being crushed. She bent forward, her fist hard against her breastbone. She could taste the grit in the air, smell the stink of scorching, hear thunder in her ears. Slowly she straightened up and forced herself to read on.

I hope one day to meet that person, to find out more about those last moments and whether Naz had any final words.

We went to lay flowers at the site near the tunnel where there is one of the big ventilation shafts, like a brick turret on top of the ridge. Now it's a huge bank of tributes, a riot of colour: bouquets, wreaths and ribbons, cards, photographs and messages. People had travelled from miles away to show sympathy, not just relatives and friends but complete strangers. They'd come to stand by us.

Our hearts were broken in two.

Our son was the sun in our lives. That light has gone and we are still lost and cold in the dark that has followed his death. Naz is with Allah now and at peace.

Holly's throat hurt as though something was stuck in it. Her eyes filled. She pressed them with her hand. She remembered stumbling through the wreckage of the coach calling to Jeff, asking about Naz. *He's in a bad way.* Walking into Jeff's

264

room at the hospital, finding him like that, broken. Holly asking after Naz and Jeff shaking his head. *Not long after you'd gone.* Jeff had closed his eye then. He hadn't even bothered to look at her again when she'd said goodbye.

God, she was so tired. The response to the site was snowballing. Just over three months since the attack and more people seemed ready to share, eager to publicize their stories.

Another coffee would help.

'We're going up.' Her mum was in the doorway.

'Yes.'

'It's after eleven.'

'Fine.' She tried to keep the irritation from her voice. She was six years old again and not allowed to stay up too late.

'You look exhausted.'

'Mum, please.'

Holly's mum raised her palms and her eyebrows.

'Night,' Holly said, before she got any more of a lecture.

Holly's palm itched. Her right palm. Crazy.

She waited until her mother had finished in the bathroom and heard the click of her closing their bedroom door, then went into the kitchen and made a pot of coffee. She washed down some painkillers with the first cup.

The next post was from Amelia Thornicroft, Caroline's daughter.

All I feel is this hard ball of anger inside at what has happened. How can people talk about forgiveness when fifty-six people died, and sixty-eight more had

265

horrific injuries, because a guy got on a train and deliberately blew himself up? That is just evil. Pure evil.

Most people, they probably know someone who's died and they think they can sympathize, but this is nothing like that. This is about murder, about a psychopath massacring people, ripping everyone's lives apart. It is f***ing awful and no one who hasn't been through it themselves has the slightest clue.

I wish I believed in God and in Heaven and Hell because then I could imagine him burning in Hell for all eternity. And I could imagine my mum in some amazing Heaven instead of just being gone for ever.

Holly wondered about the language but only for a moment: given the brutality of the bombing who would actually give a fuck?

She kept on working. She didn't want to go to sleep. When she slept the dreams came. Savage and bloody and shameful.

Kulsoom

Kulsoom had Googled the Kilsby Tunnel bombing and the first link was to the memorial website. She hesitated. She felt sick, haunted by what might be there, but still hungry to see it.

She jabbed the touchpad and the home page loaded.

There was a banner across the top, a photograph of flowers laid by a field with a simple message underneath.

This website, maintained by survivors, commemorates the events of 17 April 2015 when 56 people lost their lives and 68 were seriously injured in the Kilsby Tunnel Bombing.

Kulsoom clicked on the media page and found a fact sheet to download, photographs, and links to articles and features about the bombing. She hit the browser back arrow and from the home-page selected testimonials.

The screen filled with photographs, row after row: all of the victims.

Kulsoom swallowed. It was horrible. So horrible. She wanted to run. To curl up and hide. She scanned the faces. Most of them were smiling. There was a name underneath each portrait. She chose one at random. Caroline Thornicroft.

A new page loaded with a brief biography at the top. Posts had been added to it. The first, from Caroline's daughter, was so angry it made Kulsoom squirm. She didn't like thinking of Saheel as a psychopath, as evil. She remembered what Dad had said, that what he did was evil not who he was. But Kulsoom wasn't sure she really believed that. It was like an excuse or something. She was his sister, the same genes and everything, the same background, but she didn't want to blow people up. And shouldn't people be judged by what they actually did?

She read the next entry.

Posted on 3 July 2015 by Trevor Thornicroft

Caroline was the love of my life. We'd been married twenty-three years. We'd almost raised our kids and were looking forward to the next phase of the journey together.

Caroline was never meant to be on that train, she'd booked a seat on the 10.15.

I had a series of missed calls from my daughter Amelia. I rang Amelia and she told me she'd phoned her mum and Caroline sounded very stressed. She'd said, 'Whatever happens, remember I love you and Paddy and your dad.' Then the connection was lost. When we heard reports of an explosion on a train on the West Coast line, news of casualties, I felt sick with worry. But I hung onto the thought that she wasn't on that train.

We got the phone call just after nine the following morning.

Caroline had spoken to Amelia at 12.11. And by then she was obviously concerned about Saheel Iqbal.

Kulsoom stopped when she saw Saheel's name again, she felt the heavy sadness inside. She sighed and read on.

I'm so proud that Caroline tried to stop the attack, along with other people. But I can't bear to think that she knew what was coming and that in those last minutes she must have been so very frightened. I still don't know why she was on that train. I've gone over and over it.

The three of us are clinging to each other, like we're on a life raft, lost at sea. When Caroline died the ground beneath our feet disappeared. I miss her every minute of every day. She was my heart. Mi corazón.

268

Kulsoom Googled the last word. It was Spanish for 'heart'. Caroline Thornicroft had been a Spanish teacher. Kulsoom scrolled down to read the comments, then jumped as the front door slammed. She saw Arfan out of the corner of her eye and banged the lid of the laptop shut.

'Ooh! What you up to?' Arfan said, pulling off his rucksack as he came in. 'Watching pornos?'

'Don't be gross,' Kulsoom said.

'Why you so freaked, then?'

'None of your business.'

He shrugged. 'Weirdo.'

Kulsoom didn't care: as long as he wasn't going to find out he could call her all the names he wanted. 'Weirdo' wasn't so bad anyway. Sometimes he said it and it was almost like a good thing, a compliment.

She sniffed and he looked at her. Could he tell she'd been crying?

'There any pizza?' Arfan said.

'Cheese, double crust.'

He switched the oven on. 'You want a slice?' he said.

He usually had a whole one to himself. He never let her have some. She had to get her own. She nodded. 'OK.'

'Just one, mind,' he said. 'No taking the mick.'

And she smiled.

Jeff

The twins had come for tea. His mum and Sean were having a night out. Nana could have gone round there to babysit but Jeff suspected she thought it would do him good to see them.

They had been sending him notes and cards. Jeff could imagine his mum, the twins going on at her, 'We're bored, what can we do?' and his mum saying, 'Why don't you draw a picture for Jeff?'

There had been a series of get-well-soon ones at the beginning.

The latest offering was just a big smiley face with sequins and glitter all over it. Some hugs and kisses on the inside. The glitter came off on his fingers, sparkling everywhere. Faye had put a little note inside, purple ink on light green paper:

Dear Jeff,
I am sorry you can't do things any more but we will look after you for ever.
Lots of love
Faye

Crap. That's how they all saw it. End of the line. The thought of another fifty years' being 'looked after' made Jeff want to string himself up. Probably his own fault. Wallowing in all the shit, feeling sorry for himself. More than sorry.

270

Devastated and furious. Posting on the website had helped and later having the guts to read some of the other posts. It was like he had been trapped behind a glass wall, suffocating, and he'd finally broken through to the other side and let some air in. People commented on the posts, messages of support or thanks and sometimes requests for information, and of course you couldn't just ignore them so these little conversations started. Although his situation hadn't changed, he felt a bit more connected, part of something, part of that group.

Naz had died and he hadn't, and he didn't know why it had fallen out that way. It was so random. But when he felt the despair and the sense of hopelessness he also felt increasingly guilty.

'Did you like the card?' Violet said, after fish fingers and crinkly chips and peas had been polished off and they'd left Nana to wash up.

'Loved it,' Jeff said.

'And my letter?' Faye said.

Jeff said, 'Yeah, ta for that.'

'And you can live with us when Nana gets too old,' Faye said.

'Who's old?' Nana called through from the kitchen.

'You are!' Violet jumped up and ran through to her.

'I'm going to be OK, Faye,' Jeff said. 'I can still do stuff.'

'How?'

Jeff wiggled his fingers, pointed to his head. 'I've still got a brain,' he said. 'I can still play my

271

games, use the computer, think, talk.'

She looked doubtful. 'Well, when you can't–'

'I can.'

'So what are you going to do?'

'I don't know yet. But I'm not going to just sit on my bum for ever, feeling sorry for myself.'

Faye giggled.

'Can I have that in writing?' Nana called out.

'I'm not talking to you,' Jeff said. Christ, he loved her but he'd go mental if he had to stay here indefinitely. People managed, didn't they, got adapted housing for wheelchairs? For the first time the thought of a place of his own seemed attractive. Not yet but eventually. Get his independence back. Not that he'd ever actually lived alone. And he'd no idea whether he'd ever be able to afford it. But maybe with the compensation money, if he could get work, find someone to share with...

Faye put *The Simpsons* on the telly and sat on the floor. Violet came back and sat beside her.

It's a second chance. Jeff had read that in a post from one of the survivors. He couldn't remember exactly who now. He had dismissed it at the time because it hadn't felt like that to him. Not one bit.

But now if he didn't take it as a second chance, what did that make it? Just a dead-end? He'd talked about that last week with the counsellor. She never put words in his mouth, just asked him to expand on things, and sometimes she gave him some hard facts to help him understand common responses to experiencing that sort of trauma.

Facts and figures, like the fact that most people

will experience an acute stress reaction following a trauma, and it's usual for their symptoms – like flashbacks, numbness, hyper-vigilance and depression – to last up to six weeks. But one in three people will not be able to get over those symptoms and will continue to experience them, the condition known as post-traumatic stress disorder. Jeff liked that. You always knew where you were with numbers, with statistics.

She asked Jeff to imagine himself in five years, in ten. In an ideal world what would he like to be doing?

He found it impossible to talk about having a family or any of that side of things so he stuck to work. 'I'd like to be working in the games industry, making a living. That's what I wanted to do before. And I still do, I guess.'

'Good,' she said, and left it at that.

Planted the seed.

After the twins had gone, he checked the website. There was a new post about Rhona Gillespie, who'd been in their coach.

Posted on 17 July 2015 by Margie Gillespie
Rhona was a wonderful daughter, a loving mother, a joy, and she will live in my heart for ever. There are times when I get angry that she's gone and I'm still here. That a wee girl has lost her mammy and that I have had to bury my only child. It's so very hard. I've had some counselling, and I use medication as well because I can't cope with it all on my own.

I got a phone call about six o'clock that evening from the Manchester Children's Hospital. Maisie had been taken in with an asthma attack and they hadn't been able to contact Rhona. Could I come? I couldn't understand why Rhona wasn't there.

I live in Glasgow so it was midnight by the time I got to the hospital. Maisie was sleeping. All I could think of was that Rhona must have been in some sort of accident. The hospital offices were shut but I talked to the night sister and she rang the emergency departments in Manchester but there was no one of Rhona's name listed. I couldn't catch a wink.

It was all such confusion in the morning. Maisie was well enough to go home but I'd no keys for Rhona's flat. I called her work. The person I spoke to said, 'Haven't you heard? Oh, my God, haven't you heard?' She told me that Rhona and two of her colleagues had been on the train that had been blown up. I'd not even heard about the bombing. I fainted. The nurses were brilliant, making sure I had somewhere quiet to sit, getting me the helpline number. The person I spoke to said, 'Is there anyone with you?' I began to cry. I said yes. And then they told me.

I was in total shock. I can't remember much about the next few days. I wanted to view her body because I wouldn't believe it if I didn't see her for myself. They'd arranged it so her injuries were covered and I could see the good side of her face.

I felt so sad for Rhona and me, and for wee Maisie, who had to leave everything she knew and come to live with me. And I feel so sorry for all the other victims and their families. I've filled the house with photographs of Rhona now, all different ages. That's how I want to remember her. Not as a broken body in a mortuary.

It's hard looking after Maisie, not just suddenly being a parent again but also because I worry so much. When she goes anywhere, I worry that something will happen to her. The counsellor said it's quite a common reaction. They call it hyper-vigilance. It's like I'd failed to protect Rhona so I'm terrified I'll fail Maisie too. It haunts me. I try and hide it. I do tell Maisie I'm sad and that it's OK to be sad sometimes but I don't like to tell her that I'm scared. All the time I'm scared. And I hate that because it's like they've won. I wish it would stop. I just have to keep going, though. For Maisie. And for my Rhona.

Jeff closed his laptop.

He'd got something gritty in his good eye. He blinked but it didn't shift. He took off his glasses. There was a mirror on his chest of drawers and he peered into it, saw a speck against the white of his eyeball. He wet the tip of his finger and got it out. A piece of glitter. *We will look after you for ever.*

Not if I can help it, you won't. No way.

CHAPTER EIGHT

August 2015

Holly

Agata rang as Holly was getting ready.

'The website,' Agata said. 'Has it been down? Is it the server?'

Holly felt a squirt of guilt. 'No... I...'

'I sent in some comments last week but nothing's up.'

Holly was short of breath, too warm. 'Yeah, I'll sort it.'

'The last update was the seventeenth,' Agata said.

For fuck's sake. 'I know! It's just there's a lot, there's so much–' Holly broke off. She sat down each day and opened the laptop, and it was just overwhelming, dozens of emails, all the posts and comments to moderate, all the decisions they expected her to make. She'd start doing one task, then more messages would arrive or someone would call.

'Are you OK?' Agata said.

Holly didn't say anything.

'Holly?'

'The thing is, I'm... I'm...' She was filling up, which was the last thing she wanted. 'I don't think I can do it at the moment.' *I'm rubbish, I can't even do this.*

'Oh,' Agata said.

'I think I need to step back a bit. Just, erm ... take a break, you know?'

'Right.'

'Try and find someone else to take it on for a bit,' Holly said.

'I could have a go, if you want. It's Word Press, yes?'

'Yes,' Holly said.

'I could take over for now, see how it goes,' Agata said.

'You're sure?'

'Yes. No problem.'

Holly felt light-headed. She closed her eyes.

'OK. I can email you the admin password. I know there's a big backlog of messages, posts and comments.'

'Don't worry,' Agata said. 'Where are we up to with the reunion?'

'Still undecided,' Holly said. 'Maybe it's too soon – maybe we should wait until after the first anniversary.' The topic had been debated for a while now. Sometimes she thought it was a stupid idea getting survivors, their families and the bereaved together. For what? To rub their noses in it? Compare scars? Other times she was one of those desperate to connect with people who had been on the train. To actually meet in person. 'I just don't know,' she said.

'Well, there's no hurry,' Agata said. 'We can keep talking, see what people want to do.'

'I'll email you, with the rest. Probably later,' Holly said. 'I've got to go out now.'

'Anything nice?'

'A christening, my nephew.'

'Aw, that's great. Have a good day,' Agata said.

'Cheers, you too.'

Holly set down the phone and picked up the eye-shadow. She leant in to the mirror but her hand was shaking so badly it was impossible to put it on. She would have to go barefaced. She had thought of buying a hat with a veil to hide the scarring on her cheek, then hated herself for the vanity. She was alive, wasn't she? How could she be so trivial, so superficial?

The front door slammed; the house vibrated.

Holly was hurled through the air ... her arm was wrenched back. There was a rushing noise in her ears, like a rainstorm, or a river... She heard crying and someone screaming, 'Help me! Help me!'... And everywhere red, pieces of red. Like meat.

Breathing too fast, she felt the dizziness blacken her vision. She cupped her hand over her nose and fought to slow the panting.

'Ten minutes,' her mother called up. Then, 'Holly?' when she didn't respond.

'OK,' Holly called.

She looked at her reflection in the long mirror by her wardrobe. She wore a lemon-coloured, A-line, short-sleeved dress. She had a silver and gold braided bracelet on her left wrist, an attempt to draw attention away from the shock of her stump, her right arm ending in an ugly point, the skin puckered and shiny.

She imagined the photographs, they'd have to position her behind someone so as not to distract from the happy occasion. She decided she would wear her jacket after all and cover up, even if the black linen would look heavy against the yellow of the dress. That way no one would be confronted with her injury. None of Oliver's friends would feel obliged to mention the bombing or ask after her health.

She wriggled her feet into her gold sandals and went downstairs.

Her mum was brushing hairs off her father's jacket shoulders and he was complaining. They were all decked out, Mum in a lilac chiffon suit and a lilac and navy hat, Dad in his navy pin-stripe with a white shirt and pink tie.

She wanted to weep.

Her stomach churned.

Dad went out and got into the car. Her mum was unplugging her phone, all charged up so she could take lots of pictures.

'You've got your keys?' she asked Holly.

'Yes,' Holly said, 'I'll lock up.'

At the threshold Holly froze, the keys clamped in her hand. A wall of fear descended. Her heart thumping, palms sweating, dryness in her mouth. Blinded by the blur of panic.

Meg was on the floor, the blood bubbling from her mouth, a stake protruding from her throat. Rhona, her face half gone, head all mashed in at one side. Choking smoke. Black suns.

'Holly?' Her mum was beside her.

Holly was cowering, her arm over her head, rocking to and fro. 'I can't go, I can't go. I can't.' Terror running under her skin, like snakes, biting at her heart. 'I can't. I can't go out. I just can't.'

CHAPTER NINE

October 2015

Kulsoom

They had to do an exercise for RE: take news stories and change the words, so if it was something about Christianity you changed it to be about Islam or Judaism or Hinduism or one of the others.

Everyone had printouts from newspapers over

the last three months and also a list of websites, like BBC and Al Jazeera and CNN, to look at. A lot of the Christian stories were about child abuse but also some about poverty and food banks and global warming, and most of the Islam ones were about the war in Syria or terrorism and the shooting on the French train.

Dad had got her a laptop at last that she could use at home and also send her homework to school.

Mum was still in hospital, in a special unit. She wouldn't eat, and until she gained some weight, they wouldn't let her come home.

Arfan was studying for his A levels at a college, not school, and if he got the grades he was going to do a diploma in accountancy. Kulsoom thought it sounded like the most boring subject in the whole universe but Dad said he would be able to work anywhere he wanted with a skill like that. Arfan saw some of his old friends and sometimes came home late and Dad grounded him but Arfan sneaked out when Dad was asleep, after midnight. Still naughty when he felt like it.

The kids in her new school thought Kulsoom was shy because she kept to herself. Art was OK. Mr Peavey wasn't as good as Miss Weston but he had given her an A in every single piece of work so far. School was worst when it was subjects she hated, like maths. Then she got bored and lonely. Break time, she usually went to the library or the art room because you were allowed to do that, which was cool.

Now she was looking through the printouts and the papers and she saw this little box on one of the *Guardian's* pages: *Have you or your family been affected by terrorism? Tell us your story.*

There was an email address.

Kulsoom stood up, turned round, then sat down again. Could she? It would be so amazing to tell someone. No one ever wrote anything about her trying to warn the police: it was like she was invisible, and that part of it hadn't happened. If people heard about it, if they found out, what would they say? People might think she was brave. Maybe some would think she was wrong to snitch on her brother. She didn't think that.

Her family would hate it. She knew they were ashamed of Saheel and what he'd done, that they could never make it right, but if Kulsoom talked about what she had done, that would show everybody, wouldn't it? That she'd tried to help. That someone in Saheel's family had tried to stop it. She would ask them to keep her name a secret. And the police wouldn't like it, probably. That decided her. She opened her email and typed in the address.

Jeff

'Close your eyes,' Violet squealed. 'Close your eyes.'

Jeff obeyed.

'Now open them.' Faye, sitting on his lap, instructed.

'"Happy birthday to you,"' they were all singing, mostly out of tune, gathered in his nana's backyard.

The breeze blew out one of the candles as his mum carried the cake to the table but it sprang back to life again.

Jeff blew out the candles and they relit.

'Trick candles,' Faye said. 'Everlasting. You can't blow them out. Never.'

Jeff blew again. There was the momentary absence of flames, then they reignited.

Everyone laughed.

'Here.' His nana reached out, pulled up the candles and put them into a glass of water.

'You'll ruin them!' his mum complained.

'Rubbish,' Nana said. 'That's what you have to do. You'd know if you'd read the instructions.'

Sean looked at Jeff and rolled his eyes. Jeff smiled. The two women couldn't be in the same space for five minutes without bickering. Some things never changed.

'It's Minecraft,' Violet said, pointing to the cake.

'So I see,' Jeff said.

'Nana came to ours to do it so you couldn't see.'

'It's great.'

'I made the edge,' Faye said.

'Will you make a game like Minecraft in your course?' Faye said.

'I wish. Bestselling video game of all time. Seventy million copies.' He shook his head. 'Maybe one day. Not yet, though. Only just started.'

Jeff cut the cake.

He'd begun a distance-learning course, coding

and games design. He could do everything from home at times that suited him.

'Drive me around again.' Faye pressed the joystick on the wheelchair and it moved back.

'Not now,' Jeff said. 'I'm eating my cake. Go and do handstands.'

'Yes!' She jumped down and the twins began to hurl themselves up against the back gate.

Jeff opened another bottle of cider

'Jeff, look!' Violet called. She was upside down, walking on her hands. 'Time me.'

'One elephant, two elephant, three...'

Jeff rolled a fag and his mum got her own out.

'Have you been to that group yet?' his mum said. 'The one at the hospital.'

For amputees.

'No.'

'At least think about it,' she said.

'I am.'

'Leave him be, it's his birthday,' Nana said.

'I know it's his birthday. I gave birth to him.' Her voice rose. Sean put a hand on her arm.

Jeff ignored them and clapped the twins. 'Can you do a walk-over?' he said.

'No,' Faye said.

'I can,' said Violet. She tried and failed.

He'd loved to do that as a kid, hands to feet to hands. He felt crap for a moment. The deep bitterness never far away. He distracted himself, calling to the twins, 'Handstands again. I'll take a picture.'

When they'd gone Jeff sat out a while longer, smoking and drinking and messing with his phone, while Nana flitted in and out until it began to rain.

In his room, he played a few rounds of *Grand Theft Auto* and finished the last cider.

He made sure to set his alarm. He had somewhere to be in the morning.

Jeff had lost Holly's number when he'd lost his phone. He hadn't heard from her since she'd stood by his hospital bed when he was off his tits on morphine. She hadn't said anything about getting in touch, just walked away.

For long enough he'd left it. How could the attraction between them survive what had happened? And now he was crippled. Disabled – everyone made a point of calling it that. He knew why and didn't want to disrespect anyone but that was how he felt: crippled, physically and emotionally, by the bombing.

Still, the business with Holly felt unfinished. He wanted to talk to her, see if there was anything left, and if not, if it was just dead in the water, crippled too, then he'd forget it. It was one of the things that made him angry or miserable, the what-might-have-been. And then he felt stupid because when you boiled it down it was just a couple of hours on a train and a bit of banter. Hardly the romance of the century.

He found her in the phone book, the family anyway. They still had a landline, just two entries for Jukes in the city and only one in Northenden. He didn't ring, too risky: he needed to look her in the eye. If she was still at home. Maybe she'd moved, gone back to her event-management job. That could be why Agata was running the website.

Jeff couldn't eat breakfast: he was too wound up, his head and guts bad from his birthday boozing. He called a taxi, a wheelchair-accessible one, to take him to the address. Nana was out meeting a friend in town, so he wouldn't have any explaining to do to her.

When they reached Holly's street, Jeff asked the taxi to let him out at the end. Number sixteen couldn't be very far along.

'You want us to come back for you?' the cabbie said.

'Yes. I'm not sure when,' Jeff said, 'but I've got the number.' He held up his phone.

Jeff hadn't used the electric wheelchair much yet, mainly going up to the mini-market and back for milk and baccy. He had a sort of apron that covered his shorts and hung down the front of the chair. He wasn't ready yet to ride around flashing his stumps. He got enough sideways glances as it was.

The houses were terraces, biggish ones, the sort that had cellars and, he realized, with a sinking heart, steps up to the front door. His plan to roll up to number sixteen and knock withered and died.

He reached the house. White wrought-iron gate, path, steps. Six stone steps.

He got through the gate and wheeled to the foot of the steps. Stranded.

The house looked deserted: no lights on, no windows open. Those fancy white slatted blinds in the downstairs windows, stained-glass panels in the front door.

He launched his browser, searched for the BT

phone book, found the entry and keyed in the number. The phone rang. No one answered.

Jeff waited. It cut off.

He tried again.

'Hello?' she answered, on the fifth ring.

'Holly? It's Jeff.'

'Oh,' she said.

Not 'Oh, hi,' or 'Oh, great,' just 'Oh.'

'I've, erm ... I've been wondering how you are?'

'Bit busy at the moment. Can I ring you back?'

She was going to hang up. 'No, I'm outside,' he said.

'What?'

'Outside your house.'

The phone went dead.

'Holly?'

A motorbike went past, too quickly for the side-street, and Jeff smelt the tang of petrol it left in the air.

Should he go? Did she want him to go? He was sitting there like a right prat.

Then he heard the turn of the lock and she was there, looking down at him.

Not smiling.

Her hair was all bushy and tangled and she was wearing red checked lounge pants and a white vest. No bra. *God.* Bare feet. The stump of her right arm plain to see. She had her eyes screwed up against the light, and her forehead was creased in a scowl.

His heart gave a thump.

'Why are you here?' she said. Not exactly greeting him with open arms. 'What did you come for?'

Holly

He went red. Then she felt like a right bitch.

'I wanted to see you,' he said. 'I've been thinking about you.' His face blazing.

'Don't bother,' she said.

He rubbed his chest as though he'd got indigestion.

Someone walked past, a hipster with a dog on a lead, and glanced their way.

She didn't know what to say.

'We could get that coffee,' Jeff said.

Her face itched. She pressed at the scars. 'Jeff, I'm, erm...' She waved her head towards the house. How to tell him to go away, how to do it nicely. *Fuck off. Fuck off, please.*

'I'm not that great,' she said. 'I should...'

'We could walk,' he said. 'There's a park near here.'

'I can't,' she said. 'Sorry.' She hadn't been out. It was always tomorrow she'd try. And then tomorrow came too soon.

'I get it,' he said, disappointment flat in his voice. 'We're all fucked up now, aren't we? I just thought...' His eyes were that same sapphire colour, angry now. 'I'll go, then.'

'I'm sorry,' she said.

'Yeah.' He pressed the stick and his wheelchair spun round. His hair had grown again, he didn't have it as long now, just below his chin. He spun back. 'The website,' he said. 'It's been good. A life saver.'

'Thanks.' Her eyes stung.

He gave a nod and turned the chair again.

She went inside, shut the door and sank to the floor.

She'd left him. Left him with Naz. In the dark, in the wreckage.

And now she'd sent him away.

You are such a fucking coward.

She'd never see him again. *Fuck!* She banged her fist against her forehead. *Coward. Idiot.*

She pulled herself up, grabbed her keys from the hall table and flew out of the house.

He was at the corner by the kerb, on his phone.

She ran.

'You might want to put some shoes on,' he said.

She gave a nod, 'Wait here,' and ran back.

She found trainers, always Velcro now, no more laces, put on a sweatshirt, got her phone and some money. She worried he'd be gone when she got back, or that she'd be paralysed again and unable to leave the house, but she managed.

She was jumpy, jittery as they went to the park, anxious when they had to cross the road, tensed at each passing car. Anything could happen.

Her mouth tasted metallic.

She felt too tall, walking beside him, was eager to sit down. She showed him the way to the picnic tables. She sat astride one of the benches. Jeff stopped at the end of the table.

'There's no café,' she apologized.

'Shame. I've an epic hangover,' he said. 'Birthday.'

'You drink too much?' she said.

'Got legless.' She caught the twitch at the corner of his mouth and laughed. How could she laugh? How could they joke about it? People had died.

'Will they give you prosthetics?' she said.

'They think so. Eventually. Not sure what. You?'

'Yes. Just a dummy, for now. Less of a horror show.'

'People think I've come out of the army,' Jeff said, shaking his head.

Parakeets flew above, their cries strident.

Her heart was skipping too fast. She'd been wrong to come – it was too much.

'You not working?' he said.

Shook her head. 'No, I've been... I'm not very well.' She started crying. She didn't want to cry. She wiped her face. 'Sorry, I'm...'

'It's OK,' he said. 'It's OK, babe.' He caught her hand. 'I know.' His hand was cool, soft. She stared at his stupid tattoo. 'You want to go back?' he said.

'Soon,' she said.

'OK. Just say the word.'

An ice-cream van came down the road alongside the park and stopped at the entrance nearby.

She sniffed hard. She hadn't brought any tissues, which was another stupid thing.

'Ice cream?' she said.

'Go on,' Jeff said. 'Cornetto.'

She bought two, had to tell the man serving to wait a minute – she couldn't take them from him until she'd sorted the money out and been given her change. He got flustered when he saw why and talked too much but she blanked it out.

While they were eating the ice-creams, Jeff told her about a course he'd started. He hoped in the long run it might lead to a job. He was living at his gran's.

'I get flashbacks,' Holly said. 'Random times.'

He nodded. 'You had any counselling?'

'Some... I...' She shook her head. It had been so hard to talk about. Not at first when she was busy on the website and taking all comers but as time went on it became almost more real, scarier. She knew she should go back and get help. She had promised her parents.

'I've been reading the accounts on the website. It was Caroline who first got suspicious, right?' Jeff said.

Holly thought of the photographs on the memorial page, Caroline, Rhona and Meg, Lisa, little Eddie and Evie. All the others from the different coaches.

'Yes. She told Naz. He'd been speaking to her when I was going to the shop and that's when he said to move out.'

'And you told me,' Jeff said.

'Yes, and I was out of there but–'

'I'm sorry,' he said.

'No.'

'If I hadn't stayed to help Naz–'

'We still could have died,' Holly said. 'Look at all those people in coach C.' She remembered those last moments. Before she was thrown through the air. 'You pushed me back,' she said.

'I don't remember.' He looked away.

There was a giddy feeling inside her. She wished

she hadn't eaten the ice cream. 'I should've stayed – after,' she said.

'No,' he said. He looked back at her sharply. 'You couldn't have done anything.'

'But if I'd–'

'No,' he said again. 'You went to help. Meg. And Rhona.'

He must have read her story on the website, too.

'I couldn't do anything for them,' Holly said.

'You were there. You know what that means. They weren't alone.'

They didn't die alone. Like Naz didn't die alone.

She shivered. Watched a toddler being carried on his father's shoulders. 'I'd like to go back now,' she said.

'Cool.' Jeff got a rollie out, lit up. He wheeled away from the table.

They walked back, him telling her some story about how games now made more money than the movies or the music industry. And that the twins wanted to be gymnasts.

Outside the house, he rang for his taxi.

She was anxious to get inside now – he picked up on it, said he was fine to wait on the pavement. 'It's OK for me to come again?' he said.

Those eyes bright and warm. She hadn't asked him about his eye. He'd worn a patch in hospital. Could he see OK now? He seemed to manage. 'Yes,' she said.

'Cool. Give me your number.'

She rang his phone. He saved it.

'See you then,' she said.

He rolled out onto the pavement.

She went inside, relief at being home making her weak-kneed.

He'd called her 'babe'. Was that OK? Did she want him babe-ing her?

She got a text straight away: *You still owe me coffee xxx Jeff*

He rang the next morning, woke her up. 'Have you seen the news?'

'No, why?' Her bowels turned to ice. Another attack?

'It was in the *Guardian*,' he said. 'Now it's every-where. The bomber, you know he had a sister? Well, she found out what he was going to do. She reported him.'

'Oh, my God!'

'She was only thirteen.'

'Thirteen.'

'That's why they evacuated Euston,' Jeff said. 'The intelligence they talked about, it was her. She found a video on his laptop. We should put a link to this article on the website.'

'Yes.' Holly swallowed. 'Could you let Agata know? She's probably already on it but...'

'Yeah. Cool.'

When he had gone, Holly went downstairs. She stared at the television, the black rectangle re-flecting her silhouette. The remote control was on the sofa arm, where her mother always kept it. Holly looked at it for long enough, then turned away.

Another day, maybe. A different day.

CHAPTER TEN

November 2015

Nick

There was no way Nick was driving in and paying through the nose to park in the city centre, and he didn't use trains or trams, so they were on the bus. Half the people who got on had to stop and pet Boss – he loved the attention. No PTSD for the dog, though he didn't like fire or loud bangs; he'd hide from any sign of flames or smoke. It was impossible to know if he'd been nervous like that beforehand. With all the fireworks going off this time of year the only place that he was happy was under Nick's bed. Spaniels had been bred as hunting dogs, originally; you'd think resilience to pops and bangs would be in their genes.

Cleo had been badgering Nick to come today. She and Lisa's parents would be there. He got sick of her ringing up and asking about it so he told her, no, it wasn't for him. She said she accepted that but still gave a little sigh of disappointment, like he was letting her down in some way. Letting Lisa down.

The family wanted to visit the cemetery again while they were in Manchester, go to the Garden of Remembrance where Lisa and Eddie and Evie's ashes were. Nick had agreed to do that with them, and told them that the Chadwick did reasonable food so they wouldn't expect an invite back to the house after.

'When you're ready to sort things out,' Cleo said, 'could you please give us chance to look at Lisa's things? There might be keepsakes...'

'Of course,' Nick said. All the jewellery would go to Cleo anyway instead of passing to Evie. He didn't know what he wanted to keep. Cleo had asked if it made it harder, all the reminders of them in the house.

Of course the reminders hurt. Eddie's box of cars and tractors, Lisa's coats on the rack in the hall, her hairbrush, Evie's teddies. Each item was a fresh cut. But the pain was part of being alive, wasn't it? Him practically unscathed while they were dead.

No more than he deserved.

The bus reached Piccadilly Gardens and a cold, sick feeling filled his stomach at what lay ahead.

He asked the driver when the next bus back would be.

Twelve minutes' time.

They could wait. He shouldn't have come, should have stuck to his guns.

Boss looked up at him and whined.

'Don't you start,' Nick said.

The dog watched the pigeons hoovering up scraps from the pavement. His tail going.

There were too many people. The place was swarming with them. It was too noisy.

A beggar, a young lad with grimy clothes and brown teeth, crept up to Nick. 'Spare some change for my bus fare home?' he said.

For fuck's sake.
Nick turned away, whistled at Boss and headed through the crowd, his eyes fixed straight ahead.

Kulsoom

Kulsoom had been in such big trouble when Dad found out that she'd been speaking to a journalist. Well, he'd had to find out because he had to give his permission before they did anything because she was a minor and there were contracts to agree to and he went totally ballistic.

'That will not be possible,' he said, all cold and hard into the phone. And he just exploded. He'd never – well, hardly ever – shouted like that at Kulsoom, at anyone, and she wanted to curl up in a tiny ball and disappear. Or be wrapped in an invisibility cloak, like Harry Potter, or be able to transport to a different galaxy.

But she made herself stay there and she didn't cry. When he stopped and finally, finally, let her speak, she said, 'People should know what it's like. They should have a chance to hear about us too. You always said that talking about things, talking about differences, about everything, was better than fighting.'

'This is different.' He pinched at his nose, sat down in his chair.

'No, it isn't,' she said. 'You want us to hide and be quiet, like I don't have any rights because I'm a girl, because I'm a child. So my side of it

295

doesn't matter.'

'I'm trying to protect you, Kulsoom.'

'No. You're trying to shut me up.'

'These people,' he said, 'you're nothing to them. You are just material to be used and exploited, to sell papers.'

'It's one reporter,' she said, 'one paper, exclusive. And they won't use my name or my picture. If you don't let me do it now, then as soon as I'm sixteen or eighteen or whatever' – which was years and years away – 'then I'll leave home and do exactly what I want.'

He gave a huge sigh, and got a cigarette out. 'Why?' he said. 'Why are you so hell-bent on this?'

'Because it's important. Because people should hear what it's like to be a family of a terrorist. No one knows our side of it. It's like we don't exist.'

She saw his hand was shaking and she looked away.

He went outside and smoked the cigarette, then came back in. 'And your mum? What will this do to her?'

'I could warn her. She doesn't use the TV lounge much anyway.' It would mean visiting again, which Kulsoom hated. Her mum, so weak and haunted-looking, trying to make conversation. Asking about school and homework and then Kulsoom could see Mum was going to cry so Dad said they had to go, that Arfan needed a lift to football, which was a big fat lie, really, but Kulsoom was glad he'd said it.

Now he looked at her for ages, then said, 'Let me sleep on it.'

'Yes!' She ran and hugged him, holding her breath against the stink of smoke.

When it came out, Kulsoom bought a copy, and when all the other papers repeated the information she downloaded the articles from them and printed them out. She made a scrapbook because you never knew if you'd lose your data and this wasn't stuff she wanted to keep on the cloud. For all she knew she was on some watch list for having connections with terrorists.

Kulsoom hadn't done any animation since it happened. It was like the two things got mixed up, like clothes running in the wash and everything white coming out grey or pink. So her film project, it was like Saheel had blown that up too.

Then she saw this amazing short on YouTube, done by two sisters. It was just about a long, boring day but it was so funny.

She thought about maybe using her penguin again but putting it with a really different character, like the penguin is badass, brave and sarcastic, and then the other one, maybe something skinny and angular, like a stick insect or a spider, could be really scared and a bit useless, and they'd have adventures.

She'd need some Plasticine, and pipe cleaners, and those googly eyes for the spider. If she used ping-pong balls she could have sticky black dots she could move in between frames to change the expression and have different-sized ones for when the spider was really, really scared, or sad or cross.

And maybe they'd meet because of a crisis and

have to help each other to escape.

Dad could take her to the craft shop on Saturday. He wouldn't mind.

She knew nothing would ever be the same after what Saheel had done. And that Mum might not get better, even though Dad said she would and to give it time. But Kulsoom could still do this.

There were some things the bomb couldn't destroy. Not if you didn't let it.

Holly

In the Lord Mayor's Parlour at Manchester Town Hall there was the buzz of conversation, people finding each other, making connections. Over by the buffet her parents were talking to Caroline's family. Holly was beginning to relax: she had worried that the whole thing might fall flat, a load of damaged and bereaved people coming together and feeling awkward, freaked out. But it was fine.

The room was beautiful, the richly carved wood panelling on the dado contrasting with bright green paint above, where portraits of mayors and councillors hung. There was a sumptuous woven carpet; the high ceiling was latticed and elaborately decorated. A marble fireplace, tall, arched windows and huge chandeliers added to the sense of grandeur. Tables were set out here and there with plenty of space for wheelchair-users to get through and for people to stand and talk.

At one end of the room was a stage, and at the other, exhibition boards carried a display copied from the website with photos of those who'd lost their lives and short statements from their relatives. Beside the display was an advice stall with information on resources available, support groups, how to access counselling, medical and legal assistance. There were also lists for expressions of interest. People who would like to be part of the discussions to create a permanent memorial, those who were happy to have their contact details available for the media and so on.

They had decided to keep this first meeting informal, the emphasis on people being able to chat, to listen, to mingle and to raise ideas for what, if anything, they'd like to see happen in the future. They'd arranged some background music to create an atmosphere, some light classical music that Agata had downloaded.

Holly glanced at the time.

Twenty minutes.

Agata came over. 'Are you going to have something to eat?'

'After,' Holly said. She was due to do a formal welcome speech, which would be followed by a minute's silence in memory of the victims.

'Nervous?' Agata said.

'Petrified.'

'You'll be fine. It all looks great.'

It did: white linen on the tables with floral arrangements, sprigs of rosemary, fragrant pink roses, dried honesty, with its oval see-through seed pods, and white gypsophila.

'Holly?'

She turned to see a small woman, her red hair threaded with grey, glasses on a chain. 'I'm Margie, Rhona's mother.'

'Hello. You've come all the way from Glasgow?'

'Got here last night.'

Holly put out her hand and Margie took it in hers. 'I wanted... I've only just got the Internet at home. Maisie will need it, of course, but the library's been very good, teaching me how to use it.' Her eyes were travelling over Holly's face, searching.

'Let's sit down a moment,' Holly said.

Jeff was passing as they moved to some spare seats and he caught Holly's eye. She smiled at him.

She couldn't imagine being able to cope in any other social situation at the moment, but this was different. Bigger than her own problems. And she owed these people.

She knew what Margie needed to hear, even if she'd read the gist of it on Holly's page.

'Rhona was sitting at the table behind us, the other side of the luggage rack,' Holly said, 'with Agata and Felicity. I didn't hear her get the phone call about Maisie being ill but I know she'd left the carriage by the time we were evacuating people. And she was on her way back when we stopped in the tunnel.'

Holly remembered the shouts. Barking. Crying.

'The bomb went off.' Her mouth was dry and she cleared her throat. 'I managed to talk to Jeff but he and Naz were trapped behind some seating. I left the train and the first person I saw was Meg. She died while I was with her and I was

300

going towards the back of the train when I found Rhona.'

Margie nodded, her nose red at the end.

Holly stopped for a moment, gathering control. 'I knelt down and she was... I think she was trying to talk but she was very badly hurt.'

'Her head.' Margie gestured to her own temple.

'Yes. I sat with her, stroked her arm. I don't think it was very long. She was still trying to talk. And then she just stopped.'

'Thank you.' Again Margie took Holly's hand between the two of hers.

'How is Maisie?' Holly said.

'It's hard for her.'

'Yes.'

Agata came up then. 'Mrs Gillespie?'

'Hello?'

'I'm Agata, I worked with Rhona.'

'Oh, yes. Please...' Margie pointed to a spare chair.

Holly glanced across the room and her stomach flipped. Nick was just outside the doorway. 'Excuse me,' she said to Margie.

'Of course, I'll see you later. And thank you.'

As Holly reached the doorway Nick was walking away along the corridor. He had a dog with him. It looked like the dog that had been on the train.

'Nick?'

He looked round. 'Hello,' he said, wary. He had shadows under his eyes, his hair was unkempt and his clothes past their best.

'I'm glad you came,' she said. 'I was so sorry to hear about Lisa and Eddie and Evie.'

301

He gave a curt nod, his jaw working.

'And I wanted to say thank you,' Holly said.

'I didn't do anything,' he said.

'You pulled me under the train, you strapped up my arm.'

His eyes darted to her stump and away.

'I couldn't have got under on my own and I had blast injuries, internally, so if I hadn't got out when I did, if you...' She shook her head. 'Thank you.'

'OK.'

'Is this Boss?'

Nick grunted. The dog wriggled, wagged its tail.

'Are you coming in?' Holly said.

'Guide dogs only, according to the jobsworth downstairs,' Nick said. 'So, if you could tell my sister-in-law...'

'Sod that,' Holly said. 'Come on, both of you. My parents want to meet you.'

He looked over her shoulder and his face changed, a twist of revulsion around his mouth, a glare in his eyes. Holly glanced back and saw he was watching Naz's family greeting Jeff.

'Forget it,' Nick said, blood in his face.

'Wait–' Holly said. 'Please?' But he didn't. He marched away. The dog's claws clacking on the parquet.

Unnerved, she waited a moment, then returned to the room.

Jeff

'You were with Naz?' Naz's father said.

'That's right,' Jeff said. They'd found space near the huge fireplace in the room. Naz's parents and his sister had pulled up chairs facing him.

'Naz started evacuating the coach,' Jeff said, 'and we were helping, Holly and me.' He nodded over to where he could see Holly talking to an older couple. One of them seemed familiar... He looked very much like Diana – he must be her twin brother.

'We got everyone up and on their way and reached the seats where Saheel Iqbal was. He was on the left facing us and Caroline was on the other side, on the right. Naz said he'd be OK on his own but we stayed and...'

Jeff looked down at the patterned carpet.

'...Caroline had just moved and Naz told Iqbal he would try to find a seat for him. That was when the train stopped. In the tunnel. Iqbal stood up.' Jeff's pulse increased. 'He started muttering and then shouting.' Jeff heard his voice waver. 'Then the dog that was there started barking and the baby was crying and Iqbal was yelling. Naz was trying to calm him down, but he kept shouting. He had his rucksack in his arms. Naz was in front of me.'

Jeff heard Naz's mum's breathing change. She was crying.

'Then there was this huge bang, this pressure.' Jeff closed his eyes. He coughed. He opened them again and glanced at them. Their faces were set in sorrow. He looked back down at the carpet. 'The next thing I remember was being trapped, in the dark, with a lot of smoke, and soot. I was on my back and Naz was sort of this way across me.' Jeff sketched the direction. 'His shirt–' Jeff sniffed.

No one said a word.

'His shirt and jacket were gone. I heard him groan, maybe twice, but he didn't say anything. The next thing I remember was Holly calling to us and she had a flashlight on her phone. It was pitch-black and when she used that, shone it up over the top of the seats that were blocking us in, I could see that Naz was still breathing. And I couldn't see any injuries. There wasn't any blood or anything.'

'That's right,' Naz's father said. 'He looked perfect.'

They would have been able to see the body, Jeff realized, unlike many of the other families.

'And then I kept talking to him, to try ... well, just talking and I held his hand and I had my arm across his chest. He was shivering.' Jeff bit his lip. He felt burning at the back of his eyes. He looked up at the ceiling, all its fancy panels, and sniffed hard. 'I don't know how long it was but then the shaking stopped and he let out this breath. He was so brave.'

'It means so much,' said Naz's mum, through her tears, 'that he was not alone, that you were with him.'

The town-hall clock chimed twice, two o'clock, and Jeff wheeled closer to the stage to hear Holly speak. She looked beautiful in a purple dress and she'd had her hair done in cornrows. The scars on her cheek were still thick and angry, but Jeff couldn't remember her without them now.

This was such a big deal, her coming today. She said the tranquillizers helped but she still didn't go out much.

Now Holly's dad tapped his phone on his glass and the chatter faded. People sat down, moved forward or turned their chairs around to face the stage. The music stopped.

All eyes were on Holly. Speech in hand, she walked up to the steps that led onto the stage. Then she stopped. She looked at Jeff and began to shake her head, her eyes stark with fear. 'I can't,' she said quietly. 'I can't.'

Fuck.

No one moved, then Holly's mum walked up to her. Holly was trembling. 'Mum, I can't.'

The room was thick with tension, apprehension, pity. Jeff saw his mum shaking her head at his nana.

Fuck.

Heart thudding, Jeff wheeled forward and put out his hand. 'Holly, give it to me.'

She handed the sheets to him.

'I need a microphone,' he said.

Holly's dad went up onto the stage and took the microphone from its stand. He brought it down to Jeff.

'I'm going to read Holly's speech for her,' Jeff

said. 'Sorry you can't all see me – the disabled access needs a bit of tweaking. But just in case you were wondering what I look like, if you've not met me, think Johnny Depp but a younger, better-looking version, with more charisma and less legs.' People laughed and gasped, the joke puncturing the tension.

Jeff got out his glasses and put them on. What the fuck was he doing? This was like the worst idea ever.

He began to read: 'I'd like to thank you all for coming today but I wish today hadn't happened. I wish the bombing of the ten thirty-five train from Manchester Piccadilly to London Euston on the seventeenth of April 2015 hadn't happened either. I wish I'd never got on that train. I wish no one had. I wish I'd never met any of you. Whether you're a bereaved relative or a survivor or supporting a victim, you will know how very hard this has been. How unfair. How devastating. There is no silver lining. There was not one single good thing about that experience.

'Fifty-six people lost their lives: partners, husbands, wives, mothers, fathers, children, sons and daughters, brothers, sisters and friends. A senseless waste of life. Sixty-eight people sustained serious and life-changing injuries.

'The one thing we can give each other is understanding. We all share the terrible experience of being victims of a terrorist attack. If there was a button here that we could press to go back and change that day I'm sure we'd be fighting to be the first to press it. But we are where we are, and all we can do is go on.'

Jeff turned a page, the paper rustling over the microphone.

'We go on and make the best of it we can in the name of those who lost their lives. We go on as best we can because we had a second chance. We support each other because we care, because our humanity is greater than the inhumanity of that attack. People have exchanged stories on the website and, perhaps, here today, too. Stories of compassion and bravery, and simple human kindness.

'One phrase that has been used again and again is, "They weren't alone. I'm glad they weren't alone." All those people who rescued other passengers, strangers, who stayed–' His throat closed. The paper shook. He breathed in and out. Coughed. '–who stayed with those who were badly hurt and waited with those who were dying. Offering solace and comfort. Simple human kindness. I'd like to thank all those people. All the ones we've heard from and all the ones we don't even know about. I'd like to talk about two of the people who were in my carriage that day. Caroline Thornicroft, who first realized something was wrong and reported her fears.' Jeff looked up, and saw Caroline's husband pull his children, one either side of him, closer. 'And Naz Dawood. Naz was working as a cleaner that day. He tried to evacuate coach B and isolate the bomber. He tried to calm the situation and he gave his life in the process.' Jeff could hear someone crying, then the sound of traffic from the square outside. 'There is someone else we should remember and we should thank. She isn't here today, and we don't know her name, but Saheel Iqbal's sister

307

was just thirteen years old, a child, when she found out what he was planning. She alerted the authorities immediately. Her life has been torn apart just like the rest of us. She and her family have been bereaved, like so many others here.

'We are here today, together, aching for those who have gone. We can get support and strength from each other to go on, to keep going on, to go on for those who are lost. In their names. There is no closure. No back to normal for any of us. We are devastated. But we are here and we are together. And we go on in their names.'

Several people were crying now. Someone blew their nose.

'We are now going to have a minute's silence to remember them,' Jeff said.

It had begun to rain. Jeff listened to the spattering at the windows, the rumble of a bus outside. He thought of Naz fetching drawing paper for the little boy, the landscape shooting by, the train clattering through fields and trees, past pylons and villages and canals. Of Holly arguing with him and spilling water on his lap. Holly touching his arm. He remembered running up the ramp to Piccadilly station.

Then the music started again.

And people began to talk.

ACKNOWLEDGEMENTS

Thanks to my writers' group: Mary Sharratt, Sue Stern, Olivia Piekarski and Anjum Malik, for keeping me on track. To my daughter Ellie Preston for on-board research. To my editor Krystyna Green, Grace Vincent and all the team at Constable, and Little, Brown, for bringing my books to life. And to my agent Sara Menguc, who supported me every step of the way.

The publishers hope that this book has given you enjoyable reading. Large Print Books are especially designed to be as easy to see and hold as possible. If you wish a complete list of our books please ask at your local library or write directly to:

Magna Large Print Books
Magna House, Long Preston,
Skipton, North Yorkshire.
BD23 4ND

This Large Print Book for the partially sighted, who cannot read normal print, is published under the auspices of

THE ULVERSCROFT FOUNDATION